Praise for *Power Woman*

"*Power Woman* is a captivating journey through the exciting adventures of the main character as she explores her newfound strengths and abilities. This book kept me engrossed from start to finish, leaving me pondering its themes long after I turned the final page. A must read for anyone seeking adventure and inspiration."

Tami Christensen, Author (*Life on the Run*),
Marathon Runner, CPA, Software Developer

"A fun book about a woman marathoner turning into 'Power Woman.' It incorporates some significant reality about a woman fitting running into a busy life, all while raising a family. As a former marathon runner, I can relate to this story, which is an easy and exciting read."

Gabby Anderson, Represented Switzerland in 1984
in the First Women's Olympic Marathon Race in Los Angeles

"*Power Woman* is an interesting read with some dramatic plot lines and inspirational themes. An easy and entertaining read."

Mike Gastineau, Pacific Northwest Sports Radio Personality, Author
(*Sounders FC, Fear No Man, Mr. Townsend,* and *The Polish Prince*)

"An entertaining, highly creative story of an elite athlete who discovers she has super powers and finds herself saving lives. Amid the heroism, she must confront greed and opportunism. Pure fun to read."

Don Pugnetti Jr., Author (*A Coat Dyed Black*)

"Get ready for a roller coaster ride of entertainment in this inventive and entertaining story. It is a rip-roaring read that never slows down, a page turner that keeps you guessing and second guessing until the last gunshot."

Robert Bruce Woodcox, Author, Pulitzer Prize Nominee—
Fiction, Founder: ighostwrite

"I found this book to be entertaining—a creative immersion of fantasy in a suspenseful and compelling story."

Tina Shoemaker, President, Gig Harbor Film Festival

"*Power Woman* is the story of Tami Powers, a marathon running mom and accountant who develops super powers and is coerced into teaming up with a national TV Network. Tami saves friends and strangers alike from danger, and must fight to clear her name, protect her family, and protect her friends from the mob. A very fun story."

Tracy Cram Perkins, Author (*Dementia Home Care*), International Book Award Winner.

"21st century strong role models are rarely depicted as maternal, ethical, empathetic, and humble females. *Power Woman*'s Tami Powers does all that and leaves the reader longing for the whole story to ring true."

Cara Tobias Ingram, Author (*The Lost Angel*)

POWER
WOMAN

POWER WOMAN

BY LEE JORGENSON

*To my wife, Marianne Jorgenson, for her support
and patience throughout the process of someone disappearing
for long periods of time to write a book.*

To the worldwide community of runners out there: You rock!

PROLOGUE

Tami Powers was up to her ears in steamy diapers and living on the ragged edge of sleeplessness. A young mother and caregiver to her four babies, she was working full time from home as an accountant, attending a CPA exam prep group two nights a week, and married to an absentee (going to graduate school, working nights) husband. She was overwhelmed, deeply depressed, and trying desperately to get her feet back on the ground. So, she dug deep into her Idaho farm girl roots and started getting up at four-thirty in the morning and running. And running some more.

Her daily jogs invigorated her and restarted her life. Women would say, "You must be so exhausted, dear."

To which Tami would reply, "I've never felt better, more alive in my life." She fell in love with running to the degree of extending her distances and began running marathon races. Over time, she ran close to one hundred marathons, in all fifty states, and suddenly she was gifted with Super Powers.

From Los Angeles to NYC, in times of conflict and danger, she developed the ability to react in nano time, overcoming insurmountable odds and dangerous, ugly situations. Now, she not only kicks ass on numerous underworld gangsters, street thugs, and escaped parolees, but she also rescues babies and battles corporate intrigue, all while training to become an elite nationally competitive runner, and inadvertently establishing herself as a national network media sensation.

Throughout all the adventures, a strong family identity is her sustaining force. She supports her community, and founds and funds a philanthropic foundation. She trains and qualifies as a marathon runner for the Universal Games and is invited to work with the Diplomatic Security Service using her talents to help protect our American athletes at the games.

Author's Note: Tami Powers' character is based on the real-life adventures of Tami Christensen, a remarkable and gifted woman who resides in Gig Harbor, Washington and Coeur d'Alene, Idaho.

CHAPTER
1

Three cattle rustlers, two of them convicted felons, the other an escaped parolee, sat on horseback under ten-gallon hats, staring down their mountain trail into a valley of opportunity below. They were hungry, thirsty, horny, trail weary, and, to their surprise, a gathering was happening on the barren, high desert floor they called home.

Spud licked his chops, turned to Puck and Skunk and blurted, "Well, I'll be damned, boys! It's a drunkard's dream, right in our own backyard. Let's git on down there and have us some fun." His two sidekicks could find nothing to disagree with (as usual), so three sets of spurs jangled as they poked the sides of their horse's bellies and started sidestepping down the trail.

The delicious aroma of the BBQ smoker was wafting about, and after an austere three months of working cattle, eating beans and living rough in the eastern foothills, a hot meal and some female companionship gave all the boys a sense of urgency.

Soon they were loping along, and Spud ran a crusty bandana over his perspiring brow while squinting at the scene in front of him. He saw no security types, no guard dogs, and no other possible bad asses—and that appealed to him even more.

———

Our movie shoot had gone well. We were wrapping up production after three weeks of nonstop filming, and the July weather in Southern Utah had been spectacular. The days were long and hot, and the nighttime skies were inky black and plastered with stars. Our shoot was situated on the back side of Zion National Park, remote, but beautifully scenic wilderness to everyone.

We were filming a medium budget oater, and apparently the environment had inspired us to the extent that our British director, Malcolm Sparrow, declared we would complete filming late on Friday afternoon. The end of shooting, ahead of schedule and within budget meant a party on Saturday. A real cast party, for many of us our first.

The large, military-style tents we were billeted in were jumping with anticipation for our whoop-de-do. There were two tents, one for each sex, but there was no shortage of fraternizing between the two.

Our movie set consisted of a dusty town square, with facades of a General Store, Sheriff's and Telegraph Offices, Saloon, etc. The compound was surrounded by a barbed wire fence and had an entrance gate on the east side. Back behind the town square was all the logistical stuff, i.e. horse coral, maintenance/storage tents, water truck, showers, camp kitchen, generators, and more tents for editing, production and costumes. Our rustic digs may have been part of Malcolm's decision to throw a party. Whatever. We were a motley cast, a mixture of novices, mostly extras, with a few career leads thrown in. We were living in a boot camp and having the time of our lives.

———

Malcolm had sent the caterers off to St. George the previous day for provisions, and the festivities were set to kick off at three on Saturday afternoon. Audio was doing music for us, personnel had some activities lined up, and there was rumored to be a trick rider/roper dude show up for some authentic Western entertainment. Nobody cared; all we wanted to do was drink margaritas, and stuff ourselves at the buffet. After dark, Malcolm had promised to show some unedited cuts of our flick on an outdoor screen.

Two-thirty on Saturday rolled around and catering opened early. Malcolm was busy working on something in his private tent. Most of the support type older dudes had gone into town on their own. Our well-liked CPA Tami Powers had taken off on one of her daily twenty-mile runs. She preferred going out early in the morning, but Malcolm needed some wrap up financial reports. So, she waited around and worked up a balance sheet and P & L's before jogging out a little after one. Rumor had it she'd run in almost a hundred marathons. She was a little older than most of us, was very friendly and although married, the guys thought she was still hot.

Soon after catering rang the cow bell, most of the cast was there in the public square, hanging out, cocktail in hand, and starting to nosh. There was the aroma of marijuana and barbeque floating about, and we all were looking forward to a capital afternoon and evening.

———

To everyone's surprise, our isolated party scene was interrupted half an hour later by three hairy, desperado looking dudes riding into the compound and dismounting just past the bar. They let their reins dangle to the ground, and the horses looked like they were too tired to move anyway. We erroneously assumed they were the trick ropers Malcolm had hired. After dismounting, all three of them sauntered over to the food table and began helping themselves. And jeez, help themselves they did, each one of 'em taking enough to feed a small army. Then they strutted over to the bar and ordered Todd the barman to get some water for their horses and bring them a bottle of whiskey.

"I don't have any whiskey, just margaritas, and I don't water horses. Who are you guys anyway?"

The mangy bearded dude called Spud, narrowed his eyes and gave Todd a mean look, then shocked everyone by pulling a .45 revolver out of one of his holsters. He pointed it at Todd and told him to get his ass around from behind the bar. Todd was dumbfounded, but when a bullet whizzed past his ear, he had little choice but to oblige.

"Drop your pants for the ladies, and start spinning around real pretty," Spud told him.

Todd just stood there, staring at the grungy stranger, and finally said, "No way in hell, man."

This made Spud hopping mad, and he aimed his gun and shot Todd right in the foot.

Spud might as well have set a cannon off. Todd howled in agony, and crumpled to the ground while everyone began to scream and scramble around. Sidekick Puck fired a couple more shots in the air and shouted for everyone to get their asses down on the ground. Then the rednecks grabbed their plates and stomped over toward the fire pit and the half ring of Adirondack chairs surrounding it. Spud put his plate down and grabbed Amanda, our lead actress by the hair. He pulled her up off the ground, then fired some more shots.

Standing there for a minute, he looked around, spit some tobacco juice on the ground, and while holding a shaking Amanda bellowed at us, "y'all keep your dumb asses face down in the dirt. And if any of youse tries anything stupid, her ass is grass!"

———————

We rolled over as soon as his little speech was finished, and he just stood there, staring out over all of us lying flat on our bellies. Snickering, he called out to Skunk while jerking his head toward the bar. His partner got up, walked over and grabbed a couple bottles of tequila. On his way back to the chairs he kicked the bartender in the leg, told him to stop whining. Then he reached down, and grabbed our makeup woman, also by the hair of her head.

"Git up, honey, yer comin' with me."

He slouched down in a camp chair, and pulled Linda onto his lap like Amanda was being forced to do with Spud. The boys stuffed their faces, threw the plates at the firepit and turned their attention to the women and the liquor. Puck broke a seal, cracked a bottle open, sucked in a long pull, and handed it off. Then he began to paw Linda enough to start her shrieking at him; he responded by slapping her face hard and ripping open the front of her blouse.

The three dirtbags liked that a lot, and just for fun whizzed a few more shots over us. One of their bullets hit the coffee urn, and hot, brown liquid began to spray around. All in all, it was a very weird scene, with about forty of us laying prone, and Amanda and Linda staring down the barrel of real guns in real time.

They were, of course, traumatized, and now Spud got the bright idea that the girls should take off more of their clothes and entertain them with some table dances. Amanda told him to piss off, so he picks up his .45, aims carefully, and shoots the bartender in other foot. Looking back at Amanda, he pushed her off his lap while ripping the front of her summer dress apart, and there she stood in a set of matching pink Etsy lingerie.

The young women, humiliated, terrified and fearing for their lives tried to resist, when in a diabolical irony, the rockabilly music audio had set up kicked in and engaged remotely. Now the boys were tapping their toes and pointing guns at the girls, who were in their underwear and being forced to begin their sickly twisted dances for our uninvited guests. The three goons sat and glugged raw liquor while watching the girls gyrate. Soon their eyes began to glaze over, but that didn't stop Spud from grabbing Amanda and jerking her back onto his tented lap as her brassiere fell to the ground.

Every now and then one of them kept firing off a round. A couple of the women had crawled over to the bartender and were trying to minister to him. No one else was moving much, afraid of drawing any attention and getting their own feet shot off. Also, it was turning uglier with the rednecks, who by now had grabbed a couple more females from close by and were getting drunker and raunchier by the minute. Finally, Spud told his sidekicks, "It's gettin' late, boys. Pick which woman you want to take along; we gotta head out afore dark."

———————

Just north of our compound, Tami Powers, a superb athlete, who had in fact run almost one hundred full marathons followed her downward sloping trail around to the right. As she began her descent back into camp, she was scanning the terrain carefully having heard a lot of loud explosions in the last hour. Besides violating the quiet solitude of her mountain run, she knew Malcolm hadn't sprung for any fireworks at the party and fearing trouble, had herself on hyper alert.

Rounding the last angled curve on the trail, she gazed down at what was supposed to be a social gathering and was shocked to the core when she saw the crew all sprawled in the dirt, and three grungy strangers pawing at her women friends. A purple rage welled powerfully inside her chest, and she jogged in place for a few seconds to gather herself and survey the situation.

————

Could any four people have been experiencing the polar opposites of consciousness than Tami and the three degenerate bullies she was observing? Tami: here now, bursting with intense energy, her muscles flexed but loose, her mind taunt and ready for action. The boys: sated, approaching mindless drunkenness, distracted, their vision becoming blurrier. Would they even see her coming?

————

Solidly centered and with deadly purpose, Tami ratcheted up to a sprint, then hurdled the low fence at the camp's perimeter. In no more than four or five giant strides, covering some two hundred yards, avoiding and dodging our prone bodies, she came to a halt standing directly between number one and number two hillbilly. They both looked up dumbly, and Spud said, "hey babe, you is good lookin'." He sat gazing at a set of long, tanned, athletic legs in running shorts and a tank top, whose mop of brunette hair was still whirling and whose green eyes flashed down on him.

That was all he got out of his mouth, as Tami reached down, striking like a cobra, and knocked their hats off. In the same motion she grabbed scuzzy beard number one and scuzzy beard number two, one in each hand, and snapped their heads together like she was cracking a couple of walnuts. The thud of bone-on-bone would have been sickening if it wasn't for these two dirt bags, and both Spud and Skunk slumped into unconsciousness.

This motivated Puck to sober up rather quickly, he dropped a bottle of Hornitos on the ground and attempted to simultaneously get up while pawing at his pistol belt. Tami sidestepped in front of him, waiting until he was standing semi erect and then delivered a full frontal and spectacularly accurate kick to his groin. Puck groaned, and as he leaned forward in pain, Tami blasted him with an elbow smash to the back of his neck. He toppled forward to the ground, where Tami kicked him in the temple. Ole Pucker was dead quiet after that.

Everybody was still in shock, and half the cast and crew had yet to realize they were now liberated until Tami called out, "parties over kids, you can get up now." Amanda and Linda grabbed Tami in a bear hug while sobbing hysterically. Tami embraced them tenderly and finally suggested they go back to the women's tent, get some clothes on, and try to collect themselves. Amanda snatched her summer frock and bra off the ground, covering herself as she turned to leave, but not before spitting in Spud's ashen face. Tami sent someone off for duct tape, and she and two or three of the guys secured our unconscious outlaws hand and foot.

The camp nurse was kneeling, tending to Todd. Malcolm had heard all the commotion from his executive tent and had been standing quietly in the shadows watching throughout. He emerged quickly out to the firepit and began to take charge. Tami ignored him, and as the compound was so remote there was no cell phone coverage, sent him off in the Jeep Cherokee to get the Sheriff and an ambulance. The cast was now milling about in disbelief, murmuring quietly, the females were livid, not to mention everyone else. Some of the girls went back to the tent to be with Amanda and Linda. Tami looked around surveying the scene, kicked Puck in the side one more time, took a deep breath, and exhaled. Feeling everything was under control, she calmly walked over behind the bar and poured herself a margarita.

———

Malcolm meekly rode off in the Cherokee, and all he could think about was the extraordinary events that had just occurred. First, the astonishing invasion by the three rednecks, their obnoxious, abusive behavior, and the ruination of his well-planned (at no small expense) party. But most of all, the superhuman response he had witnessed of Tami springing onto the scene. Her athletic figure literally bounding, vaulting in like some kind of dervish, rescuing everyone, and preventing who knows what other type of carnage.

He quickly reviewed his own behavior to make sure he could not be accused of any malfeasance or negligence. One can't be too careful anymore he knew all too well, and wasn't it the producer's responsibility to have hired security for the set while they were shooting? <u>Christ,</u> he thought, *I can't do everything.* He felt assured that he could defer any liability away from himself, and therefore, was at no personal or professional risk. Then his mind turned again to this afternoon's other worldly action, and he continued to be awe struck by what had just happened.

How was it vaguely, remotely, conceptually possible that any human being, let alone a slender woman in tennis shoes, could just leap some forty feet at a time, six to eight feet off the ground, land light as a feather on the balls of her feet, and into the heart of a very dangerous confrontation? Then immediately and authoritatively take control of the situation by singlehandedly disarming and dispatching the criminals. All while being seriously outnumbered and unarmed.

"That woman is a real-time, real-life heroine," he said aloud to himself.

She had saved the cast and crew, especially the females from brutal horrors, and had done it all with her bare hands, feet, and one elbow— a situation so dangerous that he himself, a grown man, had withdrawn and stood watching from the sidelines. "Did she see me?" he mused aloud. "Probably not, and thank God I had the mental clarity to take out my phone and film the entire episode."

His mind continued to churn. Wasn't this going to bring him a pretty penny when he sold it to the networks! No one had ever seen anything like this in real life, real time. Tami was a super woman, a unique heroine, and he had it all on film. He bounced down the rutted road until he hit Highway Nine, turned right, and headed for civilization.

He would alert the Sheriff, then the local media, as soon as he could get a cell signal. He would let the local news and TV affiliate get out the initial reports, then he would start to contact the big boys. All of them, New York, LA, Chicago, Houston would be competing for his video. "Let 'em get to it," he said to himself. "I'm sittin' on a gold mine here."

He continued to refine his thoughts while driving along. *Everyone needs to be notified, then I should get back to camp and play greeter, create a presence. As soon as they're gone, I will sit Tami down under the guise of a post-incident follow-up interview. Convince her the producers want it for the insurance people. If I can get that I will not only have live footage of the actual confrontation, but also an in-depth exclusive interview with the heroine herself. Double my damn money!*

CHAPTER
2

Malcolm got as far as the small town of Hurricane and pulled into the local Police Station. He burst into the foyer and shouted that there had been a shooting and numerous assaults just north of the national park. He was so loud and strident the sleepy dispatcher almost fell out of her padded office chair.

"Calm down, sir," she was finally able to blurt out. "Exactly where and when did this happen?"

"We're shooting a movie just north of Zion. It's about fifteen miles up an access road off Route Nine. Three guys busted in on our camp as we were starting our wrap party. They shot up my bartender, attacked several of our women, and stole some of our food and booze before we were able to subdue them. Where's the Chief of Police? We've gotta get back out there!"

"Again, please calm down, I have already radioed him. He's on his way to the station right now. Why don't you start from the beginning and tell me exactly what happened?"

"Are you kidding, lady? Then do it all over again when the Chief gets here? Where the hell is he anyway?"

Five minutes later, Bill Marks, Hurricane's Chief Constable, strode into the station house, and stared at a wild-eyed Malcolm Sparrow.

Bill got to work immediately. "State your name, sir."

"Malcolm Sparrow. I am directing a movie which was permitted by the Utah Film Commission's Satellite Office in Saint George. Our set is located just north of the east end of Zion National Park. We were proceeding with our wrap party today, when three desperate men rode into our set, and began to cause trouble. They stole our food and demanded whiskey from my bartender. When he said he didn't have any, they shot him in both feet. Then they grabbed some of my Tequila, started getting drunk, and accosted our women. They were fondling them and acting in a very disgusting manner when we were able to disarm them and render them unconscious."

Bill looked at Malcolm's slight frame and thin wrists, then asked, "And how'd you do that, sir?"

"One of my people surprised them, and she was able to knock them all out. We've got them secured now, and you need to come out arrest them right away!"

"She?"

"Yes sir, our accountant, Tami Powers."

"Okay Malcolm, you wait here, I'm going to call my deputy in, and we will follow you back out there."

"Well, hurry it up, would ya? We should get back out before dark, and you should also call animal control because they rode in on three horses, and we have enough to do taking care of our own stock."

Again, Bill cocked his head before speaking and looked closely at Malcolm Sparrow. "Don't interfere with my investigation, sir. Do you understand me?"

"Sure, sure, and we also need an ambulance for the shooting victim. I would call out there and see how everyone is doing, but there is no cell service."

Chief Marks picked up his radio and called out to his deputy on a suspected 76-5-103 for aggravated assault telling him to report to headquarters ASAP. Then he radioed the EMTs and told Malcolm to go wait in his car, and they would follow him out to the camp site.

———

A bored weekend reporter for the Saint George Sentinel had her feet up on the public desk in the deserted newspaper office reading a John Grisham novel, when her radio monitor began to crackle. A 76-5-103 is a major event, so she jumped up, grabbed her worksheets and cell phone, and headed out to the car.

Malcolm returned to the Cherokee, sat down, and immediately took out his phone and googled the local newspaper. He got the weekend hotline of the Sentinel and was able to hook up with the reporter as she was leaving for Hurricane. He introduced himself and began to brief her on the situation.

"See if you can stall the cops until I get there. I'm only about ten minutes away, and I can follow you to the site."

"Will do," Malcolm replied. "I am at the police station in Hurricane right now."

While Bill Marks was waiting for his deputy to arrive, he thought it wise to call in a sheriff's unit from St. George for back up. Then went in and put on his bulletproof vest, loaded up extra ammo, and went back to the outer office to wait for everyone.

It took about half an hour to assemble the troops, but soon enough they were ready to convoy out to Malcolm's camp. Bill was annoyed to see the Sentinel reporter show up, but there was little he could do about that. He assigned a volunteer deputy to drive Malcolm's Jeep to make faster time, and they pulled out with sirens blazing.

————

It took another half hour to get to the camp, and Malcolm was the first to jump out as soon as they arrived. He rushed over to Tami, who was parked in a camp chair next to Amanda and Linda, sitting guard over their prisoners. He attempted to give her a hug, which she brushed off, so he just stood there rather awkwardly.

"We are all safe now," he gushed.

Tami and the ladies ignored him and got up out of their chairs to deal with everyone. Most of the crew were standing around talking, a few drinking; the three hooligans were still lying on the ground, unconscious.

The cops were a little cautious at first, but when they saw that the situation was under control they began to relax. Approaching Tami, and eyeballing her prisoners, Bill sent his deputy off to get a bucket of water. When he returned, Bill doused the thugs, and they began to stir back to the living. Jessica Landry from the Sentinel was busy taking pictures in the now shadowy light.

"What happened here?" Bill asked Tami. She explained what was going on, and when Bill asked her how the outlaws were subdued, she paused long enough, unsure of just what to say, for Malcolm to butt in.

"This young woman singlehandedly subdued these criminals," he said. Jessica had her cell phone out, and it was absolutely running on video.

"I just caught them by surprise," was all Tami would say being intentionally vague, which allowed Malcolm to continue babbling.

"She strode in here, grabbed those two guys, and banged their heads together, knocking them out. Then when the other guy started to get up and come to the defense of his buddies, she knocked him out too. She was magnificent!"

"Are there any other witnesses here to the actual events that occurred today?" Bill asked.

Amanda and Linda were now dressed in jeans and tees and couldn't wait to corroborate Malcolm's story. "We were just starting to get our wrap party going, when these three @#$%^&*'s came in here and started all this trouble. That guy shot Todd in both feet, pointing to Spud. Then they grabbed us and started molesting us and were groping us all over. It was terrible. Tami came and rescued us just in time, because they were talking about taking three of us women away with them. Tami basically jumped up in their faces and kicked their asses! She saved all of us."

"All right, everything seems secure here now," Bill Marks said. "We are taking these three perps back to town and booking them. EMTs are taking your bartender to the hospital for the night. Animal control is coming to look after the horses, and I am going to leave a deputy here for security overnight. He has a two-way radio with him, so there shouldn't be any more trouble. I want you four, Malcolm, Tami, Amanda and Linda, in my office at ten a.m. tomorrow morning to make official statements. Any questions? No? Then we're out of here."

Jessica Landry, who was not under the jurisdiction of the cops, decided to stick around. She was only a cub reporter but was smart enough to know she was sitting on the biggest story to hit Hurricane since forever. Malcolm had lots to talk about, as did Amanda and Linda, and the rest of the cast were slowly coming out of shock.

Tami remained stoic and non-committal. The events of the day were something she would rather ignore, better yet suppress completely, as she was still not quite sure of what had actually happened. Not only the physical events of the day, but how it had all happened so quickly and so spectacularly.

CHAPTER
3

Jessica left after half an hour, taking along plenty of live footage of the crime scene, but also some quality copy from her interviews with Malcolm, Amanda and Linda. She needed to get her scoop to press for the Sunday Edition, and was afraid this would push the sewing bee news to the back page. Tami had all but disappeared out of sight.

Malcolm loaded the Voice Memos App on his cell phone, and it was set to record as soon as he pressed the red button. Tami was still laying low until Malcolm rousted her from her quarters an hour later. "When I was in town," he told her, "I called one of the producers, and she suggested, actually ordered, that I sit down with you, and get your take on what happened here today."

"I don't want to talk about it," Tami said. But Malcolm reiterated how important her statement was and Tami sighed in resignation. "This is essential for the protection of the company, but also all that we have accomplished out here the last three weeks."

She could see that she was going to have to make a statement of some kind anyway, so she started considering her options. In the meantime, Malcolm began making more small talk to get her going. Where was she from, how long had she been running, had anything like this ever happened to her before, etc.? Finally, he sensed she was beginning to relax, and pressed record on his VM App.

Tami began with her childhood in southern Idaho. She was a farm girl from a small town, her parents were Mormons, and she had lived an agro/rural childhood life. In addition to herself there were three brothers, and her family was quite close. Grandma Powers was much more worldly than Tami's parents and exposed her to many of the niceties of life: Travel to exotic places, fine lodging and dining, silk scarves and girly intimates. Her memma's influence had opened her eyes to so many things off the farm, and "she became a major influence in my life." Starting college opened Tami's eyes in other ways, and by her sophomore year, she had divorced herself from the Mormon religion.

"I didn't start running until later in life. I was a young bride with four children, an absentee husband, and was so overwhelmed I just started running out of desperation. The running blended so well with my lifestyle and sedentary accounting career, that I immediately fell in love with it. I began to get up at four a.m. every morning to jog for a couple hours. It became my time, and I continue to rise at four in the morning and run for a couple hours a day.

"It is my passion and has shaped my life and my values. I became interested in running marathons, and so far, I have run nearly one hundred of them in every state in America, not to mention Mexico, Canada and Europe. Running has taught me endurance. I am rarely sick, and have developed steely discipline and devotion. I have had to organize my life to accommodate my running habit, which has shaped everything I do.

"When I am running, I feel powerful, almost omnipotent. There is the normal rush of endorphins after any workout, but they don't compare to the personal sense of fulfillment, satisfaction, and intensity I have come to know when I am in the zone out on a road or trail. It is more than just running; it is the spiritual and physical knowledge that I can do or accomplish anything I set my mind to. When I am not engaged with my family, running, or working as a CPA, I practice Asana Yoga and Tae Kwon Do."

Malcolm was impressed; he brushed his longish hair over his right ear and focused on Tami's story. This was fantastic copy on a very personal level from a person who was otherwise very reticent. It was obvious to him that running was the conversational pivot into her personal life. Now he needed to steer her into a discussion of the day's events.

"Tami, will you describe to me in your own words what happened today, and how you were able to do what you did?"

"To be honest with you, I am not sure what happened," Tami said, biting down on her lip and pausing reflectively. "While I was out on the trail, I kept hearing noises that sounded like gunfire, but they were coming from our camp. I was concerned, and as I was finishing my run and headed back, I looked down on the set, and saw what was happening. Somehow, Amanda and Linda just reached out to me. I could feel the pain in their bodies and souls and what they were going through. I got very upset, and simply reacted. My running instincts intensified, and suddenly I was flying to their rescue. That is probably why everything worked so well. I was in those guys faces before they saw me coming, and wham, I was banging their heads together. It was like for a short amount of time I was all powerful."

"And nothing like that has ever happened to you before?" asked Malcolm, who had never run so much as a mile in his entire life.

"No not really. I mean whenever I'm running a marathon, I hit the wall around twenty miles and must dig down deep to finish the race, and that was the feeling I had today. Just dig in and get to it. Amanda and Linda were in real danger."

"Tami, you bounded into camp today like a two-legged gazelle, jumping forty yards at a time. And six or eight feet off the ground. Have you ever, or are you now on anabolic steroids or any other performance enhancing drugs?"

"Absolutely not."

"You would be willing to take a lie detector test to that effect, Tami?"

"Only if necessary. Just remember, whatever a person might take to improve their own personal performance, it is still hard work that is the key to success."

"Do you have anything else to add before we conclude this interview, Tami? I feel like I should be calling you TurboTam or Killer T or something heroic. Hey how about T Pow?"

"Please just call me Tami, and no, I'm not sure what really happened out there. I'm just super glad I was there for the girls."

"Thank you so much for your time. Go rest up, we've got an early start with our statements and all tomorrow morning."

"Sure, or maybe you'd like to get up at four-thirty and come running with me?"

Her offer was predictably declined.

After talking with Tami and she had departed, Malcolm rewound the interview, pressed play, started to introduce himself and state that he and Tami Powers would be taping a conversation to dutifully record the events that had occurred earlier today, June 3, just north of Zion National Park, southern Utah. The interview sounded so good, however, he was afraid he might damage it somehow with a voice over, so he let it be.

––––––––

After a quick stop for morning lattes, Malcolm pulled into the parking lot of the County Precinct in Hurricane at the allotted time of ten a.m. Tami had been up since four, ran eighteen miles, showered, and, as usual, was miles ahead of her sleepyhead buddies. Bill Marks greeted them, had a team present to take individual statements, but saved Tami's account for himself. As a man, he was impressed not only with her natural beauty, but what she had accomplished yesterday. Long auburn hair, flashing green eyes, sparkling white teeth, an attractive yet unique, angular face, natural smile, all while standing a lithe five foot ten. She looked both vulnerable yet deadly efficient at the same time.

"Please state your name, age, and home address." Continuing, the story of her heroics fascinated him, and he wanted every detail she could recall. In her typical style, Tami was modest and self-effacing.

Her account was minimal, i.e.-she saw trouble, felt the urgent need to come to the aid of her co-workers, and simply reacted. Everything happened so quickly she was able to minimize the danger, and subdue the troublemakers, and that was about it.

"But Tami," the sheriff interjected when she finished her story, "you singlehandedly subdued three very dangerous felons. We've had warrants out on all three of these guys for the last six months and you just leap in there, or should I say catapult in there, and put all three of 'em out on the deck. Ho hum, eh?"

"Well, Sheriff, like I said, it was just my reflexes taking over. In addition to being in good shape physically, I practice Tae Kwon Do, which is a defense discipline oriented around footwork. So, it aligns closely with lower body strength and agility."

"But your reflexes are nothing short of miraculous, Tami. You hop-skipped in there, leaping superhuman distances. How is that even possible?"

"I am a professional runner, sir. I am a long-distance runner. When I'm out on the road, I am relaxed but focused. It's hard to explain, but I am hyper aware and yet oblivious at the same time. I am in tune with my body, my immediate environment, and kind of dial everything else out. Unless of course a situation develops like yesterday. Then my reactions became instinctive. Everything intensified as if I was supercharged, and everything else was in slow-motion."

"Has anything of this magnitude ever happened to you before, Tami? And for the record, I would certainly not recommend you injecting yourself in such dangerous situations as this again. That's what we in law enforcement are here for."

"Yes sir, I know that. But we were all just out there in the middle of nowhere, and our group was in extreme danger, so I reacted."

"You reacted so quickly, in such a spectacular fashion, and that was why you were so successful. Your adversaries were overwhelmed before they could respond to you. I have everyone's statements, and the District Attorney will be preparing charges. We are done for now, but you will probably be recalled to testify once the trial starts. If travel is a problem, we can facilitate a zoom arrangement for you."

"Thank you."

"You're welcome, Tami, and I just want you to know that I think you are a spectacular young woman."

"Thank you, sir."

CHAPTER
4

Malcolm led everyone back to the car, taking a minute to speak with Tami on the side and handed her the keys. "Tam, I've got some details to wrap up here in St George, could you drive everyone back, and tell Joe (Malcolm's assistant director) to finish off those last four reshoots we talked about. I will probably be here for a couple of days. When I get back, we can wrap things up as far as being on location."

"Sure Malc."

"By the way, you may want to pick up a couple editions of this morning's paper, You're the headliner."

"Whatever."

———

Malcolm called for an Uber as soon as the van left and headed for the closest Marriott Hotel in St George. He checked in, taking care to grab a paper on his way up. Inside the room, he turned on the TV, looking for a midday news update. Tami covered the first three pages of the paper. The scene of the crime was dissected, the three criminals were profiled, and Tami's rescue was heralded. And heralded and heralded. Malcolm licked his lips in anticipation. He spent the afternoon relaxing at the pool, then had an early dinner so he could go to bed at nine and be up the next morning to start calling the East Coast.

———

The alarm went off at five a.m.; Malcolm turned it off, called room service for a pot of coffee and an order of sweet rolls, waited until five-thirty, and started calling. He had connections with World Broadcasting Corporation at their Headquarters in NYC, and when the receptionist picked up, he asked for Mr. Ben Benson.

After an almost ten-minute wait, Malcolm heard a voice on the line. "Benson here."

"Hi Ben, this is Malcolm Sparrow; I'm so glad I was able to get through to you. Yes, doing well, thanks for asking. Say Ben, I have some of the most extraordinary footage you have ever seen. Might you be interested taking a look?"

"Whatcha ya got, Malcolm?"

Malcolm began to relate Tami's story. "It's local at this point, Ben, but I am directing a feature film down here in southern Utah. Our set was invaded two days ago by three armed desperadoes. Things got very ugly with these louts boozing it up, molesting our female cast members, shooting one of our caters. I have footage on my cell phone of our staff accountant, a young woman whose name is Tami Powers, bounding into camp forty or fifty feet at a leap, six to eight feet off the ground, and personally confronting and subduing these criminals. You have never seen anything like it. This will go big time viral, everyone in the country will be locked onto this woman."

"Sounds interesting, why don't you send me something?"

"Sure, Ben. I want you to know that you are the first person I have contacted. Not only do I have a fifteen-minute film of the action, but I also have an in-depth interview with her. I will send you a sixty-second center-cut clip and, if you like it, I can sell you the video for one million dollars. And this needs to happen today. To reiterate, you are the first person I have reached out to, and if I don't hear back from you by noon, I will pursue other opportunities."

"Just send the clip to my secretary, Malcolm, and I'll take it from there"

"Thanks, Ben; it's on the way. And I'm sure I needn't remind you of my copyright protections."

"Please don't insult my intelligence, Malcolm. I'm going to connect you to Gianna now."

"Sorry Ben, no harm intended, just covering my backside."

"No need. I gotta go."

————

Malcolm's phone rang back in an hour. "We're interested, Malcolm. Where and when exactly did all of this happen?"

"Saturday afternoon. We are shooting a Western northeast of Zion National Park in southern Utah. Our set is in a very rural location, and it just happened, that's why I'm being so urgent with everything. Keep it current, eh?"

"I'm a National News and Operations Director, you dumbass. I know urgent." They discussed the details for another half an hour, and Malcolm had himself a deal.

"Please wire the money in my name to the Chase National Bank on First Street in St. George, Utah. As soon as it hits the bank the video is on the way, and after that, if you are interested in the interview, I'll be at this number."

"The money is on the way, and don't approach anyone about the interview, until we talk again."

"Yes, sir."

————

Malcolm showered, pulled on some clothes, and walked six blocks to the Chase branch. He was the first customer in the doors when they opened at ten a.m. and checked in with the receptionist. She directed him to have a seat in the lobby, and he picked up yesterday's Sunday paper while he was waiting for the manager. He could not get enough of reading about the happening on his very own movie set, and now his footage was going national. The wire was received in about twenty minutes, and all he had to do was forward his video to Ben Benson.

Tami was going to be a star tonight at five-thirty on almost two hundred fifty WBC television news outlets throughout the country.

"How would you like to process your deposit sir?" the manager asked Malcolm.

"Checking is fine."

"That's quite a sum of money, sir, to leave in an uninsured account."

"Thank you for your concern, but I'll be back in London in a week, and my banker will deal with everything then."

"Very well, then, and thank you for banking with Chase."

"You're welcome; have a good day."

And just like that, Malcolm had made himself one million dollars.

It's a good thing she's out in the backwoods, and unaware of what is going on, Malcolm thought. *I've gotta keep her in the dark, until I sell her interview, blame that on a leak by the producers, and then sign on as her Agent. She/we will make a killing. Everybody in the country will want a piece of that woman. No pun intended.*

After a late breakfast of American bangers and eggs, Malcolm packed his meager baggage, checked out and walked downtown to rent an SUV. As he drove out to the camp, his mind was spinning like a merry-go-round on acid. He would strike camp as soon as he got there, but the most important item of business was his handling of Tami, and he knew her to be independent as hell. Also knew she would be upset that a video got released without her permission, and that would be hard to blame on the producers. She would surely know the video came from him personally. Not to mention the interview, which wasn't even released yet.

But Malcolm was also aware that even if WBC didn't want his recording, the tabloid rags would jump on it. He had to be careful to wrap up the movie shoot efficiently but was confident they already had enough footage that his editors would have plenty to work with. He would take some location shots, strike camp and have Joe hand deliver the final tapes back to Burbank. He had already ordered a charter to bus the crew to St. George, from there he would focus his time and energy on taming Tami.

———

Taming Tami was a task Malcolm in his ignorance wasn't remotely qualified for, but having dispatched his other duties, he requested a sit down with her as soon as she was packed to go.

"Hi Tami. You don't need to worry about the bus; you can ride back to St. George with me."

Trying her best to keep her distaste of Malcolm out of her voice, she replied simply, "Whatever."

"Actually, Tam, there have been some developments you should know about."

"Whatever."

"Don't be petulant, my dear; I am here to help you."

"How can you possibly help me, Malcolm dear?"

"Well, there are major events about to happen, and you should be the first to know. Developments that affect you personally and will also bring some major PR to the film we just shot. The producers are very happy about that."

"What are you talking about, Malcolm?"

"Tami, I was in my tent doing some strategizing, when I heard the commotion going on in camp, and as I got dressed and headed toward the meeting area, the three stooges were shooting the place up. Well, I took out my phone and started filming so we would have some evidence to submit to the police, when out of nowhere, you came bounding into the scene, and saved everyone's arses."

"If you took footage of the crime scene, I didn't hear you saying anything to the cops in town about any video yesterday."

"That isn't important, Tami. I did happen to get a call from a friend of mine while I was in St. George, and after I told him the fantastic story of what happened to us, he wanted to see what I had on my phone, so I sent him a copy of the vid. Tami, he released the footage to WBC News, and just before I left town this morning, I got a call saying they were going national with the video. It is going on the news tonight throughout the country."

"What the hell? You just did what you piece of crap?"

"It all just happened so fast, and you are going to be famous, my friend. You will be America's sweetheart, America's heroine!"

"I'm not your sweetheart, and who did you just happen to get a call from?"

"None of that is important, hon. What you did was nothing short of miraculous, and you are going be appreciated by everyone, especially every woman in this country. You saved lives here, Tami, and the American public should know about that. You are fantastic, and America is going to fall in love with you."

"I don't want America to fall in love with me, Malcolm. I want to live my life, run twenty miles every morning, raise my kids, and enjoy my privacy."

"Tami, by tomorrow morning you are going to be inundated with contact from more people than you even knew existed. People are going to want to make movies about what you did, they will want to talk to you from every media market in the country. TMZ will be calling, *Cheers! America* might want you in NYC this week, the offers will be endless. You will need representation Tami, and I am here for you."

"Oh jeez, Malcolm. What did you do? You just happened to talk to someone from WBC News? That is bullshit! You leaked this whole scenario, and now you want to cash in on me? You are a slimeball, and I don't want anything to do with you. Not now, not ever!"

"Tami, Tami, please. You totally misunderstand me. Don't you think what happened here would eventually leak out? You saved the lives of some very intelligent young people in this camp. Do you somehow believe they are going to leave camp, and not say a word about what happened to anyone? Trust me, they can't wait to get out of here and share. You can bet Face Book, TikTok, Instagram are going to light up like Times Square, and you will be the star of the show. You have the wrong take on this whole thing. I love you; we love you; everyone loves you. What you did was superhuman, you saved people from imminent danger in the most fantastic manner Tami, and that will take on a life of its own. Trust me. I am just trying to forewarn you that a lot of attention will be coming your way when we get back to civilization, and I think you might need some professional assistance handling that. Again, please allow me to be here for you. I have an agency agreement right here, please sign it for us."

"Malcolm, Malcolm." Tami breathed out a heavy sigh. "It's not that I don't appreciate everyone, but it is the opposite of what I want for my life. I am as close to a professional career runner as is possible. That is what I do. It is my Zen, and when I run, I am transported to another place. A place of peace, calm and personal power. I wouldn't give that up for all the acclaim in the world. I saw something going on, I reacted to help my sisters, and that's the end of it. Plus, if I ever did benefit from an interview or an appearance or anything of that sort, I would donate all the proceeds to a Children's Hospital somewhere, and I'm not signing anything."

"Tami, please listen to me. You have the most honorable of intentions, and I know and respect your desire for privacy, all I'm trying to tell you is this might be out of your hands. Can I make one suggestion?"

"Like you wouldn't anyway?"

"Let's get back to St. George this afternoon and we can book flights out for the morning. Stay on my dime at the Marriott Hotel and check out the news and see what happens. If you want to split, fine. But just give it one night, won't you please?"

"Okay, Malcolm, one night and tomorrow morning, I am back in LA. I will be home with my family in Pasadena by tomorrow afternoon."

"Great, Tam. Let's just play it by ear, go out and have a nice dinner, and see what's shaking."

"Okay, but for Christ's sake, will you please stop calling me Tam!"

————

Malcolm made sure they were back in St. George around three, so they could freshen up, and watch the evening's early news. He rented the best suite on Marriott's sixth floor, with a room down the hallway for Tami, and ordered a couple bottles of French champagne. He checked his phone for messages and took the time to return a call from Ben Benson.

"Allo Ben, Malcolm here," he said in his most charming British accent, "whazz up?"

"Malcolm, I called to tell you the committee of News Directors went crazy over your video. As I told you before, we are featuring it as our lead item across the country tonight starting at five-thirty p.m. This story is one of those heart warmers that will capture everyone across any market and demographic. The story is so big I took the liberty to call our affiliate show *Cheers! America* and give them a sneak peek. Not only will they profile the story tomorrow afternoon, but they also want Tami and one or two of the girls she saved on Friday's show. They will fly you all first class to New York, limo you to the Plaza Hotel, limo you to the studio. You will have union scale renumeration, and two hundred fifty dollars a day per diem.

"Wow, Ben that sounds fantastic, I can't wait to tell everyone. We are back in civilization now, and they are all coming over to my suite to watch tonight's national news on the tellie. I'll get back to you." Malcolm hung up, and quickly confirmed with Linda and Amanda that they could come. He also reached out to as many of the cast as he could get ahold of that there would be a party in his suite tonight, and that he had delayed the bus's exit back to LA. Also, Malcolm thought, turning down a trip to the Big Apple would be harder for Tami with all the girls here. He called room service back, ordered a banquet bar setup, "and have it here as soon as possible," he barked.

———————

Malcolm Sparrow had one more call to make and rang up his producers. "Yes ma'am, we are all safe, and back in St. George, thank you. I do have some very exciting news for you."

"What is that?"

"So, I took some footage of the incident back at camp and shared it with a friend of mine at WBC News and Streaming. He loved it, and it is going national tonight at five-thirty on the most watched news program in the country."

"That's fantastic Sparrow, and did you get a plug in for our movie?"

"I ain't finished boss! We have been offered the lead slot on *Cheers! America* this Friday. I will be able to plug away at length on their afternoon show."

"Malcolm, you are inspired today. What else have you got?"

"I'm going to need a few pounds sterling in order to pull this off."

"How much, Malcolm?"

"Well, I owe a stipend to my friend for setting things up. I will have to reschedule numerous personal appointments, plus chaperone Tami and three or four more of the staff to New York."

"How much, Malcolm?"

"One hundred grand should cover it."

"One hundred thousand dollars? Are you kidding me?"

"No ma'am. I mean we don't have to go, but where are we going to get this kind of national exposure for free for our movie? Wouldn't it be worth taking some money out of our advertising budget? We will save a ton in the long run, and also get a good, early jump on our release."

"You're probably right. When do you want the money?"

"If you could wire it in my name to the Chase Bank on First Street here in St. George, I will make it all work."

"All right, it'll be there in the morning." And the phone hung up.

What a bunch of jerks, Malcolm thought. Give them the deal of a lifetime on a silver platter, and they want to look up your arse every which way about it.

CHAPTER
5

Most of the crew was hanging out at Malcolm's suite early, so at five twenty he hid them and the banquet bartender in the bedroom, and when Tami arrived, all twenty-five of her admirers jumped out and shouted "Surprise."

Tami was taken aback, began to redden slightly, and glared at Malcolm. But everyone hugged her then queued up to the bar for another drink when Darryl Moore made his intro on WBC's premier evening time slot.

Seated behind the highly respected national news desk, he opened the show with; "Welcome Ladies and Gentlemen, we have an exclusive segment for everyone out there tonight. It's like nothing you have ever seen in real life, real/time before. A violent and intrusive confrontation occurred this weekend, along with a remarkable rescue by an unarmed and extremely brave young woman.

A film cast and crew were shooting in southern Utah, just north of Zion National Park, and they began to proceed with a wrap party on their isolated set last Saturday afternoon. Suddenly three armed, desperate, and wanted criminals rode into their camp on horseback and began to terrorize everyone with obscene threats and handguns. One of the admin team, the staff accountant, was out jogging and came back to camp amid all the chaos. You will be absolutely amazed to see her reaction to the situation. And I want to assure you that the film clip you're about to see has not been altered in any manner."

Malcolm's video began rolling, and after some brief footage show-ing the entry into camp along with their aggressive behavior, it cut to Spud shooting Todd in the foot. Then it continued with their drink-ing and acting like depraved fools. The scenes showing the female cast members under dire duress had been handled delicately by the net-work's editors. They blurred out the X-rated scenes and the exposed body parts of the ordeal, but still portrayed the crux of the situation. And then out of nowhere, Tami bounded into the party like a turbo jet in runners and subdued the situation.

The video had been edited down to two minutes, but the essence of all the happenings had been captured to near perfection with wide angle spans, close ups and professional lighting. Especially concerning Tami, whose superhuman efforts were, of course, the feature of the video. It culminated in a full frontal up shot of her standing in her New Balance jogging shoes, tank top and running skort, with her arms crossed while looking down in disgust at her fallen foes.

———

The crowd watching TV in Malcolm's suite went bananas at the end of the clip. Everyone was shouting and jumping around, as most of the attendees hadn't actually seen Tami kangaroo into camp because they were all lying face down in the dirt. Tami sat stoically on a barstool at the side of the room. Soon enough, the young women were attacking her with hugs and kisses, when Malcolm stood up and raised his hands to quiet everyone.

"Kids, allow me to share some spectacular news. I received a call earlier today from *Cheers! America*, and they have invited us to appear on their show this Friday." And the cheering, fist pumps and jumping up and down started all over again.

"Please, please let me finish. They have offered to fly us first class from Las Vegas to New York City. We will be picked up in a chauf-feured limo and stay at the Plaza Hotel. Also, there will be a healthy per diem. Now, unfortunately not everyone can go, but of course they want Tami, Amanda, Todd and Linda. I can get one more person in, and shouldn't it be Stephie, who was brave enough to risk her own life to administer to Todd while the arseholes were actually still shooting away? What do you say, gang?" Malcolm wrapped up his speech with a broad smile.

The girls were obviously excited, all except Tami. She remained seated on her barstool throne, lonely and aloof, shook her head, and swore to herself quietly.

Malcom again shushed everyone, and asked, "Are we going?"

"Of course," the women shouted, but Malcolm looked over at Tami and saw her lack of excitement. Just the opposite.

"Tami?" he asked.

"You all go on without me," she said. "I've got to be getting home."

The ladies murmured, and Malcolm addressed them as a group. "I'm afraid this is an all-or-nothing situation. If Tami doesn't go, then the deal is off, so I guess you'll just have to convince her."

Tami shot Malcolm a death look, and tried to make it to the restroom, but the ladies were having none of that. "Please Tami, please Tami. Please." This went on for twenty minutes, until Tami finally weakened and said yes on one condition.

"What is that?" asked Malcolm.

"I want to be sure everyone is healthy after this ordeal, both physically and emotionally. If any of the girls or Todd needs any kind of therapy, I believe the producers owe it to them. And I will not consider going if there are any personal issues to be resolved."

Again, Malcolm spoke up. "How ironic that we were shooting a film about desperadoes, when three desperadoes invaded us. And because of them, and this beautiful woman here," motioning to Tami, "we have a unique opportunity to go to NYC. We have the chance of a lifetime to promote our very own work. To share our stories and benefit from our labors and possibly advance not only our movie but own our cinematic careers. This is a rare gift indeed, and I hope we make the most of our opportunity. Are any of the concerns Tami has so graciously addressed a problem that would interfere with this opportunity of a lifetime for any of us that are present here today?"

Of course, Malcolm was surreptitiously recording the audio of the gathering in his hotel suite.

A chorus of "No's" answered Malcolm's question, and he continued on. "I think we all realize that however unfortunate our situation was, especially for Todd, it was an isolated event, which the odds of occurring were probably over a million to one. I assure you that Todd's medical bills will be taken care of, as well as any disability compensation due him, and if anyone else has any need for assistance, or counseling please bring it to my attention now. No? Ladies and gentlemen, it sounds to me as if we are going to New York City!" And a chorus of cheers and nods of approval erupted at Malcolm's unofficial cast party.

Of course, Malcolm would not only be advancing his career, but also his bank account as his contract included a written addendum to share in a percentage of the movie's proceeds.

"And I am also happy to announce that in addition to receiving union scale for our time in New York, there will be a one-thousand-dollar bonus paid to us by our producers, for your support in promoting our movie while on the CA show."

Everyone was, of course, even happier now, especially Malcolm and the producers. Everyone except Tami, who was fuming, and Todd, who was wondering how he was supposed to navigate NYC on crutches and big, gray protective boots on both feet.

Tami grabbed Malcolm and dragged him into the bedroom of his suite. "I will go to New York with you this one time, mainly because of your assurance that everyone will be taken care of properly, but don't you dare put me in this kind of situation ever again. I will walk out of your sorry life, and you will never see me again."

Malcolm hung his head and stepped forward as if to give Tami a hug, but she was gone. Long gone.

———

It was Wednesday late afternoon, and the Alaska jet liner hit the runway smoothly at Kennedy International. Of course, there was a sign holding driver at baggage claim, and an executive assistant from *Cheers! America* waiting for them inside a slick, black stretch limousine.

"Welcome to New York City," she purred, while opening a chilled bottle of Nicolas Feuillant champagne and pouring a glass for her guests. "I hope you enjoy this selection; it is for our VIP guests only." They did.

After fighting their way over the Queensboro Bridge, and on to towards Central Park and the Plaza Hotel, the show's aide informed them of their itineraries: "This evening is yours to enjoy. I have printed out a list of recommended restaurants. There are also some club suggestions for those who wish to party and/or a menu of entertainment opportunities available to you. I have envelopes containing cash for your per diems which I will hand out.

Tomorrow, we have a mandatory briefing at our Times Square studio. The limo will be here to pick you up at eleven AM, please be in the lobby at ten forty-five. Friday, the limo will bring you back to the studio for makeup, prior to airing the show. You are the only live guests in the appearance queue.

That's about it. Once the show has aired, your flights are booked back to Las Vegas on Friday evening. Should you decide to extend your stay, you must reschedule your own itinerary, and procure your lodging. I'm sure the Plaza would be delighted to accommodate you if they have rooms available. Please make your decisions as soon as possible. Also, all CA guests receive a twenty-five percent room discount at the hotel. That about it, I'll see you at tomorrow's briefing if there are no more questions. Fine then, welcome to New York City."

Malcolm had plans to visit friends, Tami was meeting a NYC marathon buddy of hers. The ladies and Todd were going out for Italian somewhere around Times Square and maybe look for a club after that.

Tami was lying low, but Malcolm didn't care. He had gotten her here and been paid handsomely for his efforts. He had begun to realize that Tami's presence on CA was going to greatly reduce the selling price of his personal interview with her, but what the bloody hell he thought. I'm up 1.1 mil and staying at the Plaza, so life isn't all bad.

————

After spending an hour on the phone with her family, Tami stopped in at the Frick Museum for a brief visit, then continued to her friend's condo on the Upper East Side. She was excited to renew acquaintances, especially since her buddy was trying to convince her to attempt to qualify for the upcoming Universal Games. She wasn't personally persuaded she was ready, however, with all the dedication and determination anyone would ever need and having run her best ever time this year in the Boston (3:03); her friend knew she just needed a little more prodding.

As Tami Ubered up Fifth Avenue by Central Park, she savored the memories of her NYC marathon experiences and couldn't wait to get back there for an extended run. She would have a pasta dinner with Anne Marie Stein tonight, and they would hit it, like seasoned running pros, for twenty some miles all over the park in the morning.

Maybe Anne Marie, a long time New Yorker and a willowy thirty-seven-year-old divorcee, with a pronounced New Yauk accent could help Tami understand what was happening to her life. Where had this superpower suddenly come from, and did it have plans to stick around?

And for how long? Would it affect her normal running? Would it affect her qualifying? Would it enhance her race times? She desperately needed help to cope with her feelings, questions and anxieties.

The last thing she wanted was to be turned into some kind of super freak by the national media. Anne Marie met her at the door, they hugged for a long interlude, and Tami began to cry softly in her pal's arms.

As the two friends shared a home cooked meal, they talked nonstop. At the end of the evening, the BFFs and marathon runners concluded that her intervention was an isolated event. Probably created in equal parts adrenaline, emotion, stress and maybe even the thin mountain air.

Tami felt a lot more comfortable appearing on national TV after talking it over with a trusted friend and confidant. This evening helped even more than her daily chats back home with her husband and gave her fragile confidence a boost going forward. I'll be okay she thought when they parted company.

She and Anne Marie agreed to meet in the morning at five-thirty outside the Plaza so they could run the Park. Then Tami would use her per diem to treat for lattes and breakfast.

Dawn broke clear and was supposed to warm into the high eighties, but they were starting early enough to avoid the heat and humidity. Anne Marie was on time and due to the early hour found a parking space. The women stretched their hamstrings for couple of minutes and took off at a brisk pace. This was heaven for Tami, and she felt strong as they found the southeast entrance to the park and headed north up the cobblestone pathway.

Tami and Anne Marie were jogging easily through the light foot traffic, in that beautiful weightless gait of experienced runners, when their trail merged onto Fifth Avenue. They were still traveling north, and about halfway past the grand steps of the Metropolitan Museum of Art complex, approaching 87th Street, when suddenly a blood curdling scream split the quiet morning air. Stopping and turning towards the commotion, the scream sounded again this time even louder. The sparse early morning crowd had also turned to the monolithic apartments, and the cell phones began to come out.

Looking up at the sizeable building before her, Tami saw a woman and what looked like a two-year-old child framed by their apartment window on maybe the twelfth floor, both of them screaming at the top of their lungs. As Tami stared, the woman was desperately holding onto the leg of a squirming child. Tami realized the toddler, left unattended momentarily, had somehow managed to unlatch a living room window. Proceeding to climb through the unscreened opening, the baby was now about fall to their death when they were grabbed just in time by a caregiver. But suddenly the woman's grip loosened, and as if in slow motion, the screaming child began to fall to the cold, hard, filthy cement below.

Tami felt a surge of adrenaline, her legs strengthened and the next thing she knew, she was doing her leaping/bounding thing, catty corner over a startled car and driver, and across Fifth Avenue from where she and Anne Marie stood. Boom, boom, and just like that Tami caught the stricken, tumbling child in her arms about waist high and cradled the baby to her breast.

There was dead silence on the street, which doesn't happen very often in New York City.

Spontaneously some applause started slowly, and then everyone began cheering. Anne Marie ran to Tami and the baby and held them in her arms, while the screaming continued. More phones on the street were filming.

Tami was overcome with emotion, Anne Marie was crying, and then some people in the crowd who had apparently seen this week's WBC News show, realized who had caught the baby, and started chanting "Tami, Tami, Tami." The loud, throbbing chorus went on for a long time.

CHAPTER
6

Tami and her crew could hear the applause and white noise as they waited in the green room of *Cheers! America's* state-of-the-art studios in Times Square. The girls were ready to go with excited anticipation. Malcolm was licking his chops at being in front of the cameras, and kept reminding everyone to plug their movie. Tami would rather have been at a public hanging than about to face a national TV audience. Especially after yesterday's event which had made all the news shows in New York on Thursday evening and did little to help an attempted low-key approach to her newly found celebrity status.

She and Anne Marie had extracted themselves from the near fatal accident scene yesterday morning, but not before she had had to be grilled by the NYPD rep. Then a NY Times reporter grabbed her for another interview, after he had procured some footage of the rescue from a crowd member. Again, Tami was not a very exciting interview candidate. Finally, she and Anne Marie finished their run in silence and returned straight to AM's condo. They had to drive past the entrance to the Plaza to get turned around, and Tami was aghast to see a clutch of reporters and a couple of news vans outside the hotel hoping for an exclusive with the new media star.

The women got back to the condo, Anne Marie popped a couple of Diet Cokes, and Tami collapsed on the couch in a daze. She was teary again, asking Anne Marie, "what's happening to me?"

After a couple hours of decompressing and trying to rationalize a life that was quickly moving into the fast lane, Anne Marie, never one to mince words, summarized their time together as best she could.

"Tami: girlfriend, I believe life as you know it has changed. You have a supernatural gift, and the good news is you are using your abilities for the greater good. You have already saved multiple lives, and you could rescue many more. So put your big girl panties on, and deal with it, *capiche?*" Tami, overwhelmed and confused as she was, still appreciated the wisdom of Anne Marie's words.

———

After talking with her husband that night, who agreed with Anne Marie, she went to bed, slept fitfully, got up at five-thirty a.m., and ran for two hours on the hotel's treadmill. Back in her room, she showered, meditated for an hour, and ordered a goat cheese omelet and a side of fruit from room service. She dressed for success (Tami style) and now found herself sitting in the CA green room waiting apprehensively to face America. Her mind was spinning in otherworldly angst.

———

Tobin, Michelle and Mara, who was sitting in for a vacationing Garett, took turns welcoming their guests to the casual set stage of the show and did their best to make everyone comfortable. The conversation started with a summary of the events on the movie set, which was a designed approach rather than focusing the whole segment on Tami. After Malcolm and the girls had related their stories, comprised mostly of the young women praising Tami, and Malcolm pandering his soon to be released masterpiece of a B-grade movie, Robin turned her attention to Tami. Sitting quietly and suppressing a nervous twitch, Tami turned a smiling face to Robin and her interview began.

"Ladies and gentlemen, in case you are one of the few people who might have missed it, we are going to run the clip again that has gone viral from WBC News, across the internet and social media, of Tami's spectacular intervention in the Utah high desert."

The two-minute video ran, and Robin asked, "Tami, how can words describe what has happened to you in the last couple of weeks? Maybe

Malcolm should shelve his current project and make a movie about you. Not only did you display extraordinary courage out there in the badlands, but then you come to the City for our program and create another amazing miracle. Saving a child's life and that family from devastating tragedy. How do you do what you do, young woman? Not only the undaunting courage you display, but the miraculous physical talent."

"God has given me a rare gift, Tobin. I don't know how long it will last, and it is nothing I can overtly control. But when I am in the face of danger, which has happened twice now, and both times while I have been out running, my body simply reacts to rectify whatever danger is present. I am not afraid, I am simply hyper alert, and react accordingly.

Things happen so quickly that whatever the danger, it is over before I even realize I am involved. I believe that the strength I have acquired through running, both mental and physical strength, has equipped me to just react instinctively. But I am very glad that I have been able to be a positive force. While I wish no personal gain or notoriety, if I can continue to be a sanguine influence in society, well sign me up."

The whole set was quiet for a moment, reflecting on the power of Tami's statement, when Michelle Strong finally offered up, "Tami, I know many NFL teams who would love to sign you in an instant, and I would be happy to represent you."

"Michelle, I am honored by your offer but the imminent danger there, would be to my physical person out on the field with those behemoths."

Mara interjected, and asked Tami to share with their audience a little about her personal life.

"I was born and raised on a farm in rural Idaho and Tami continued her personal mantra, ending with, I love my family, and love to run. I run early every morning and have run in almost a hundred marathons in every state in the union."

"How old are your children?"

"They are five, ten, thirteen, and seventeen."

"How in the world do you find the time to manage all of that?"

"Competitive running teaches one the management of space and time. I have applied those same principles to managing mine and my children's lives. Running is my passion and my private time. It is when I reflect on things, when I organize and plan my life, when I rejoice to be alive and create all the positive energy I can for my life and my family. It is also essential to master time management in order to run a systematic household. My life is synchronized from the moment I get up in the morning until late in the evening after dinner. My older children are big enough now to help when I am away running in a marathon on weekends."

"Do you plan to continue working in your professional field of accounting, or will you just work parttime around the tax season now?"

"Oh no, I will work full time out of my home office. I have a roster of clients who keep me busy."

The esteemed hosts were again at a loss of how to relate to this extraordinary woman. Finally, Tobin recovered to ask Tami about her feelings and experiences of late. Namely, her abnormal feats of physical strength, acrobatics and bravery."

"Tobin, I do not like or approve of the term abnormal. I am not a freak of nature, merely, as I have stated earlier, when I'm running, and am confronted with something dangerous, it takes me no more than a nano second to compute what is happening, then my mind and body merely react. I can feel my legs power up, feel an intense energy surge through my body. I instinctively respond with lightning speed which allows me to do what is necessary in split second time. It is as if the rest of the world is operating in very slow motion. That's about all I know to date. Is this temporary? Will other runners somehow acquire this talent or ability. I don't know."

"Tami, I keep saying the word extraordinary, but it has been an extraordinary pleasure to have you and your team on this show. I hope you are willing to come back periodically and give us updates on your activities and continued success. By the way, are you still living in Idaho?"

"No ma'am, our family has moved to the Los Angeles area to better facilitate my running and my husband's career. I would look forward to coming back for a visit. Also, thank you very much for your hospitality, for providing a forum for me to share these newly personal experiences, and for giving us on the film crew more time to spend together."

————

That was it, and Tami and friends segued off stage right. They were back in the green room and refreshments were offered at a bar and buffet table. Tami helped herself to a Diet Coke, and Anne Marie came backstage. She and Tami hugged. "You were beautiful, girl. You did very, very well, I am so proud of you." She met the rest of the cast, except Malcolm. He was already into the scotch, and in a snit about the snub his movie had gotten.

————

Tami and Anne Marie went out for an early dinner. "We might as well eat at the Plaza; they have been so pleasant on this trip," Tami said.

"I am so damn proud of you girl," Anne Marie said once they were seated. "You ran an emotional marathon today, and when you hit the wall, you ran right through it. I want you to hear me really good, will you listen up for just a minute?"

"Yes ma'am."

"I have a bachelor's in business management from Tufts University and a master's degree in marketing from NYU. I would love to represent you; I feel like you will be totally inundated without an agent. If you don't want to work with me, please hire someone you know well, has business management experience and you trust implicitly.

I'm not interested in churning you, or making money, I am well taken care of from my divorce and my client base. But you are going to need someone to front for you. The money you are going to make from the movie alone will pay for your kids to go to any school in the world. I don't need to live in New York, I can move to LA. But I will keep my NY contacts functioning. There is enough action in LA to keep you busy for a long time. Why don't you go home and bang the shit out of your old man, take your kids to Disneyland or something and think about it. This thing is absolutely uncontained, and I am here for you, Tami."

"What movie are you talking about?"

"The one they are going to want to make about your life."

"Oh, that one. I'll think about it, and thanks for your support and advise."

"You're welcome, and please do. You are a real live super heroine woman, not some bullshit cartoon character. Your potential is world changing. It is over the top. The big top, so you ponder that one for a few days, my love. You conquer evil or adversity single handedly, and without any bat mobile or spider outfit, yeah?" If I were you, I would move to a gated community or a high rise building with security. People will be knocking on your door, and not just good people. There are a lot of douchebags out there."

"Trust me, my mind is running a three-minute mile right now. I just want to get home and be with my family and decompress. I'll call you,"

"Please do, and if I can help you, I will be there in a nano second. T-Pow."

"If we are going to work together, please just call me Tami."

CHAPTER
7

Tami packed, put on an oversized pair of sunglasses and a Covid-style face mask, and heard her phone beep as a call came in. She checked her screen and deleted what was the third incoming from Malcolm that morning and went down to the lobby. After checking out, she jumped in an Uber with Amanda and Stephanie, and they headed for Kennedy. Tami was flying direct to LA; the other two young women, aspiring actresses, were connecting in LA to Seattle. Linda was staying longer, spending time with some family members who had driven over from Pittsburg. Malcolm was extending his visit to the Big Apple for business considerations.

Their flight was long, if uneventful, Tami had preloaded some psychological research sites on her iPad and spent part of the time reading about feats of hysterical strength and the hypothalamus gland. I am in excellent physical shape, she thought, with a remarkably resilient physical frame and joints, so maybe my amygdala is enlarged or something. That was the summation of all she could conclude about her ability to bound about like a turbo charged cheetah.

A little before eleven in the afternoon EST, Malcolm stepped into one of three elevators and pressed the button for the twentieth floor in the WBC Production Offices on West 61st Street. He checked the time on his phone and was pleased to be five minutes early for a one-on-one sit down with Ben Benson.

"Good morning, Sir," Malcolm said in greeting, as he was shown into an executive meeting room by the receptionist.

"Gianna, could you please get us a couple of coffees? Thanks. Malcolm, you take anything with that?"

"Cream and sugar, please."

"My friend, you're looking reasonably well, how's the city treating you?"

"Thanks, having a time of it. What's on your mind?"

"Business opportunity for you. What we think is important enough to call a meeting with you on a Saturday morning," and Ben took a sip of his black, free trade coffee.

"Always like those, what're you thinking about?"

"Well Malcolm, in the first place thank you for bringing Tami Powers to us. The response and ratings we have received from showing your video have been sensational. And after we were able to air Tami's second event, the rescue here in NYC, we are about to offer her a unique package. We would like to sign her to a futures type contract, whereby she is exclusively connected and contracted to us here at WBC. Can you deliver her to us, Malcolm?"

There was a pause in the conversation, and Malcolm's body language shifted perceptibly. "Ben, I am in negotiations to represent her, but currently, we do not have a formally signed agreement."

"Malcolm, I'm sure you are acutely aware of the future earning potential of this woman."

"That's obvious, Ben, however she is an intelligent, active and fiercely independent young professional. On top of that, she has no commercial ambition. She's content to do little more than maintain her current lifestyle. But I am continuing to work her from the angle of how much she could contribute to society, charities of her choice, etc."

"We all thought, and you had given me the impression that she was already signed."

"Could happen this afternoon, Ben."

"By all means, let me know as soon as it does." With that, Ben Benson stood up, took a last sip of coffee, told Malcolm Gianna would show him out and excused himself. Malcolm slumped in place, uttered a silent curse at independent women, and took out his cell phone. His call to Tami went to message, Gianna knocked softly on the thick glass doors, and Malcolm's bowls tightened as he knew his very profitable window of opportunity had just evaporated.

––––––––

The Alaska Jetliner touched down without incident in the middle of Los Angeles' massive airport, and Tami's family was waiting for her outside of her exit door. She was so excited to see them, and hugs went all around. They loaded up, and Tami asked her older daughter to sit in the front seat with Dad, so she could schmooze in back with the younger kids.

"Mom, you're a star," they chorused. "We saw you on TV and everything."

"Oh, that wasn't anything special. I feel better and am having more fun here with you right now." Tami's phone kept ringing, so she just shut it off.

But everyone was still very excited and wanted to hear all about her adventures. It was no family secret how strong and disciplined their mom was, and yet, the whole of last week had been over the top for all of the Powers family.

While the younger children jostled to be the closest to her, they all chatted and she told them every lurid detail, finally, Tami was able to turn the conversation around to their friends, teachers and activities. She thanked everyone for holding down the fort while she was gone, and then they stopped at a Ghirardelli Ice Cream shop for cones. Big ones.

Back at home in Pasadena/La Canada, an affluent suburb in the northwest corner of greater Los Angeles, Tami almost cried when

Scott pulled into the driveway of their Western-style ranch home. The large corner lot was unchanged, but well-tended. She couldn't wait to get up the walkway, through the double, arched alder wood front doors and decompress.

This home was her comfort zone, and often the large rectangular window boxes in the family room called her to their sunny, cushioned enclave that looked out over the back garden. Here she could work on her laptop, relax and recharge. It was the home and hearth she had missed so much. Not to mention the people inside it. "I'm back to earth," Tami thought to herself, as everyone began settling themselves, had a snack, and started getting ready for tomorrow. Finally, she and her husband were alone. They embraced, opened a bottle of wine, and began a chat that lasted well into the night.

Scott Powers, Tami's ruggedly handsome, scientist husband was becoming more fully comprehensive of what was happening in his wife's world, and how that related to his own reality. They sat casually, semi facing each other on the soft leather sofa while he gave his love a foot massage, and she spoke at length of what/how she had been able to accomplish on her trip to the Big Apple. I.e., concerning her newly realized supernatural power, and how that new status might affect themselves and the children. They talked about the future, safety and security of their home and family. About how the kids had coped in her absence, etc., finally they went upstairs, and Tami fell into the sleep of the dead.

———

The next morning was a Saturday, Tami had already risen at five a.m. and jogged around the Rose Bowl complex five times. She knew she could be back in time to cook breakfast, but she was resolute as ever that her lifestyle would stay status quo. It was hard earned, well defined, and she would fight to the death to maintain it. She loved her family more than life itself, they were her foundation, her rock, her essence, and were worth fighting for. They in turn loved her, and that was all she needed and wanted in life, except for providing for her kids, and getting up early to run like a well-oiled machine. If there was an opportunity or challenge presented through her new gifts, it would have to be compatible with her core values. Period.

———

Back home, Tami shucked off her running clothes, freshened up, and climbed back in bed to see if Scott was awake yet. They spent some marital play time and dozed off together. She got back up, showered again, went downstairs and was stirring pancake batter for a late breakfast when her phone rang.

<h1 style="text-align:center">CHAPTER</h1>

Tami looked at her screen and saw a call coming in with a WBC News ID from a New York area code. She was ambivalent about taking the call, but was so appreciative of their hospitality in New York, she picked up and said, "Hello, this is Tami."

"Good morning, Tami, this is Ben Benson calling from New York City. We had so much fun hosting your segment on *Cheers* this past week, I wanted to personally call and thank you for taking the time to visit with us back here on the East Coast."

"Gosh, Mr. Benson, it was a lot of fun being back in the city again, and I wanted to thank you anyway for taking care of us so well. I was apprehensive at first to be in this kind of spotlight, but I got over it as your staff put us completely at ease. The young women from our cast were out of their minds with excitement to be on your show. They will never forget their experience."

"Tami, and please call me Ben, I am going to be at our WBC West Coast headquarters this next Tuesday, and I was hoping I could give you a quick tour of our facilities there, and we could grab a bite of lunch, either in our facilities or somewhere close?"

"That could work, Ben, might I bring my daughter with me? She's seventeen and was absolutely gaga that I was your guest on *Cheers*."

"We'd be happy to offer her a glimpse into the television, news and variety industry. Maybe, she might even be interested in an internship at some level?"

"She would be excited to spend some time over there for sure."

"Tami, we want you to know how much we respect your values and the beautiful relationship you have with your family. What I'm trying to communicate, is that we would very much enjoy discussing an ongoing relationship with you, on your terms of course, and perhaps we can break down some options on our visit."

"What is a good time for you on Tuesday, Ben?"

"I'm at your disposal, Tami."

"We will meet you at WBC Headquarters in North Hollywood, at ten AM. It's just down the 210 freeway from us."

"I look forward to meeting you personally. Drive into the main gate, and security will have a VIP packet ready for you."

"Thank you."

Ben hung up and called his Director of Human Resources at home. "Rachael, sorry to bother you on a Saturday afternoon, but I need a complete background file on Tami Powers, her husband, her family, where they live, how much money they make, where their kids go to school, her college GPA's, the whole nine yards, and I need it by Monday morning. This is a top priority project. Get one of your best people in there now, and then give them Monday off if you want. But I'm counting on your team to gather as much information for me as you can. My flight leaves for the West Coast Monday morning, and it will give me some reading material on the plane."

"I'm on it, BB."

"Thanks."

After a raucous breakfast with the fam, plans were made to spend the day hiking in Griffith Park, followed by dinner at their favorite Mexican Restaurant on La Cienega. While everyone was getting ready to go, Tami stole away, and called Anne Marie. She related her conversation with Ben Benson, and Anne Marie translated that she was probably going to get an offer.

"What should I do?"

"First of all, I am going to scan and email you a standard representation contract. It renumerates me at ten percent of your non-accounting income, plus extraordinary expenses. I already told you that if you needed me to move to SoCal, it would be on my dime. Just listen to what Ben has to say, and then you and I can discuss it Monday evening. I don't think he would be offering Carrie an internship if he wasn't going to make a move. Sign our contract, shoot it back to me, and tell him you want to talk it over with your representative and we will get back to him. Thank him for his offer and let him know you are grateful for his interest in you and your family."

"Will do. Carrie is going to be thrilled."

"That's great, but don't sign anything until we talk again."

"Got it."

———

Tenacious wanker that he was, Malcolm tried Tami another half a dozen times without getting through to her on Saturday. By this time Tami had blocked his calls. Early in the afternoon, he went into the Plaza Bar downed a couple of Bloody Mary's, and idly twirled the swizzle stick from his drinks while his mind digested the last couple of days. Although he had made over a million dollars on the side in the last week, he was depressed and annoyed that he had been unable to sign Tami. I should have put more pressure on her back at camp while I was interviewing her, he thought. Even more so, he was annoyed that Ben had not given him a little more time to grab her. How much bloody money did I make WBC, and Ben cuts me out of the deal like I'm a leper.

Checking out of the Plaza, he marched his roller bag over to Fifth Ave, turned right, then left on 57th, and walked into a Tiffany's Jewelry Store. Half an hour later, he strolled back onto the street wearing a $125,000.00 solid gold Rolex Cosmograph Daytona on his left wrist. That began to raise his spirits.

————

Malcolm had decided to spend a couple more days in NYC and see if he could do anything with his recorded interview with Tami before he had to head back to LA and finish supervising the editing of his film. He hailed a cab up to West 66th and checked into The Phillips Club. The PC is a residence hotel, great location across the street from the Lincoln Center, smallish, nicely substantial, and much more affordable than the Plaza. He stashed his bag and decided to go out and do a little bit of carousing on this sunny Saturday afternoon. Buying the Rolex had been a bonus, but he was still digesting his remorse at blowing the Tami deal. Call it his anal DNA, but the million plus bucks he had deposited into the bank, was a mere pittance compared to what he could have made had Tami inked with him. That drew a gray pall over his afternoon.

He took off walking south on Columbus, was distracted by the sights, sounds, and people watching on one of New York's busier thoroughfares. There was literally not a street in the city that didn't have some nugget of entertainment value. Do you ever hear of people walking the streets of downtown Los Angeles he thought? Soon enough he was in Hell's Kitchen and thirsty again. Looking around, he spotted a joint across the street, he walked over, and opened the door to Luca's Ristorante on 52nd St and Columbus. He had walked about fourteen city blocks and was a little winded. It took Tami about ten miles of running uphill to even think about being short of breath.

————

Luca's was classic NYC Italian. It was a deep rectangular layout, with a Maître D's stand inside the doorway, then there was seating on the right side of the room, and the front of the left side. The kitchen was located at the back of the right side of the eatery. The bar was tucked at the rear of the left side of the darkly paneled room. It sported half a dozen cocktail tables and a dozen barstools. The restrooms were in the back corner past the bar space. Malcolm strolled in and grabbed a seat on one of the stools. It was three forty in the afternoon, and Luca's was maybe a third full. Happy Hour didn't start until four.

"Bombay Sapphire with a splash of tonic, please."

The barkeep spun a monogrammed cocktail napkin down on the bar and poured Malcolm's drink. He was sitting right in front of the bar's well, so all the barman had to do once he poured the drink was reach out and set the cocktail down. The Sapphire tasted delicious, and Malcolm's mood began to elevate. He looked around the room like you do in any new watering hole. The back bar was an ornate affair of carved oak, with a mirror behind the lineup of liquor bottles. He peeked around the bottles, checked himself out, and decided he was a bloody dashing bloke. There were numerous framed photographs on the walls of famous Italians prizefighters; Rocky Marciano, Primo Carnera, Jake LaMotta, etc.

A handsome free-standing glass fronted cabinet of aging wine stock stood against the back wall, and some photos of Italian soccer teams and their standout players filled up the rest of the space. The lighting was low, his barstool had a padded seat and back and was very comfortable. He settled in, sipped his drink and in half an hour, ordered another one.

A baseball game played idly on TV over the bar, and a soccer game on another one. He absentmindedly watched the soccer ball being punted back and forth and wondered how anyone in their right mind could get excited about the sport. It was so boring compared to a riveting afternoon in the cinema. People were dribbling in and out of the bar, and around five, things started picking up.

Just as he was about to leave, a thirtyish couple seated themselves on his left. Italian to the core, and apparently regulars, as the barman automatically sat a couple of drinks in front of them, and a few minutes later, brought an order of crostini, with bruschetta, some prosciutto and grilled bell peppers. They were a handsome duo, dressed upscale casual for a night out together. The woman sat next to Malcolm, and her dark hair was pulled back with clips. She had olive skin, a Roman nose, and full, brightly painted lips. She smelled like lilac or something good.

Malcolm ordered another Gin and Tonic and asked the barkeep to make it a double. His drink came, and a food menu was placed next to his tumbler. He continued to sip, starting to feel the premium liquor's effect, and tried to decide what to do for dinner. He was in the mood for a good steak and took his phone out to google some locations. And right then another couple came and took the last two barstools on the other side of Malcolm.

A well-appointed Italian couple of course, stepping out on a Saturday night, and Malcolm made little effort to disguise his British superiority by giving them an unsubtle once over. The man was six feet tall and burly, with thick, hairy forearms. His wife also sat down next to Malcolm. She was lighter skinned than her counterpart to his left, but also olive complected. She had on a sleeveless cocktail dress of which she was pleasantly spilling over the bodice and sported a beautiful rock on the wedding finger of her left hand. They got the same treatment as the other couple, a glass of white wine for her, and something dark and on the rocks for him. Malcolm was checking the woman out in the barback mirror until their eyes met and she looked away. Ten minutes later Malcolm slightly slurred his words as he ordered another double. The barkeep looked at him, and said "okay pal, but you need to order some food."

"Bring me some calamari then," Malcolm said. He sipped his fresh drink when it came and was getting bored as well as slip sliding nicely down the road to alcohol induced oblivion. Malcolm was six feet tall, and while he was slender, he had always been able to hold his liquor well. As he waited for his appetizer, he picked up his cell and made a reservation at Morton's Steakhouse, which was only a mile or so across town. His plate of food finally came, and just in time, as his blood alcohol level was now well beyond where it should have been.

Suddenly, the man on Malcolm's left looked across him at the gentleman on his right and said, "Hey, wasn't I in the 101st Airborne with you?"

The two men got up, stood a few feet behind the bar, and began to reconnect. This left a bored and tipsy Malcolm sitting between two attractive women who were both ignoring him.

Malcolm turned to the woman on his right and introduced himself. "Allo, I'm Malcolm Sparrow." The woman raised her eyebrows and turned her head to discourage any further conversation, but Malcolm would not be detoured.

"I am a movie director, perhaps you saw me on the *Cheers! America* show yesterday?"

No answer. Mick, the barman, was trying to catch Malcolm's eye and was vigorously shaking his head. No, no, no was the message. Everyone saw him but Malcolm.

"Reason I ask, is because I am an international connoisseur of cinematic beauty, and I think you are spectacular."

No answer. The barman was now preoccupied at the other end of the bar.

Malcolm reached over and took the woman's hand. She stiffened. "Take the female hand for example, some learned men have said the mere touch of a beautiful woman's hand will open a man's heart." He began to caress her hand. "Do you model, by the way?"

The woman pulled her hand away and turned her head again.

Malcolm, warming to the task and feeling no pain, placed his right arm around the back of her barstool, and reaching out with his left hand, gently turned her face back to his own. "The reason I ask, is that you are exquisite, and in a most classical manner. You are the paradigm of feminine beauty."

The woman again jerked away again, but not before her husband interrupted the conversation with his war buddy and stared in disbelief at Malcolm. He nudged his new friend, who had already been aware of the situation.

The married woman got off her barstool and started walking back to the ladies' room, her high heels clicking rhythmically on the tile floor. Everyone but Malcolm was aware of the tension in the bar. He was so oblivious he naively thought this was also a good time for him to visit the Loo. He extricated himself from his barstool perch with maximum effort and began wobbling back to the men's room.

The two Italian gentlemen who had shared their military training time, some of the most physical training the armed forces can offer, were also currently connected to several different Italian fraternal organizations in and around the city. Organizations that command respect. They looked at each other, turned as one, and followed Malcolm to the men's room.

As they entered the latrine, the gentleman whose wife had been accosted grabbed Malcolm by the neck and hurled him against the back wall of the two-stall room, while his partner latched the heavy door closed. As Malcolm turned slowly, dazed by the unexpected attack, he received a crisp sucker punch to the gut. This caused him to begin regurgitating about half of the expensive liquor in his belly, and as he was about to puke, the muscular Italian grabbed Malcolm by the scruff of the neck, shoved his upper body toward the urinal and flushed it on Malcolm's head while he was vomiting. To say the least, this all but destroyed Malcolm's buzz. The Italians had a belly laugh together.

"Hey lover boy, let's get a look at that nice watch of yours," Italian gent#1 requested.

While Malcolm was now dripping wet from the shoulders up and his mind was still foggy, he was conscious enough to realize his dire predicament. He slowly took off his expensive new watch and handed it to IG#2. Of course, a couple of made guys who steal things for a living recognize value when they see it, and IG#1 took the watch, looked it over, and put in on his wrist.

"Tell you what we're going to do, lover boy. Thank you for giving me this beautiful watch of yours. Now me and my buddy are going to finish beating the shit out of you, and then we're gonna throw you in that stall back there. Then we are gonna to go get our wives and go out for a nice dinner, and we don't ever want to see your sorry ass again. You unnerstand me?"

Malcolm, still groggy, but clearing, had the presence of mind to say, "Wait a minute, please. I intended no insult, and I have something for you that is far more valuable than my watch."

"What is it?"

"My name is Malcolm Sparrow; I am an international film director. I apologize if I got out of line back there in the bar, but my mind is a virtual whirlwind of activity. I am evaluating talent at all times. You might have seen me on the *Cheers! America* show yesterday."

"Whatta you got for us, pal?" IG#1 said without a clue what Malcolm was talking about.

"Have you heard of Tami Powers, the crazy woman who can jump around and save people? Everybody is talking about her."

"Yeah, what about her?"

"I have an original interview with her on tape that is worth thousands and thousands of dollars. I have an appointment on Monday at one in the afternoon with the national *Probe* tabloid magazine in Brooklyn. They are going to buy my tape. You can come with me, and I'll split the money with you, if you just give my watch back. Sorry if I was a bid obtuse with your wife, I've been drinking all day."

IG#1 and IG#2 paused and looked at each other. Their wheels were turning. Didn't this clown just get major stupid and earn a severe beating, or might he have something even bigger for them? If they could get a cash payout from Brooklyn, they both knew they would keep the watch anyway.

"Where you stayin' at, Malcolm?"

"The Phillips Club on West 66th."

"Okay, tell you what we gonna do. What time is your appointment?"

"One o'clock."

"We gonna keep your watch for the weekend, then we gonna pick you up at twelve noon on Monday in front of da Phillips Club. We'll drive you over the bridge, and if you can make a big enough deal, we split the dough, and you get the Rolex back. That work for you? But if you don't have no deal on Monday, then we get the watch and you gonna go for a swim in the East River. Got it?"

"How do I get in touch with you if the *Probe* people change the plans?"

The guys looked at each other and started laughing. "Hey man, Romeo might want to get in touch wit you this weekend."

"Yeah, maybe you should give him your old lady's number."

"For sure, ha-ha. You just be on 66th Street at twelve noon, you asshole." They both glanced in the restroom mirror, IG#1 washed his hands, adjusted his collar and they walked out of the john together.

CHAPTER
9

Malcolm spent ten minutes in the Loo pulling himself together. He squatted down in front of the electric hand dryer, blasted it, and that helped. After four cycles of the dryer, his hair and clothes looked presentable. He smoothed himself out, draped his longish hair over the bump on his forehead, splashed a dash of Mennen skin bracer on his face. As he headed out of the bar, a manager came in search of him.

He walked back to his bar stool in one piece, to the amazement of the other patrons, looked around at everyone, and ordered a cup of coffee with a shot of Bailey's in it. Then he called the bartender back over and ordered a round for the bar. People nodded at him in amused awe at his resilience. The two Italian couples had already moved on.

Malcolm knew he had just avoided serious bodily harm, but somehow, this seemed to energize him. No one ever seemed to take him seriously, but he had just had an interlude with a made guy's wife, in a public saloon no less, had gone into the Loo with not one, but two goons, and talked his way out of danger. He had in effect, perhaps subconsciously, created a real time drama of his own to film mentally. Now he had a personal dilemma to solve, and knew that he was up to the task, knew he had to be smarter and more creative than his new tormentors. He seemed to be unaware at the time of the old axion about God taking care of babes and drunks.

After a second fortified coffee, and another round for the house, Malcolm tipped his bartender a C-note, and asked for a cab to be called. When he got back to his room, he jumped in the shower, and in ten minutes crashed on top of the king-sized bed.

———————

Sunday morning at about ten-thirty Malcolm stirred, rolled out of bed, brushed his teeth, and put on some casual clothes. The elevator gave his stomach a flip on the way down to the lobby and he strolled next door to the deli/mini market to get some coffee and breakfast. He was starving.

His mind was churning while he ingested a couple demitasses of espresso, and a bagel with lox and cream cheese. "Ah, you've done it this time, Malcolm old boy," he said aloud. Several people close by were staring at him. He chuckled, finished his repast, and walked outside into the sunshine. A plan was formulating in his mind, and he knew it would have to be a good one to best these two ruddy mates.

The first thing he did was google the closest Chase ATM, and then walk the seven blocks over there. He should have been hungover, but Malcolm was eerily calm and prescient. Arriving at the ATM, he started pressing buttons and extracting money. The withdraw limit was fifteen hundred dollars so he had to go through seven cycles to finally walk away with ten thousand five hundred dollars.

Back at The Phillips Club, he asked for the Bell Captain. It took George Palmer half an hour to free himself from his duties. Sunday noonish was weekend checkout time, when he made almost half his weekly income. But he was finally free for a few minutes, and Malcolm was waiting. They met at the back of the public lobby, and Malcolm asked if George was working tomorrow.

"Yes sir. My days off are Wednesday and Thursday."

Malcolm pulled out three thousand dollars in folding money and handed it to George. Then he said "I need your help tomorrow. I will double this money, if you can explicitly follow the instructions I will give you. They are not difficult, and depend mostly on timing, but must be executed exactly as I say. Can you do that?"

George was a fifty-one-year-old man who had worked for gratuities his entire adult life. He was holding the largest sum of money he had ever received at one single time for his services. This startled him and raised his blood pressure, but he kept his emotions in check. Malcolm liked that.

"Ain't no illegal shit going down here, is there?"

"Absolutely not. Some gentlemen will be coming here tomorrow for a meeting, and after my sit down, I need to adjust my schedule, that's all. Works for you?"

"That's sounds easy enough, sir."

"Okay, let's sit down for a minute, and I am going to write you a short list of exactly what I need you to do."

"Yes sir."

————

Not being able to do much else until Monday morning, Malcolm went up to his room, and took some time transferring his Tami Video and Interview footage from his phone into files, which he emailed to his laptop. It was now two-thirty in the afternoon EST, and he clicked his cell phone into contacts and made a call to Canarsie in southeast Brooklyn.

"May I please speak to Donovan?"

A woman's voice shouted out for Donnie, and in a few seconds, he was on the phone.

"Hallo."

"Mr. Templeton, this is Malcom Sparrow; sorry to disturb you at home on Sunday. My timeline has moved up, and I was wondering if we could iron out some of the details of our transaction, and finalize tomorrow at our appointed time?"

"Not a problem, I've got an hour before the kids come over." So, the two men, one the buyer, the other a seller, and notice they were not referred to as gentlemen, hashed out their transaction. When they were done hashing, all that remained was for Malcolm to show up tomorrow with his merchandise.

———

Malcolm clicked off, called Morton's the Steakhouse again, and made an early reservation in another name, since he had stiffed his appointment the night before. Pleased with himself, he decided to take a leisurely bath and finish his book by David Mamet, *On Directing Film.*

———

Dinner was delicious. One Sapphire Martini to start the night, but only one. He loved his filets of mignon, and this one was fat, juicy, expensive, cooked to a perfect medium, and served with scalloped potatoes. It was the best meal Malcolm had enjoyed in some time, and he congratulated himself on his urbane choice of establishments. He passed on dessert, left a generous tip and Ubered back to the Phillips Club. George was just getting off duty as he entered the lobby. They conversed for a several minutes, and George assured his sponsor that everything was in order and ready to go.

Malcolm went up the lift to his suite, undressed, took his evening ablutions, and crawled into bed. He set the alarm on his cell phone to eight AM, fluffed his pillow, rolled over and went to sleep.

———

Monday morning came without a hitch. Malcolm rose, sang to himself while he showered, dressed and went down the lift to get some coffee and a sweet roll. He also needed to order a catered luncheon package, which he did, and was back in his room in half an hour. At exactly nine-thirty a.m., he rang WBC Headquarters in New York City.

"Good morning, this is Gianna in Mt. Benson's office; how may I help you?"

"This is Malcolm Sparrow; is Mr. Benson available?"

"He is leaving for the airport on a few, but I think I can grab him for you." This was the key element in Malcolm's plan, and he was silently thankful he had been able to reach Ben.

"Good morning, Ben, so sorry to bother you, it's Malcolm Sparrow."

"What do you need man, I'm just about to walk out the door."

"Just a small favor Sir," Malcolm said, and iterated his needs to Ben Benson.

"Hang up and call Gianna back, tell her we spoke, and I said for her to take care of you," and Benson disconnected.

Malcolm waited half an hour, and called Gianna, and she proved to be most cordial and helpful. After they finished their business, she told him that if Ben's trip was successful, there would be a signing party a week from Saturday night at Bistro Soirée in Beverly Hills and he was invited. He should check back with her.

Well, guess I'll know if she signs or not, he thought.

———

Done with WBC, Malcolm put in his next call to into the *Probe* tabloid people. "May I please speak with Donovan Templeton, VP of Content Acquisition?"

"I'll ring him sir."

"Templeton here."

"Good morning, it's Malcolm."

"Long time no talk, Sparrow. What can I do for you? Weren't we supposed to meet at one this afternoon to finish our deal?"

"Yes, we were. However, I have a couple of issues on my end, and was wondering if you might be able to join me here on the Upper West Side instead? I have your parking secured and will provide some luncheon."

"Where are you, Malcolm?"

"I'm staying at The Phillips Club on West 66th. They have a well-appointed professional space on the ground floor. I'm sure we would be most comfy."

"Of course, I can come over to Manhattan, Malcolm, but that is going to cut our deal in half!" And Donovan, who was a large, jovial man, issued a resounding belly laugh.

"I was actually thinking I should double the price, especially since I'm buying lunch."

"Well, why don't we leave things where they are," and the two men spent the next few minutes confirming the details of their seven-figure agreement. Which more cynical people might call blood money.

————

Done with chatting, Malcolm turned on the tellie; everything he saw bored him. He decided to take a stroll around Lincoln Center and the Fordham University campus and enjoy this sultry late summer morning. That would kill an hour, and then it would be showtime. He walked out of the Phillips Club and turned west this time.

————

After a pleasant interlude, his last in NYC, Malcolm got back to room #402, freshened up, put on his best pair of woolen slacks, and a monogrammed Christian Dior dress shirt. He Windsor-knotted a striped silk tie, slipped on his lightweight brown leather bomber jacket, and threw the rest of his gear into a roller bag.

At eleven-forty, he was downstairs in the lobby, checked his bag with George, then picked up a *New York Times* off the front desk countertop, and stepped over to an overstuffed lobby chair. He was feeling calm and confident, enjoying the anticipation of another handsome payday, and began perusing the headlines of the paper.

At five to twelve, he stepped out the front door of the residence hotel and cased the street for his associates. He waited for twenty minutes, and at twelve-fifteen, very annoying to Malcolm, who detested tardiness, a black Cadillac Escalade slowly rolled past the Phillips Club. Malcolm waved, and the head Italian stopped, rolled down the passenger window, and beckoned Malcolm over to the car. Malcolm trotted across the narrow street; the car was facing west, and the driver motioned to Malcolm and told him to get in the front seat next to him. There was only the driver in the car, and Malcolm could sense he was nervous.

"Relax man," Malcolm told him. "Everything is copasetic. The meeting has been moved here to The Phillips Club; we don't need to drive to Brooklyn."

"Get in the fucking car, asshole. Now." Malcolm was in a great mood, he had another million-dollar deal coming down, he was a respected, if not world renowned, feature film director, and was not in the mood to be ordered about like a naughty child. These Goombahs needed to be taught a little respect.

"Don't F@#%ing swear at me, mate. I've got a million-dollar deal going down in about half an hour. I am willing to cut you in on part of it because I want my watch back, which has sentimental value to me. If that doesn't work for you, then keep the damn watch, and I'll see you later. If you want to join me, the Bellman has a parking space reserved for you right there in front of the club. Go ahead and park, and you can come in and look around. You can check me for a wire if you want to. Oh, and I need the watch back now."

"Forget about it."

"Listen to me. We are going to sit down to a high profile, big bucks meeting. I have specified the payout to be in ten one hundred-thousand-dollar Certified checks, made out to cash. You will be sitting on either side of me, so where could I go, or what could go wrong? You will be my bodyguards, and you can't be wearing a more expensive watch than me. After the meeting is over, you can escort me out to your vehicle, and I will pay you off in certified paper and leave."

The driver of the Escalade was taken aback by Malcolm's assertiveness. He had left his partner standing back at the corner with the watch just in case this was a set-up, now the situation was drastically different. He thought for a minute, then told Malcolm to go stand in front of the Club, and he would pick up his partner and swing around the block.

"Malcolm, I'm telling you for your own safety, we have a third person spotting for us today, and if anything should go wrong, my partner and I may go down for petty theft or something minor, but you will never live to tell the story. I will personally choke your ass until you are dead and blue. Do you understand? Plus, my friend, we want an even split. Fifty/fifty, si, si?"

"I hear you, man."

———

The Escalade was back in the length of time it took the driver to explain the situation to Alonzo, and George motioned them into the Phillips Club's reserved loading zone. They got out of the car, and George asked for the keys in case of emergency, like if he had to move the car. This also did not sit well with the Mafiosos, but George patiently explained to them it was like they were leaving the car with valet parking.

"Whatever," one of them said, and they walked away without leaving a tip. Once they were standing outside of the car, it was obvious to Malcolm and George that both Italian men were packing.

Malcolm escorted his guests through the rectangular lobby space, and on towards the back left side of the facility which housed the dark, intimate meeting space. The Italians were casually intently eyeing every nook and cranny of the club. They were relieved to see no dorky looking, clean cut agent types loitering around the lobby. They did not like doing business on strange turf, but the temptation of such a lucrative payday whispered sweetly in both their ears.

Attempting to reassert their control of the situation, the Italians spun Malcolm around and frisked him for a wire. They took a stroll around the premises, scouted out the exits, looked in the back storage room, and finally, assured the place was clean, gave the Rolex back to Malcolm. He slipped it over his left wrist, letting it dangle obtrusively. Two catering girls from next door were putting the finishing touches on the luncheon buffet, and Malcolm asked the boys if they would care for a coffee or espresso? The beverage offer was declined, but the guys began to help themselves to the ample spread the caterers had just finished presenting. Malcolm gave the girls a one-hundred-dollar tip, told them to come back for cleanup in an hour. He looked with disgust at his "bodyguards," who were stocking their plates, thinking them quite rude to proceed before their guests arrived.

Right on time, Donovan Templeton walked in with an assistant. He and Malcolm shook hands, sat across from each other, and Malcolm pulled a laptop out of his attaché case, and opened the files for Donovan's inspection.

Donovan was both excited and impressed.

"You obviously know I have sold the rights to WBC of the action video which they have already aired nationally, but to my knowledge, Eastern Europe and South America, etc. are still in play as available markets."

"Yes, we spoke of those options."

"Also, let me point out some interesting copy I have made available to you as an experienced editor." And Malcolm scrolled the screen down towards the end of his interview, and his wrap up questions to Tami, then read aloud:

"Tami, you bounded into camp today like a two-legged gazelle. Are you now, or have you ever taken anabolic steroids, stimulants, or any other form of performance enhancing drugs?"

"Absolutely not."

"And would you be willing to take a lie detector test to that effect, Tami?"

"Only if necessary. Just remember, whatever a person might take to improve their own personal performance, it is still hard work that is the key to success."

———————

"Do you see what I'm talking about, my friend? By omitting the middle sentence of that dialogue, I have completely altered the context of the interview."

Donovan's experienced eye quickly grasped Malcolm's handiwork, and he smiled at the film director's creative smarts and strategic technique. "Good work my friend, I think we have a deal, the boss wants to get right on the foreign markets. Budapest, Prague across the pond, that sort of thing. Your editing will just be frosting on the cake."

He pulled out a rather fat envelope and handed it to Malcolm, who tucked it into the inside pocket of his bomber jacket, turned to Alonzo, and winked. He completed the transfer of files to Donovan's laptop, Donovan made sure they were successfully received, and got up to look at the buffet's offerings.

George came into the room with a bottle of Dom Perignon champagne. There were five glasses on the serving tray, and he set the tray down at the edge of the table. While Donovan and his aide helped themselves to a plate, Malcolm expertly popped the expensive bottle of bubbles, and poured out five glasses.

Malcolm's bodyguards were finished eating and after their perfectly chilled quaff, while Donovan was wrapping up, Malcolm stood and said, "Gentlemen, I've a plane to catch, can you please excuse us?" Everyone rose; Donovan told Malcolm to go ahead, he would be along presently. At precisely two o'clock, Malcolm grabbed his attaché case, signaled his bodyguards, and exited the room.

They walked smoothly through the lobby; Malcolm paused for just an instant at the front desk, thanking everyone for their hospitality, and left an envelope for the Head Bellman. The three men then continued over to the glass exit door, which slid open obediently for them.

Malcolm descended the shallow steps in front of the Club, when suddenly four sets of Klieg lights blinded him, and a WBC remote location reporter shoved a microphone into his face.

"Good day, sir, may we have a moment of your time?"

Malcolm and his bodyguards blinked into the bright lights, the Italians looked up and saw a large WBC box truck parked on the other side of their SUV. The last thing a made guy wants is bright lights and camera time. They shrunk back a couple of steps behind Malcolm, and his only words to the newsman were, "Would you mind speaking with my associates here?" Then he ducked under the arm of the reporter with his handheld mic extended, and like a greased eel, darted into the street. He jumped on the back of a delivery service Kawasaki motorcycle George had arranged for him. As soon as he was squarely on the curved back seat, he leaned forward, and the driver sped off with a roar.

Malcolm was gone. The reporter started to ask something of the Italians, and they grabbed his microphone and smashed it on the steps. "Get your fucking van off of my Escalade," Alfonzo said, and looked around for George who was standing there holding his keys for him. Again, no tip.

A very happy head bellman walked back into the private club while the Italians and the TV people were extricating themselves. He stopped at the front desk and retrieved the envelope Malcolm had left. All he had to do now, was overnight Malcolm's roller bag to the Beverly Wilshire Hotel as agreed, and he was done. He signed out for his lunch break, shed his bellman's jacket in the men's locker room, took the roller bag, slipped on a pair of new Oakley sunglasses and left through the back door.

———

At first Alfonzo, sometimes known as Alfie, was pissed off. He and Geo sat in the Escalade enjoying muted silence, but after twenty minutes or so he turned and said, "we made some serious money today, amici."

"How is that?" asked Geo, who was also not a bit happy at being played.

"We know him, Malcolm Sparrow, smart guy, eh? Now he not only owes us half a mil, but it is plus vig, and plus expenses. We must be patient, but he will come back to us. Trust me."

"Si, si."

CHAPTER 10

The Powers had an all-star family day. It would have been a good one if they had just sat at home, but after being separated for almost a month, cavorting around in Griffith Park was just what Tami needed. Scott and Tami took turns hiking with the older kids. They did some physically challenging rock climbing, while also sharing time entertaining Sadie around the playground. Towards the end of the day, Tami isolated with Carrie, and asked her what was going on in her life this week.

"Would you like to go on a business trip with me?" Solo time with Mom was special, especially since she was now a bona fide celebrity, and missing a day or two of school wouldn't hurt her. "I'm just wrapping up summer school, Mom," Carrie intoned, and Tami invited her to come to WBC Headquarters on Tuesday morning.

———

Monday was a busy catchup day for Tami around the house and her home office. Tuesday morning after her sixteen-mile run zigzagging through Arroyo Seco Canyon, Tami returned home, showered, kissed Scott goodbye, fed her boys, got them ready for a day at the teen center, and then drove Sadie to her friend's house. When she and Carrie were home alone, Carrie wanted to know what to wear. "Something nice but casual," was Tami's reply. "You will probably be mobile most of the day."

"Okay."

"Why don't you wear your nicest warm up suit?" In the car, she would explain to Carrie where they were going, and that there might be some pretty cool opportunities for her.

———

The girls arrived at the formidable WBC West Coast headquarters building in North Hollywood and were directed at the gate to the VIP valet attendant in the compound. He opened the car doors and took the keys to Tami's BMW X-7. "Gee, we really are VIPs," Carrie said.

There was a phalanx of security and several receptionists in the lobby of the well-appointed building, but one of the best and brightest young staffers was waiting for them. She whisked the Powers girls to the private executive elevator and up to the fourteenth floor. Ben Benson's ponderous executive self was seated and waiting for them in a corporate meeting room.

"Would you care for anything to drink, ladies?" He asked, while standing courteously.

"I would love a Diet Coke," Tami replied. Carrie asked for a bottle of water. The young receptionist was quick to oblige. "I have swag bags for the two of you," Ben said, producing two monogramed WBC fabric sacks. Which turned out to be filled with various souvenir tee shirts from studio productions, Apple watches for mother and daughter, various other keepsakes and paraphernalia. And finally backstage passes to any Jimmy Kameron Show of their choosing.

"Carrie," Ben said, "your mom and I will be doing some touring in the primary building here and meeting some people, what would interest you about our company? We specialize in comprehensive news coverage, but also have a couple of production lots that are filming for our streaming platforms."

"Women's sports are exciting to me," Carrie said. "I play on my high school's varsity volleyball team, could I spend some time in your athletic news department?"

"Of course. We are the West Coast headquarters but work closely with our local Los Angeles affiliate WLA12 who cover the region's sports scene extensively. Let me make a call, and I'll set up a meet and greet for you. Excuse me for a sec."

Ten minutes later Ben was back. "Heather, Todd with 12 is going out to the UCLA campus in half an hour. Apparently, they have just fired their women's volleyball coach. Why don't you ladies meet Todd on the campus, and Carrie can have a firsthand look at sports journalism. Offer to buy him lunch afterwards, and then he will take you to the LA studios and show you around. I believe Thad Tucker is there in production today. That would get you back here around two. Sound okay?" It sounded sublime to Carrie. Ben looked at Tami for her approval. She gave the nod, and said "have fun, be safe."

———

Carrie and Heather left. Carrie didn't realize they would be squired around in a stretch limo and jumped in the back behind Heather as the driver held the door for them. It took a little over twenty minutes to get to the Bruin's campus, and Heather talked a lot about how much fun it was to work for WBC. "You are out in front of everything," she told Carrie. They hooked up with sports reporter Todd in the parking lot of the campus Athletic Center. Although he seemed more interested in Heather, Carrie still thought he was very hunky.

After their interview with UCLA's Athletic Director, he offered them a tour of the building. But Todd had a deadline to meet, and they thankfully declined. Todd did know of a four-star taco truck on the way back to North Hollywood's WLA12 studios, so the three amigos stopped there for an early snack. The taco truck was in a scruffy urban parking lot off Western Avenue, and where but in LA would you find a stretch limo camped in front of a taco truck?

All the construction dudes eating lunch on picnic tables kept asking Heather for a ride, which she coolly blew off. Carrie tried to be chill too but was blushing furiously. Finally, Todd jumped in the limo with them, and the crispy carnitas tacos he had recommended proved to be delicious.

Back at the studio, Todd transmitted his interview over to the newsroom staff, and took his charges for a look around. Carrie was amazed at all the technical gear it took to run a newsroom. Todd explained a lot about the sound, lighting, modulation boards, etc. Heather and Carrie got to sit at the news desk for a few minutes and did a very quick mockup of the midday news. Todd, working with the station manager, had the tech people make a CD for them.

After all their thank yous, it was out to the limo and head back to headquarters. Carrie was floating. It didn't take a social media post to appreciate this VIP lifestyle, especially when Heather mentioned that they could be seeing more of each other, because there might be an internship offer waiting for her. Pretty heady stuff for a teenaged kid, a junior in high school.

———

Ben kept his and Tami's morning on about the same level of cordiality. He gave Tami a tour of the corporate building, including the executive offices, and introduced her around. She was a bit taken aback by the warm reception of this powerful group of senior division heads; how everyone stopped in their tracks to shake her hand, and chat with her for a few minutes. She even posed for several selfies and was thankful that no one asked for an autograph. After touring, she and Ben ended up in the executive dining room, and Ben began a dialogue with her about a relationship with WBC.

"Tami, I'm sure you realize by now, how much we would like you to be a significant part of the WBC family. After lengthy discussions with the powers that be, we are prepared to offer you a package we feel is designed to fit your lifestyle and career goals." Tami wondered how Ben might have any idea what her career goals might be but continued to listen politely.

"First of all, we would like to invite you to join our Business Management Staff here at headquarters with a position as a senior CPA. You would have a view office on the upper level of the building and be asked to work six hours a day. You would be welcome to use our facilities to conduct business with your existing client base. We have a compensation package that would start at one hundred twenty-five thousand dollars per annum, including substantial medical, vacation and retirement packages. There could also be an internship in our sports department for your daughter."

"Sounds good so far."

"Great. As a return on your basic package, WBC will retain exclusive rights to any footage of you interceding in any active conflictive type situations."

"And how do you propose to manage that there will be conflicts or anyone will have access to cover them?"

"We have a new hire in our business department who just graduated from the University of Colorado. She has her master's degree in human resources and was captain of the varsity volleyball team there. Her name is Leona Harris, she grew up here in south central LA. Her achievements and self-motivation would make an amazing success story in and of itself. She would run with you every morning at whatever time you designated or accompany you when appropriate. If anything transpired on your outings, Leona would be there to tape it. If anything happened at another time, hopefully someone would be with you, again with a cell phone and the WBC team would retain the rights to that recorded footage. Should no live images be available to us, we would create time for you to give our news teams a breakdown of the incident. Share any insights you might have as to what happened, that sort of thing.

These would be the only real conditions of your employment, except that for any original, live footage that was obtained of you actively involved in an incident, we would also compensate you at the rate of one hundred thousand dollars per episode. Not only would we compensate you handsomely per episode, those incentives would be tax exempt, in that we would also make a deposit into your prepaid income tax account. Also, we would be happy to compensate you retroactively for the last two incidents. The conditions of the prepayment would be an exclusive interview with a WBC News representative to discuss the incidents. Your original employment contract would span five years, but also be reviewed on an annual basis. I will be your primary contact within the corporation, and my door would always be open to you."

"I feel like I am being asked to be a character on LA Law or something, Ben."

"Tami, we have tried to work out a concept that would be agreeable to both of us. We want to respect your privacy, but also are cognizant of the fact that you are sizzling hot as a news source right now. We empathize with the fact that you have no desire to embrace the notoriety that has and will continue to come your way. Nor do you wish to capitalize in a monetary manner on the talents you have recently displayed. But should you elect to join our broadcasting family, our legal team would be at your disposal to help create a trust fund or foundation to aid any cause you might wish to identify with. Our offer would also open doors of opportunity for your family in the realms of education, exposure and careers. For example, if Carrie is interested, there would be a paid internship available for her."

"What if my talents, as you describe them, are ephemeral, and the last couple of weeks are an anomaly in terms of repeating itself?"

"We think so much of you as a force for the good, Tami, we are willing to take that chance. If there should be no more exhibits of your supernatural powers, we would still employ you as a CPA, but we also feel like you might find a place in our network of opportunity that would/could display your talents in the programming fields of Yoga instruction, self-defense for young people with an on-air Tae Kwon Do segment. Perhaps a serial on physical fitness for our nation's youth, or your own show with a positive news format. Start out in accounting

Tami, spend some time with us, get to know us. We are betting you will like our corporate culture here at WBC."

"Thank you for your time, Ben. I appreciate your offer. I will, of course, need to take our conversation back to my family and professional representation and get their input."

"Certainly, how much time will you need to evaluate things?"

"Oh, shouldn't take more than a day or two."

"How about we meet for lunch next Thursday?"

"That will work. I'll call you tomorrow afternoon to confirm?"

"Please do. Would you care for anything else before you go?"

"I'm fine thanks and I appreciate your hospitality with Carrie. I'm sure she had a capital time of it."

"We try to please, Tami."

———

Carrie was hanging with Heather in the archives room off the main lobby when Tami came down from her time with Ben. She thanked her for mentoring Carrie, Carrie and Heather hugged goodbye, exchanged phone numbers, and it was time to leave the building.

Carrie could scarcely contain herself on the way home, babbling on about how nice everyone was, how special they made her feel, how much fun they had had, how she couldn't wait to start her internship. Finally, Tami reminded her that every glittery thing is not gold. "But Mom . . ." Tami realized how significantly every molecule of her life was going to be tested. "I'm just asking you to relax a little bit is all, hon. I know you are excited but remember your sibs didn't get to go ride around in a limo all day like you did."

———

Tami got home and started the fixings for a nice family dinner. When things were organized in the kitchen, she timed out and called Anne Marie.

"Well, I did it."

"What?"

"Spent the day with Beelzebub."

"Why do you say that? Did they make you an offer?"

"Oh yeah. They made me an offer; they chauffeured Carrie all over town in a limo, gave us all the swag they could think of."

"What's wrong with that?"

"Anne Marie, don't you think all this is going to put an enormous amount of pressure on my life, and that of my family?"

"Well, sounds to me like it's the right kind of pressure. Tell me about the offer."

So, Tami related the details of her conversation with Ben."

"Off of the top, Tam, it sounds like a very solid offer. You have all the flexibility in the world to work in your accounting field. All they are asking is to have exclusive rights to your superpowers, which they will pay you handsomely for. And there are some fantastic bennies for your family. I would include an out clause in the contract—that is, give you the ability to opt out of the deal on thirty or sixty-days' notice, if you are not happy. We should also ask for approval for you to work from home a couple of days a week. How does that sound? Finally, we should ask WBC to clarify their expectations as far as promotional work, and any personal appearances by you."

"The opt out would give me some peace of mind and working from home a couple of days a week would be awesome, but I think I should have the option to opt out any time I want. That might also give me some leverage if I need it. Let me discuss everything with Scott this evening and I'll call you back tomorrow morning."

"Talk to him, I bet he'll agree that it's a solid offer. It seems to me like they are bending over backwards to make everything work for you, Tami. Ciao."

CHAPTER
11

Tami fed the kids an early dinner, and when Scott got home from work around six-thirty, they put Carrie in charge and went out for Mexican. Carrie was only too happy to help, she was still on cloud nine, and had been in full cooperation mode all afternoon.

To say Tami had married well would be an understatement. While his wife was totally committed to her life choices and went about managing them in a very structured style, Scott, a laid-back kind of guy, was her antithesis. Six-foot-one and rugged-looking with a bushy mustache, some beard stubble, he had sandy brown hair and deep blue eyes, a square jaw, and an athletic physique. He was a mechanical engineer and wrote code for the Jet Propulsion Laboratory in La Canada, so he worked ten minutes from home. He enjoyed tinkering with engines and drove a 911 Porsche Carrera. He also had an old Indian Motorcycle which was his pride and joy. Cupid had sent him to Tami, because they balanced each other so perfectly. Tami felt Scott was in favor of her accepting WBC's offer. He was easy-going, inclined to take things as they came, and, although he was an engineer, interestingly, he wasn't as concerned with details or disruptions as his wife.

Tami thought the offer was generous enough but having worked for a Big Five accounting firm a year before she married Scott, she was less enthusiastic about joining another national company. She knew this was her WBC honeymoon, and life would start changing as soon as she signed, but she liked Anne Marie's ideas. At least, including the opt out clause would give her some peace of mind.

————

The young "Power" couple walked into Montezuma's Restaurant, were seated at a booth in the bar and picked up menus. They both ordered Margaritas on the rocks, Tami wasn't very hungry, so the waitress suggested ordering some nachos, and they began to talk.

Scott worked in a structured environment for a large, bureaucratic organization and wasn't intimated by WBC. He felt like her offer was solid, especially the bonus structure for any of her extracurricular activities. "Tam, I would never want to put you in harm's way, but if it is inevitable that this is the path we are on, we might as well capitalize on it."

"Both you and Anne Marie feel like this is a good offer, the only thing that concerns me is if these other worldly things keep happening to me, the publicity for our family will be overwhelming. Maybe we should ask WBC to build us a castle with a moat."

"Well, that's not going to happen, I mean nobody is building us anything like that, we will just have to move to a gated community if necessary." Tami, who had already moved three times with her husband while he was working on his university degrees, through various stages of her own pregnancies, motherhood, and career, just shook her head. She loved her home, neighborhood, neighbors, etc., and when Scott so casually mentioned picking up and moving, it made her shudder.

"Scott, I love you so much, and am so thankful my aunt was here to help out while I was gone in Utah. But I never want to be away from us for that long again."

"Well, we managed, but it's not the same when you're away. I personally support everything you do, and I feel your love. We are lucky to have each other, and I know that when something comes along that I have to/get to do, you'll be there for me."

"This is what concerns me, Scott. We are one together, but that has never been a limiting factor for our individual development. I don't want any of my new whatever you want to call them, experiences, to change anything in our lives."

"We won't let that happen, I certainly won't if it is humanly possible."

"I believe our lives together, our love, and nurturing our family needs to be a carefully guarded treasure. It's within our control, and we need to be very cautious not to lose that bond. It means everything in the world to me, Scott. I can't thank you enough for being the supportive man that you are. You are always there for me, for us, and I love that so much. Not to mention the fact that you are kind of dreamy."

Scott raised his margarita glass while smiling the loving smile at her that she adored, and they toasted each other and their lives together. "You are getting kind of gushy woman, calm down and have a sip of tequila."

She made a goofy face at him and picked up her cocktail glass.

———

The next morning Tami called Anne Marie and told her she better get on a plane. "Scott and I basically approve of the deal, more so Scott, but every time we talk, things get more complicated. There is no deadline on this, so why don't you fly out and stay a few days and help me sort everything out?"

"I'll book a flight today and be there tomorrow afternoon. What are we talking about here?"

"Everything you and I talked about already, and I think the out clause will really help. But I'm concerned if these incidents keep occurring, the publicity is going to be overwhelming. If I have to move, I want those expenses paid for. If worse comes to worse, I may even need a bodyguard for myself, or for the kids. All those kinds of things."

"I hear you Tami, and I will be there tomorrow afternoon. Who have you been dealing with at WBC? Maybe I should give them a call and start a working relationship. It seems to me like we are entering some unchartered territory here, and I think you are very wise to understand that."

"Mr. Ben Benson, he's a senior vice-president, and you're right. I mean, I am perfectly happy without WBC. If they want to make money off me, then I just want my family and myself to be protected. And don't forget about Carrie's internship."

"You are preaching to the choir, Tami. Let me go, and I'll give this Benson a call, interesting name by the way, and I will text you my ETA. Sounds like we may need some type of blanket clause to cover these kinds of issues, and also you should be compensated for your first two incidents which they have made money from. I have spoken to a couple of labor attorney friends of mine, and they will be in touch to help us navigate our way."

"Benson already offered to cover the first two."

———

Anne Marie arrived at LAX late Thursday afternoon, and Tami had already scheduled a Friday noon meeting with Ben Benson. He invited them to lunch in the executive dining room and listened patiently while the two women aired their issues.

"I empathize, ladies, and I'll take my notes and pass them along to legal. They should be able to turn an updated offer around in a couple of days. Why don't we meet again next Wednesday?"

Wednesday came in a flash, and things were getting closer to completion. Legal had acquiesced to Tami's main stipulation of the no notice opt out, and also didn't fight Anne Marie's last-minute request for a twenty thousand dollar signing bonus to help cover travel expenses and attorney fees, and with Ben's encouragement to his legal department, the documents were ready to sign.

Anne Marie asked for WBC's patience for two more days so her attorneys could do a final review, and both groups agreed to meet the following Monday at two in the afternoon.

———

As is so often the case, the inking ceremony was actually anticlimactic to all the prep work that had gone into the documents, but after Tami signed on the dotted lines, Ben Benson escorted the ladies back to the executive club room and had a bottle of Veuve Clicquot, with chilled glasses ready for their small celebration.

"Welcome to the World Broadcasting Company, Tami. I feel like this is going to be a hugely successful venture for both of us." Ben drank lustily, the girls sipped.

"Thank you," replied both women.

"There is a signing party scheduled in your honor two weeks from this Saturday evening at Hans Ebersol's Soirée Restaurant in Beverly Hills, how many in your party will be able to join us?"

Tami thought for a minute, Scott, Anne Marie, Carrie, and herself. "We will be four. May I contact you if that number changes?"

"Certainly. Cocktails begin at seven, dinner at eight. We will be in private dining room number one."

"Thank you, see you Saturday."

———

Tami was thankful Anne Marie had been there to help her, the thought of having to negotiate the last week with Malcolm Sparrow as her personal rep, and the elegant champagne, made her head spin. She thanked AM and lightly braked her BMW 7 as traffic on Interstate 210 East began to back up.

"Where we going to celebrate tonight?" Anne Marie asked.

"I was thinking pizza and a movie with the kids," Tami replied.

———

Alfonzo called his Zio and asked for a meeting. It was a warm, humid afternoon in Queens and Uncle Carlo invited Alfonzo to join him at his little table on the sidewalk in front of the Italian Men's Social Club.

"Junior, I haven't seen you in a while. Everything okay? I heard there was a little dustup last weekend at Luca's."

"Ah, you still don't miss anything do you?"

"I keep an eye out for you kids, if that is what you mean. How is that beautiful wife of yours?"

"Cara is great, Uncle Carlo."

"When you gonna give me a little one? You gonna wait until I'm inna ground, then you can tell them how great an Uncle Carlo you had?"

"Any day now, Zio."

"What's on your mind then?"

"Well, I don't know how much you heard about Luca's, but I met a guy in the bar I was in the 101st with. While we was talkin', this civilian at the bar starts getting out of line with Cara. She ignores him, but then he decides to follow her back toward the john, and me and my buddy Geo follow him to teach him a little lesson, eh? So, we goes in there and start to work the guy over. He is just a skinny little shit, and while we is dealin' wit him, we notice he's wearin' a real expensive Rolex, so we take it. But the guy says, Hey, wait a minute; I got something a lot more valuable than that watch, and you can have half of it if youse don't kill me in here."

"Interesting, go on."

"So, it turns out this guy is a movie director, his name is Malcolm Sparrow. He tells us he has a tape recording of that new broad that jumps all over the place and knocks people out, and he is going to sell it to some tabloid magazine on Monday for big money. But he will give us half the money if we give his watch back to him and go wit him to Canarsie on Monday. So, we say we'll keep the watch, but we'll go wit you on Monday, and you pay us half, and you can have the watch back. So, he don't like it none, but he says okay.

"We supposed to meet him on West 66th and take him to Brooklyn. But when we get there, he says we ain't have to go to Brooklyn, we gonna have the meeting right there in his hotel. So, we go in, it's a nice place, we check everything out like for security, for him wearin' a wire, you know? In a while the magazine people show up, and he cuts a deal for one million bucks. They give him ten certified checks made out to cash for one hundred Gs, of which me and Geo figure half is ours. Oh yeah, he had us give him his watch back, because he says, 'You two are my bodyguards, and you can't be wearin' a better watch than me.' So, we let him wear it during the meeting. Then when we gets up to leave, we go out the front door of the hotel, and all of a sudden there is a WBC news truck right there, and they have all kinds of those movie lights shinin' in our faces, and then this little Malcolm Sparrow shit, he just ducks out of there. He has a motorcycle dude waiting for him out on the street, and he's gone."

"That's quite a story, Alfie."

"Well, I told Geo we done good, because now he owes us half a mil, plus vig, plus expenses. Right?"

"Yes, technically. But as they say, possession is nine tenths of the law."

"Well, I done some research on this guy. Then I had me a good idea and realized my niece Gianna works for one of the big bosses at WBC here in the city. She knows all about this guy Sparrow, told me he was in LA, stayin' at the Beverly Wilshire Hotel, and there is a spendy party in Beverly Hills this Saturday night, and Sparrow will be there."

"And you want to know how you can get your half million bucks, right?"

"Well, yeah."

"First of all, Alfonzo, paper money is very difficult to deal with. It leaves an ugly trail. What is your plan?"

"So, if we go out there and pick him up on Saturday night, we figured by Monday he would be willing to make a withdrawal."

"This is true Alfonzo. If you picked him up on Saturday night, he would be willing to cooperate by Monday. But where you going to take him on Sunday, back the Beverly Wilshire? When you walk into the bank with him on Monday morning, and he been worked on all weekend, you don't think the bank is going to call the cops right away? You also know that you can't withdraw more than ten grand in cash without filling out forms for the government on where the money come from, who is it going to? You know that, eh? And if he writes you a check, or drafts secure paper, there is a trail. Yes? Not to mention there is cameras everywhere."

"Well, yeah."

"So, you got a problem, Alfonzo."

"Yes, Uncle Carlo."

"But I tell you what I am going to do for you. For a small fee of course."

"Thank you, Uncle Carlo."

"In the first place, don't get greedy. You and your friend Geo go out to Los Angeles this week. And you keep an eye on this Geo because he is not a part of our family. You can stay in this safe house I have if you want to, I'm gonna give you the address. It's right there near Hollywood. On Saturday night, you dress up nice, and you go to where this party is. Then you wait, and late at night, you grab this Malcolm Sparrow real quiet like, and then you blindfold him, and take him to my house in Burbank. You get your watch back, and you work on this little fucker easy like, but not nowhere near his face. Then on Monday morning, Sparrow is going to call his bank and tell them to transfer five hundred thousand dollars to this account number in the Bahamas I am going to give you.

And you tell him you gave him a discount because you like him. Then you tell him that if he screws around in any way, with the cops, with the bank, the next time you are going to kill him. You are going to chop him up piece by piece by piece. You got all that."

"Yes Sir."

"Okay, go buy a nice suit, and make a plane reservation. You need any money?"

"I'm all right, Uncle Carlo."

"Remember too, doing business on the West Coast is different than us. LA is big and spread out, traffic is terrible, parking is a big problem. People are just different, and listen to me, it's against the law to carry a concealed weapon without a permit in California. So youse need to be extra careful."

"Yes sir."

"Why don't you come back here tomorrow, I'll get you set up with the house, get fake IDs for you to rent your car and hotel rooms wit. I can have a Chase checking account in your alias name for you, a couple of burner phones and I'll give you a few more ideas out of my bag of tricks."

"Yes sir."

CHAPTER
12

The party at Soirée was coming together nicely. There were eighteen guests confirmed, including Tami's four, Ben and his wife, two more senior VPs with wives, Jake Burns, VP of Corporate Security, and Heather and Malcolm, who were not a couple and not essential guests. Heather was there to entertain Carrie, and Malcolm had made it out of the goodness of Ben's heart. The rest of the guests were from WBC's senior management staff.

The menu was a six-course offering of chef's seasonal choices highlighted with an entrée of risotto, and white Italian Truffles and caviar with seared Komatsu greens. The wine choices kicked off with a jeroboam of Schramsberg bubbles and followed with Napa Valley's finest. An apprentice sommelier was exclusively attending Ben's party, and there was a three-piece string trio playing chamber music to add to the atmosphere.

Anne Marie, Carrie, and Scott were looking forward to a capital evening. Tami was ambivalent—happy to be with part of her family and her close friend, but not crazy to be a guest of honor. She had already told Ben speech making was not her thing and asked him to keep it low key in that regard.

Tami had arranged childcare for her two youngest children and sent her second child off to spend the night with his best friend who lived down the street. The Powers gang planned to leave early from La Canada, not just to beat LA's traffic, but to tour Anne Marie around a bit. She had been to LA for their annual spring marathon run several times, but those were quick, in and out trips.

Scott wore jeans, Western boots, a dress shirt, and sports jacket. Anne Marie was in a black sheath party dress, Carrie was doing her best to emulate Anne Marie, and Tami wore black leggings, New Balance running shoes, and a mid-length jumper of fall colors. While obsequiously informal, Tami was comfortable and that was good enough for her.

Three hours later, cruising into Soirée's valet parking was relaxing for Scott. Trying to find parking street parking in Beverly Hills with the town buzzing on a summer Saturday night would have been a nightmare.

Anne Marie enjoyed her mini tour of Los Angeles. They cruised the Hollywood Hills and the world-famous Sunset strip, where she saw homeless individuals in designer workout suits sifting through the sidewalk trash cans. They motored out to Malibu and back to Beverly Hills.

———

Ben and his wife arrived from the rarified air of the Beverly Wilshire Hotel to the heaven-scented air of Soirée Restaurant at seven on the dot and began welcoming guests. Soon their private dining room was a titter with animated conversation, everyone was introducing themselves, and the chamber music made for a delightful intimacy and sophistication. Dinner followed, and Carrie, who had adopted Anne Marie as her social mentor, watched closely to select the proper utensils. Anne Marie even managed to slip Carrie a couple sips of wine when Tami was otherwise occupied. Scott was enjoying himself while engaged in conversation with the VP sitting next to him about our national space program. Tami wondered if Soirée might have a treadmill somewhere she could slip away to.

———

Malcolm's acquaintances had arrived on a United Airlines flight out of La Guardia the day before. They picked up a sedan and fought traffic to the Beverly, where the Valet attendant all but sneered at their Ford Taurus rental. Alfonzo and Geo donned Covid masks and sunglasses, walked to the registration desk, and checked in. They were on a delicate mission. Using their contacts with Gianna, they knew all of Malcolm's personal information, but the delicate part was when/how to grab him and get him to the safe house without causing a scene.

Alfonzo was prepared to go to Soirée, if necessary, but they both decided it would be best to surprise him and wait in his room until he came back to the hotel, most probably three sheets to the wind.

Around eight the boys went to Malcolm's room, carefully picked his lock, and upon entry were surprised to find it vacant. "He must be leaving town tonight after the party and has already checked out," Geo deduced.

"Dammit, we can't come all this way and let him slip us again. We gotta get ready and head for the restaurant. At least we know where he is now, so we better get over there."

"We'll both dress to mingle, and wait him out, eh?" Geo said.

"Yeah, but if it looks like he is in a crowd and leaving the joint, I may have to join the party."

"Sure, if you need to go in, I will get the car, and be ready for us to take off," Geo said. They had rented the Taurus thinking it would be inconspicuous, but in the affluent climes they were rolling in, the effect was just the opposite.

Both Alfie and Geo were suited up, and doublechecked with the front desk as to Malcolm's status as they were leaving the hotel. "Damn it," Geo said. "If he is already gone, this changes everything."

"Excuse me, I am trying to reach my friend Malcolm Sparrow in room 409; has he arrived back yet?"

Click, click on her keypad, "I'm sorry, sir, you just missed him. He checked out about an hour ago."

"Thank you."

"Most certainly, have a marvelous evening," the desk clerk said while smiling roundly, and the boys left to call up their ride from Valet. "This place is probably some California tutti frutti joint, but at least it has a European-sounding name," was Alfonzo's take on the situation.

The plan was to grab seats in the bar, go easy on the drinks, order some food, hang out, case the place, wait for Malcolm to show, and somehow grab him. Alfonzo was the lead man; Geo was backup. Plans change, as they so often do, and now the boys were flying by the seat of their pants.

———

Alfie and Geo waited patiently, ordering from the extravagantly expensive lounge menu. But both the food and beverage courses were extraordinarily good. About eleven, Ben Benson's party began to break up. They could see the banquet room from the elevated cocktail table where they were sitting at the outer edge of the lounge, and Alfonzo told Geo to go call for their car. He went outside to the Valet podium, gave up his ticket, and when the car came, he tipped the driver a hundred-dollar bill.

"We might be a few minutes, is that okay partner?"

"No problem, sir, I'll park your ride over here by the exit, and leave the keys in the ignition. Take as long as you like." Perfect thought Geo.

Back inside the bar, Geo found Alfonzo sitting on the edge of his cushioned bar stool. "Shit is coming down, man. Be ready."

"I am, the car is outside, good to go."

Now the gilded banquet room doors were propped wide open, and the starched staff were lined up in attention at the exit to bid their guests adieu. The boys saw some civilians exit the room, then came a tall man (Ben Benson) and his wife followed by Tami, Scott, Anne Marie, and Carrie. Malcolm and Heather brought up the rear.

They were standing no more than twenty-five feet from Alfonzo and Geo, and the boys heard Malcolm turn to his left and importantly slur to Heather that he had called for a limo to LAX for a flight back to London tonight. Not tonight Malcolm me lad, the boys thought.

Alfie bolted off of his bar stool, strode over to the WBC party, and faced off with Malcolm. Although he had slipped his covid mask back on, the film director almost had a heart attack when he saw Alfonzo, his old friend from Luca's. The rest of the group felt the growing tension and fanned out around Malcolm.

"Place your hands on your head, sir; you are under arrest for bank fraud and interstate flight." Alfie reached into his jacket pocket and produced a bogus badge from the Los Angeles County Sheriff's Department.

"He's a phony," Malcolm was barely able to croak out, and Jake Burns stepped up to Alonzo and demanded to see the badge for validation.

Jake grabbed the badge out of Alfonzo hand, looked at it, and said, "Hey, this is showing no Official State Seal, it's bogus."

"Really?" Alfonzo mocked him and his hand slid inside his suit jacket and into his shoulder holster. As everyone flinched, he pulled out a canister of Alaskan Bear Spray. Ben Benson was especially relieved he hadn't flashed a weapon, but not so much when he hit Jake with a shot dead in the face. He whirled, missed Ben Benson, but dosed Mrs. Benson, who fell to the floor in agony, her skirt riding up inappropriately. He turned back just in time to whack the two Soirée Security Guards who were rushing head on into the scene. By now everyone was pushing back, trying to create some space and shield themselves. Malcolm was sliding out towards the front door.

Alfonzo whirled around one more time to find Tami standing about four feet in front of him. He started raising his mace cannister for another shot, but to Tami, he was moving in slow motion. Her high, front kick came from the ground up in half a split second and caught Alonzo directly under the chin with the ball of her right foot. Her kick, working like a jackhammer upper cut, snapped his head back hard enough that he went over backwards with a thud. He was out cold before he ever hit the deck, and the room went silent.

It was a moment of shocked silence, then everyone went wild, screaming and jumping around. Tami was surrounded by her family who embraced her frantically. She returned their concerned affection, and they all locked in relieved hugs. As their embrace broke, Carrie was crying and still holding onto her mom. Scott was stoic but dumbfounded at seeing his wife in action. Anne Marie, having previously witnessed Tami's otherworldly skills, was more conditioned to what had just happened.

The police were not called, as that might disturb the prestigious restaurant's guests, but no problem, Soirée's Security Guards were off duty cops. After shaking off the bear spray with damp towels provided by Soirée staff members, they revived Alfonzo, cuffed him, and took him out the kitchen exit to be booked at the Hollywood substation. That saved Soirée the ignominy of any blazing police cars flashing their sirens and lightbars at their elegant brass and glass entrance. Not only were the cops not coming, the lack of a 911 call bypassed the police scanners, which nullified any media's appearances.

Soirée's General Manager was immediately at the group's side supplicating, Anne Marie and Heather were applying more towels to the faces of members of the party who had been sprayed down. Everyone seemed to be regrouping, recovering from the ordeal.

While they were all refocusing, Ben Benson had the presence of mind to draw the General Manager aside, and request/entreat/petition/demand a copy of Soirée's lobby security camera footage. Ben and the General Manager knew each other well, actually Ben had just signed his executive credit card for eighteen thousand dollars in charges, which included three thousand dollars in gratuities. All the GM asked for in return was a favorable report concerning Soirée's Security Team. Ben was all too happy to oblige. It was a small request in return for another major exclusive breaking story for WBC News.

———

Appreciating the diversions, Malcolm by now had sidled out of the Soirée foyer and once outside, he looked over the curved driveway for his limo. Geo, his face suitably masked, was standing quietly to the right of the exit doors, and therefore directly behind an unsuspecting Malcolm. He was aware of Alfonzo's fate, and would come back for his partner later. Now, he needed to coral Malcolm.

Geo stepped forward, put his arm around Malcolm's shoulders, turning him away from the valets, said, "hello old friend," and started walking him to the tan Ford Taurus instead of a black stretch limo. Pulling Malcolm closer to him, Geo doubled his left fist and the short, powerful punch to Malcolm's jaw knocked him cold, just as the valet Geo had so generously tipped appeared to Geo's left. Malcolm was now supported entirely by Geo's strong right arm around his back and under his armpit.

"Please excuse my friend; he seems to have overindulged a bit."

"No problem, sir, I just wanted to give you the roller bag he checked with us when he arrived."

"Thank you so much. Here, let me take care of you for your always excellent service." And the alert valet helped Geo load Malcolm into the back seat of the sedan as he made himself another hundred bucks.

———

Geo drove to the safe house, used the garage door remote, parked inside, closed the door, and carried/drug Malcolm's limp body roughly inside. The house was smallish and spartan, built out of cinder blocks, and on the fringe of an industrial park. Not anything Geo would ever invite his wife to, but perfect for his current needs. He deposited Malcolm on a dumpy, single bed that was bolted to the floor in one of the three small bedrooms, handcuffed his right hand to the sturdy metal frame of the bed, removed the Rolex from Malcolm's left wrist, put it on his own, went back out to the car, brought Malcolm's bag in, and sat it on the kitchen table.

Tired after a long day, and still a bit jet lagged, he went into the kitchen and obtained a glass of water to throw in Malcolm's face, then went into another bedroom and hit the hay. It had been a little dicey, but they had separated Malcom from the herd with minimum damage. Now all he needed to do was get some sleep, and bail Alfie out in the morning. He took off his suit, hung it up, sat down on the edge of the bed, and called the Beverly Wilshire just in case.

Alfonzo was taken in an unmarked car to the Hollywood Sub Station and booked under the name of Larry Campos for disturbing the peace and impersonating a police officer. Since the drunk tank was already overflowing, he was given a ticket to appear the following Wednesday in Beverly Hills Municipal Court and escorted out the Vine Street exit. He walked a couple of blocks toward West Hollywood until he could hail a cab, asked the driver to take him to the Beverly Wilshire Hotel, and sat in the back seat rubbing his eyes. He had no idea what had happened to Malcolm, but hoped Geo was there to clean up the mess he had created.

When the cab arrived, Alfonzo straightened his clothes as best he could, gave the cabbie fifty bucks, walked quickly across the lobby, and took the elevator up to the seventh floor. He unlocked his door, walked in, and was relieved to see the message button on the house phone lit up.

Pressing the retrieve button, he heard Geo's voice, "All's well here. Our visitor is comfortable; we are at Zio's place. Talk tomorrow."

CHAPTER
13

Scott called for their BMW, and the Powers party headed out. in no time, he was driving north on the 405 to the I-10 and home. Tami was grateful she had not had to deal with the press. Scott was thankful his wife was unscathed, Anne Marie was sitting in the front seat with Scott; she was also relieved and thankful for Tami's safety. Carrie was in the back seat, draped over her mom, still in shock over what she had witnessed. All Tami wanted was to be home. Everyone was deep in thought and not saying much.

Traffic was intermittent at the late hour, so their return trip took little more than twenty minutes. Scott suggested they all turn in, get some rest and called for a family meeting in the morning after Tami and Anne Marie got back from running. Before going upstairs, he went to the liquor cabinet, and poured himself two fingers of rye whiskey. Anne Marie joined him while Tami went upstairs with Carrie. It was like putting her to bed when she was five years old again. Tami sat with her on the side of the bed and stroked her hair until Carrie started calming down.

"Mom, you were so awesome tonight, but you scared me. What if something bad happened to you? What would we do?"

"I am very careful, hon. It seems kind of dangerous, but trust me, if I didn't feel like I had total control, I would back off."

"You promise?"

"Of course, I do. I promise I will never do anything that would take me away from you."

"What made you do what you did tonight, Mom?"

"Carrie, it just happens. When I am confronted, and somebody needs help, I simply react. It just happens so fast and is over in a flash. Like tonight: trouble, a bad guy hurting people, and boom, I just reflexively deal with it. Anne Marie has seen me before, only the last time it was a little kid in danger. I don't look for trouble, it seems to happen when I am around. Does any of this make any sense?"

"You need to be careful, is all, Mom. I love you so much and would die if anything happened to you."

"I promise I will be careful. Did you have fun otherwise tonight?"

"Oh, hell yes."

"What?"

I mean, "Oh yeah, you better believe it. The dinner was so good, and it was great to see Heather and Mr. Benson again. And Anne Marie is so much fun. Mr. Benson told me I could start my internship any time. He said I would start out on the copy desk but could also go out on assignment, and Heather is going to help me get prepped up."

"Let's talk about that in the morning with Dad, hon. You go to sleep now."

"Good night, Mom." Carrie reached for a hug before the lights went out.

Tami joined Anne Marie and her husband. Everyone seemed more impressed by what had happened that night than Tami. To her it was just business as usual. Like she had told Carrie, her inner self reacted to negative situations in superhuman time. It was almost like she had no control over her body, other than the supreme confidence that she could move faster than time.

"Want a drink, killer?" Scott asked her.

"No, thank you, I'm going to bed. What time do you want to go out tomorrow, which is already today, Anne Marie?" The two women agreed on six a.m., and it was lights off for them too.

————

Tami wanted to sleep, but Scott was having none of that. He pulled her to him and gave her a huge hug. "Baby, I had no idea."

"What did you think was happening here? Does WBC pass out offers like we got to just anybody?"

"No, they don't. But it is totally different when you see it happen in real life."

"Whatever. Let's go to sleep." Tami rolled over and spooned into her husband.

Scott's mind was still going a hundred miles an hour. He was flabbergasted at what he had seen and was beginning to fully comprehend Tami and Anne Marie's concerns. The super phenomena Tami was creating, now fully fueled by the media, was beginning to dawn on him.

Tami, not as tired as she thought she might be, gave her backside a little wiggle. Scott responded with a little tickle, and she turned around and squirmed back into his welcoming arms.

————

At quarter to six, Tami rolled out of bed and into her running gear. She went to the bathroom, brushed her teeth, and was stretching when Anne Marie came down the stairs. The women ran through the quiet residential streets until they reached Arroyo Seco Parkway and were able to stretch out their legs in the open spaces adjacent to the Rose Bowl Stadium.

"I am just so glad the press wasn't there last night," Tami told Anne Marie.

"Don't hold your breath. With all those network people around, word will get out."

It was another beautiful morning in sunny Southern California, the kind of weather that makes so many people put up with the crowds and freeways and air quality to live here. The two women were enjoying themselves to the fullest. For Tami, the morning run was cathartic in processing what had happened last night. To Anne Marie, it was simply blissful to be with her friend with the light breeze in her face and their steady pace through the towering eucalyptus stands.

———

Geo called Alfonzo's cell phone about eight o'clock, and the road warriors chatted. Alfonzo had already called room service for breakfast. Geo had spent his time going through Malcolm's travel bag. They chatted for a few minutes and agreed that Geo would come pick Alfonzo up in half an hour.

———

"I'll be back in a few minutes," Geo told Malcolm.

"I need to go to the bathroom."

"There is a portable commode right there by the bed. I have to go out, so you behave yourself. No one can hear you in here, so just shut up, and I'll bring you back something to eat. You are going to be okay, but if you stir up any trouble, we will beat the living shit out of you when we get back. I mean, did you think you could just walk away from us, and we wouldn't come for you? Think about it."

"I want some coffee."

"Sure, Malcolm. I'll be right back."

Geo left, but the sickening rage in Malcolm's belly went nowhere. All he wanted to do was get away from these clowns, go back to Soirée, get his bag, and hit the airport. How he was going to pull all that off, he wasn't sure. *They can have the cockeyed watch,* he thought. *It's been nothing but trouble since I bought the damn thing.*

———

Tami and Anne Marie slowed their run as they neared the house after doing briskly paced twelve/five minute forty-five second miles. Scott was up and had the coffee pot on. He had started rummaging in the refrigerator for breakfast. The morning news was on the TV in the kitchen, and Scott poured two mugs of fresh coffee out.

"Hey Tamer," he said, "you're famous again."

"Whatta ya mean?"

"Here, I recorded a segment of the morning news, let me play it for you." He pressed the record button on the remote, and the screen jumped to the top of the morning report with some footage of a disturbance in a fashionable Beverly Hills restaurant last night. The entire WBC party came into view, and they relived the disturbance on color TV. Tami was, of course, horrified to be on television yet again, especially as her counterattack to Alonzo's aggression was filmed with her front and center taking him out. To make matters worse, the security footage also followed her and her family walking out the exit to the Beamer, with their front California custom license plate in plain view.

"That's not cool," Anne Marie said.

"Look on the bright side, AM; Tami just made a hundred grand."

"I know Scott, but aren't you aware of how easy it is to trace a license plate? You will probably have at least three news trucks in front of your house by the time we finish breakfast."

"That makes me want to puke," Tami said. "Better yet, let's give them Ben's address, and send them over to him for a scoop."

Geo asked Malcolm what he wanted for breakfast, and that he would bring him back a large coffee. He checked the tightness of the handcuff and bolted the heavy wood planked door from the outside when he left.

Sunday morning was probably the best time of the week to drive in LA and it took Geo no time at all to find his way from Burbank to Beverly Hills. He texted Alfonzo from the street in front of the hotel, and Alfie was downstairs in three minutes.

"I need to pick up some fast-food breakfast for me and Malcolm on the way back," he said.

"Everything go okay over there?"

"Just beautiful, and you ain't gonna believe what I found in Sparrow's bag."

"What?"

"Just wait until we get back to the safe house."

Geo pulled into a McDonald's drive through and ordered half a dozen deluxe breakfast biscuit sandwiches, three large coffees and they were back on the road.

The garage door trundled up and Geo pulled inside. He took the breakfast package into the house and set it on the rectangular yellow and chrome Formica kitchen table. Taking a couple of biscuits and a coffee for Malcolm, he went over and unlocked the secure room's door.

"Morning Malcolm, your breakfast has arrived." Malcolm sat up, and sneered at Geo, it looked as though he had been crying.

"Buck up, old chappie, things ain't so bad; we'll have you out of here in no time."

Although the biscuit and sausage sandwich tasted like chalk to him, he took a second bite, and sipped some coffee. In his dismal surroundings, at least the coffee buoyed his spirits.

"I want out of here, and damn it, I missed my flight last night."

"Be patient my man, you'll be back on the street in an hour or two."

"Where's my watch. Give it back to me now."

Thinking Malcolm might be mistaking Geo's good humor for some kind of weakness or sympathy, Geo walked over and told Malcolm to put his coffee down. When he did, Geo slapped his face, and walked out of the room, closing the door behind him.

Alfonzo was sitting at the kitchen table looking through Malcolm's bag, when Geo came back in and wolfed down a biscuit.

"There's nothing in here but a bunch of clothes."

Geo walked over to one of the kitchen cupboards and pulled out a pair of latex gloves, put them on, then reached up to the top shelf, and grabbed an oversized Chase bank bag. He took it over to Alfonzo, opened it, and shook out the bulky envelope Donovan from

Probe magazine had handed Malcolm back at their meeting in the Phillips Club.

Alonzo looked up in amazement at Geo. "Everything's all there?"

"Yep."

"I don't believe it. I mean, a million bucks in negotiable paper?"

"Right here! And don't touch anything unless you have gloves on."

"I mean I love Uncle Carlo, but we don't have to have him launder our money?"

"Nope."

"Let's get the fuck outta here then."

"Where you wanna go?"

"Get Sparrow ready to go, dump him somewhere near LAX, and let's drive to Vegas. We'll fly back to New York from there."

"Vegas sounds great to me. The Casinos can launder some of the money for us."

"This is almost too good to be true."

"I'll get him ready to go."

While unlocking Malcolm, Geo told him to get freshened up they were leaving. Malcolm wanted to take a shower. "In there," and Geo pointed to the little adjoining restroom. He left, locking the door behind him. Back in the kitchen, Geo sat down and looked at Alonzo.

———

"How you want to split the paper?"

"A hundred grand and the watch for Uncle Carlo, and you and me split the rest?"

"Four fifty each?"

"Works for me. But shouldn't we give him back his watch?"

"Nah on the watch, good to go on the paper."

"I think we should give him the watch back. You know, that would be a token of our goodwill. I mean if he goes to the cops when we cut him loose, that could be trouble. He don't know our names, but he knows where we hang out. He might be able to ID us."

"How is he going to explain to the cops why he is caring around a million bucks in cashier's checks?"

"I think he got the paper legally, though."

"Look through the rest of his stuff and find his personal shit. Get his old lady's address, or a girlfriend in England or something we could threaten him with. If we came all the way from New York to find him, we would for sure go over to London if we had to, wouldn't we?"

"It's in the bank bag."

Geo looked in the bag again. Sparrow's personal was stuff all there. Letters from mom, a post from his sister with pictures of herself and two kids. Some miscellaneous business correspondence.

"Perfect. Let's go have a chat with him."

Geo and Alfonzo went into Malcolm's small room. It seemed even smaller now with the two beefy men inside standing menacingly over Malcolm. He sat on the edge of the bed and refused to acknowledge them. Geo ripped off a pillowcase and held it in his hand.

"Hey buddy, we need to talk."

"Let me out of here."

"Be patient. We are just about to leave, but we want to get our business straight with you. We are going to drop you off by the airport, and we don't want to hear from you again. Got it?"

"Whatever."

"No, that is not whatever. We are going to turn you loose and we are done. Do you understand? That means we never see each other again. And I mean never."

"Whatever."

Geo cuffed Malcolm with another hard slap, and he cried out. The two Airborne Rangers were not impressed with Malcolm's tolerance of pain.

"One more time loser, we are going to release you by the airport. You are going to book a flight to England and get the fuck outta here. If you try to call the cops, or your buddies at WBC or anyone else, we have some names of your people in London. We came all the way to

California to settle our score with you. Do you think we won't go to England and mess them and you up? Do you want to see that happen, Malcolm? Because if it does happen, it will be totally on you, asshole. Am I making myself clear. Do you understand what I am saying?"

"Yeah."

"Say yes sir."

"Yes sir, but you stay from me." Malcolm was shocked at the efficiency of these clowns. They had somehow found him in Los Angeles, and now they seemed to have knowledge about his family in London.

"Just fly off to Heathrow, and no one will get hurt. But if you can't or don't want to do that, well, Alfonso can punch your ticket for you right here and now. Is that what you want?"

"No." Definitely no, but Malcolm immediately filed Geo's slip of the tongue in his mental computer.

"What are you going to do if we take you to the airport?"

"Buy a new ticket and go home."

"That would be the smart thing to do Malcolm. Don't forget that. And one more thing, we are going to keep your phone, so you don't get any stupid ideas in your head."

"You wouldn't dare," Malcolm spat out.

Geo reached over and gave Malcolm another vicious bitch slap. "What's your passcode?"

"Fuck you."

A couple more noisy slaps and Malcolm saw the wisdom of letting the boys keep his phone. Geo tried the passcode. No problem.

———

Alfonzo gave Malcolm back his wallet, then draped a pillowcase over his head, and wrapped some duct tape around his neck to secure it. Before the boys led Malcolm out, they checked the house, purged it of any prints or DNA, threw his bag in the car's trunk, and took Malcolm into the garage. They loaded him onto the floor of the back seat and split for LAX. Geo drove south on Vermont until he saw a deserted bus stop. He brought the car to the curb, and Alfonzo pulled Malcolm off the floor. He pushed him down on the bus bench, threw his valise on the ground in front of him and they sped off.

Malcolm sat up and began to tear at the duct tape holding the pillowcase over his head. He finally got it off and looked around. Sadly, no one had seemed to notice or care about a guy with his head all taped up, sitting on a bus bench on a bright Sunday morning. He didn't know where he had been abducted to, or where he was now.

Looking down, he saw his roller bag sitting on the ground, and dread engulfed him like a cloud of poison gas. Tears began forming in both of his eyes.

He had lost, stupidly outsmarting himself, and knew he was a defeated man. One minute he had been on top of the world sipping the finest champagne, nibbling caviar, the next, he had been eviscerated. Without doubt his valuable papers had been stolen. His mom and sister's information had also been in the bag, and now he had to get to LAX and buy another expensive plane ticket to get out of this star struck piece of crap of a city. He sat for a bit and cringed in agony, digesting his losses like they were kidney stones, and began to suffer the severe migraine that was settling over him.

CHAPTER
14

A news truck from NBC rolled up in about half an hour and someone knocked on the door. Scott answered it and told the male reporter to get off of his property or he would call the police. Soon there were two more trucks, one from CBS, one from Fox, who also tried knocking on the door.

Tami called Ben Benson and explained that because of the leak of the security video from Soirée, there were about fifteen reporters milling around in her front yard, and would he please get some security over to her house.

Carrie, of course knew what was happening, but Charlie, the second oldest kid in the family was pretty astonished to see so many people milling around on their front lawn as he walked home after the overnight with his BFF. As he approached the front door, one of the reporters stuck a mic in his face and asked what he thought of his mom's new superpowers. He was at a loss for words. Scott, hearing some commotion, had to go out and extricate Charlie. He burst into the house wanting to know what was going on.

"Sit down, son," Scott said. "We are about to have a family meeting. Have you had breakfast yet? There are pancakes and some scrambled eggs in the kitchen."

"I've already eaten, thanks. What are all those people doing out there?" Scott got the younger kids out of the kitchen, and everyone sat down in the living room.

"Okay, everybody knows Anne Marie, Mom's friend from New York, right? This is a little hard to explain, but Anne Marie might be staying with us for a while. Your mom has been helping some people out. She has not only been helping people, but because of her running, has been able to do it in a special kind of way."

"What kind of a way, Dad?"

"Well, it seems like mom is very strong, and has special talents that other people don't have. Not only that, but she has also been on TV a lot lately, and people are really interested in what she can do. That's why all of the television people are outside."

Charlie thought that was major cool. "Can I be on TV too, mom," he asked.

"Charlie, it's not being on TV that makes anyone cool, it's you being yourself that's cool."

"Yeah mom, but if you are like Wonder Woman or something, all our friends would think that was gnarly."

"Carrie, Charlie, Sonny, Sadie—I am honored and happy to be your mom; it is the absolute greatest joy of my life. If I can help somebody who's in trouble, that's also great, and I want to do that, but after everything is all said and done, I am still just your mom. It is so important to me that everybody understands that, no matter what, we are still a family."

Anne Marie chimed in, "Kids, the hard part is that because your mom is somebody really special, things may change around you, outside of you. Like the people in the front yard right now, or kids treating you differently at school, or you having to be super careful when you are outside your house, and never ever talking to strangers. That kind of thing."

———

Scott was ready to say something when the doorbell rang. He got up and went to answer it. It was a couple of La Canada/Flintridge uniformed policemen.

"I understand you might be having some trouble here?" said one of the officers.

"We're just trying to keep people off of our property, officer."

"Good enough. We will make an announcement that your front yard is private property, and anyone trespassing will be arrested."

"I hope the news vans aren't blocking traffic flow?"

"We'll take care of that, have a good day." The policemen were super helpful, but they kept looking over Scott's shoulder when they were talking, like they were hoping to get a glimpse of Tami.

"Will do, thank you."

———

Scott went back into the living room. Their initial family conversation had opened the lines of communication, and when Scott looked at Tami, he could see she was pretty happy with the way things were going. From there, the issues seemed to be sorting out along gender lines: Sonny and Charlie thought it was way cool to have policemen at their front door, and news trucks all over the place. Carrie was old enough and had seen enough to know what was going on, it was little Sadie who was still confused. The adults agreed she would need the most support, and possibly some professional therapy, she might even need to be home schooled. But this morning was a significant start in addressing their new lives.

"Hey, let's watch a movie," Tami suggested. Scott and the boys opted to throw a football around the back yard, and then watch the afternoon Dodgers game. Tami and the girls turned on TCM and started watching *Sleepless in Seattle*.

When the movie was over, Tami took matters into her own hands and went out to the front porch. She offered the remaining reporters some bottled water, a few of whom accepted, but then, being reporters, they immediately started firing off some questions.

"There will be no interviews today," she told them. "My friend and I run for two hours every morning, starting at four-thirty a.m. We run and talk. If any of you would like to join us, please be here at that time, and I mean to run. No motor bikes, no roller skates, no dirt bikes, no skateboards, just you and your running shoes, and no tape recorders. Thank you."

"Well, we'll see where that goes," Anne Marie said when Tami came back inside.

"Who knows, if we can get a few more people off their butts, and outside jogging, it could be a good thing."

————

Early the next morning Tami and Anne Marie were joined by Leona Harris from WBC, and the three women took off running before anyone else joined them. Leona was a strong and powerful young black woman, but she was not as light on her feet and smooth as Tami and AM. She had yet to develop that powerful effortless glide on the balls of the feet that Tami and Anne Marie were pros at. Of course, she had not been running for as long as her two companions, and while she was less experienced as a runner, she was younger and stronger than the two older women. Therefore, she was determined to keep up.

Tami and Anne Marie chatted about yesterday's family gathering, and Tami announced she was going to meet with Sadie's Summer Program director this morning. "If she can help monitor things for us, I am willing to leave Sadie where she is for now. If not, you may be starting a new career in homecare. Hey, how about home schooling her?"

"Happy to help for the short term. I can get Sadie started on her Marketing career!"

Tami and Anne Marie picked up the pace a bit to create a little privacy for themselves.

"I think I am going to opt out, Anne Marie."

"Tami, think about it. You are only just starting your contract."

"I know, but that film clip this morning really pissed me off. Benson didn't have to do that. I mean, I don't care about what happened inside the restaurant, but to flash my personal info like that was totally careless and rude. And now I have to go into work today and actually talk to the news team about what happened."

"I agree, but maybe it was an accident. I'm sure they can blur it out for later broadcasts."

"I'm sure they can too, but the damage is already done."

"Word was going to get out in time, Tami, now we just have to deal with things sooner, that's all."

"Just deal with it, right. You understand that Sadie means more to me than all the WBC's and Ben Bensons in the world?"

"Sure, I do Tami. Why else would I drop everything, and fly out here to be with you?"

"The whole thing just doesn't sit right with me, Anne Marie. I don't need it, I don't want it, I was perfectly happy with my life before Ben Benson called me."

"I know you were, Tami, but can't you understand that if you manage WBC effectively, they will be a huge asset to you and your family?"

"How, like by terrorizing my kids?"

"Tami, three of your four kids think WBC is the coolest. I agree, we have to protect Sadie, but Carrie could receive some major professional and educational benefits from this experience. Not to mention the huge socializing aspect available to her. Sonny and Charlie will be the coolest kids at their schools. Scott likes the deal. If you hadn't signed, you would be out there on your own, trying your best to deal with every Tom, Dick and Malcolm in the world knocking on your door."

"If I had to, I would just move my family back to Gig Harbor."

"What about Scott's position?"

"He would work with me, if I needed him to."

"Would he? You know this is his dream job, right?"

"Don't get in my personal stuff, please. I appreciate all you've done for me, but this is my life, and I need to figure it out on my own."

"Sorry, I don't mean to interfere, but can I please make a suggestion?"

"Sure, you can Miss Relentless."

"Ha-ha, I know you are struggling with everything that is going on. As someone who is on your team, and if I were in your shoes, I would lay low. Let things settle down. You know the press has to have instant gratification, and if you stay out of the limelight, they will move on. Carrie and I will help you with Sadie, and while you are laying low, why don't we start training you for the Universal Games next year?"

"Wow."

"Yeah, wow. Your best marathon time is around three hours, qualifying time is 2:27. You are an experienced, dedicated runner. You love to run and workout daily. You are the apex of recreational runners; don't you think if we introduced some proven training disciplines into your running you could trim thirty seconds off your best time? Not to mention we have over six months to help you qualify?"

"Anne Marie, you know what a thrill it would be to qualify. But I am a thirty-something year old woman with four kids, a husband, and a job. How could I do that?

"Well, you would have to work your fanny off. But who works harder, or is more disciplined than you anyway? Plus, if we introduced some Fartlek method into your workouts, threw in some speed work at Pasadena City College, start adding in some elevation work in the San Gabriels, I know it would enhance your performance. You could do it, Tami."

"I don't know Anne Marie. There is so much going on right now, and what the hell is Fartlek anyway."

"Fartlek means speed play in Swedish. It is a training technique that involves adding short bursts of speed work into your runs. It would be so simple to add to your routine and could produce some exciting results. It was developed by a Swedish Olympic runner in the 1930s."

"I would be so honored to compete against the world's best marathoners, but I would like to talk to Scott. This would involve so much extra time, training, and effort. I don't know if this is the right time to put anything else on my family."

"Think about it. You train every morning anyway. Are you going to stop running now? Of course not. Would adding some formal training to your workout change things that much?"

"Let me sleep on it for a couple of days and talk to my husband."

"Check it out. I'm willing to adjust my own schedule, stay out here in California and work with you the whole way."

"You are becoming my life coach, my business advisor, and my athletic trainer. Don't get any ideas about Scott."

"LOL."

———

The ladies finished their run and bid Leona goodbye until tomorrow. Tami went into the house, took a shower and started rousting her kids out of bed.

———

Mrs. Waters was young, dedicated, and had been the Director at Pasadena Childcare Center for five years. Her kids were special to her, and she and Tami already had a proactive relationship going on.

"Good morning, Mrs. Waters," Tami half whispered while knocking on her office door.

Britany Waters looked up from her desk and smiled. "Good morning, come on in."

"I know this is a drop in, but I was wondering if I could take just a couple minutes of your time."

"Sure, sure. How can I help?"

"Just wanted to touch base, maybe if you think it would be better, we could schedule a formal appointment. But Scott and I are concerned that all of the publicity I have gotten lately might have a negative effect on Sadie's environment here. We wanted to ask if you could keep an eye on her for a while. She loves spending her summers here, and we like nothing more than having her here. But if things got weird with the kids, and not just in session, but it's anything that might go on out on the playground that concerns us."

"I understand and I will monitor the situation. Most likely this age child is not watching the evening news every night, but they may have picked up on some of what's going on from their parents or older siblings. I will put the word out to look after Sadie, she is one of our favorites by the way, and if there are any problems, I'll give you a call."

"Thank you so much."

"No problem, Mrs. Powers."

"Please, call me Tami."

"Certainly."

————

Happy with her short meeting, Tami took off for West Hollywood. She collected her thoughts and began to prepare for her interview. She would be featured in a WLA12 segment this evening. She rolled into the studio lot, found her designated parking space, grabbed her bound leather attaché case, and headed for the entry.

"Good morning, Mrs. Powers," the receptionist chirped. "Mr. Benson would like to have a word with you on the eighth floor, please."

"Thank you."

Tami was escorted to Benson's suite door. She was summoned in and sat down in a plush wingback chair in front of his large mahogany desk. There was another gentleman seated next to her. "Good morning, Ben," she said.

"Morning, Tami. Thanks for stopping by. This is Carl Middleton, he and I wish to discuss a few logistical things with you, but first, I want to apologize for the sloppy work of our technical department. There is no excuse for their egregious processing of your film clip, and they have been reprimanded. Especially after the way you reacted and throttled our assailant. That was remarkable, and we are all in your debt."

"Thank you and thank you."

"You are very welcome, and Carl and I want to assure you it will not happen again. Your privacy is very important to us, Tami, and what happened is inexcusable. Moving on, I am returning to my position in New York, and while I will still be available to you, Mr. Middleton who is a senior Vice President here on the West Coast, will be your primary contact. He is tasked with the management of our Accounting Division, and you are being assigned to our cost analysis team. He will also co-ordinate any and all interaction for you with the news side, personal issues, etc. Human Resources has your contract secured in their offices and are fully aware of the agreement we have reached. Do you have any questions for me?"

"Yes sir. I appreciate your concern with my family's privacy and can assure you that the scene in my front yard yesterday was highly unpleasant. I have young children who don't need this kind of negative intrusion into their lives. The peer pressure they could experience at school would be very detrimental, and my husband and I won't stand for that. If any kind of glaring omission or indiscretion by your staff should happen again, I will think seriously think about opting out of my contract with this company."

Ben Benson, a Yale man who had been through the corporate wars with savvy and guile for many years was unaccustomed to be spoken to in this manner by a staff member. He much more enjoyed having his ass kissed but was becoming aware that today was not the day for that.

"Tami, we all live in the real world. Accidents happen, and I have sincerely apologized to you. We will make a concerted effort to prevent any recurrences, won't we Carl?"

"Yes sir."

"I have enjoyed working with you Tami and am hoping that we are parting on good terms. As I have said, you are welcome to call me anytime."

"Thank you, and yes I will continue to be in touch with you in the future."

"Very well, Carl has scheduled you for some time with News to do a live wrap up interview of our experience on Saturday night. That should take about two hours, eh? Then you two can go over the details of your future responsibilities in the accounting department. Maybe a late lunch?"

"I will be in my office on the seventh floor, Mrs. Powers, please drop by when you are finished with the production people on two."

"Sure Carl, and please call me Tami."

————

Tami was getting accustomed to her interview processes, and the makeup department personnel were friendly and accommodating. It was actually kind of fun to have people fuss over you and do new things with your hair and image. When makeup was done, Tami's stylist walked her next door to a studio and she met Candy Ekberg, news anchor of the midday show.

When the two women had conversed for a few minutes about relevant content, Candy nodded to the technicians, the digital lighting bar engaged, and Candy introduced her to the news audience and asked her first question.

"Good midday everyone, we are leading off our newscast today with Mrs. Tami Powers who has been making quite a splash lately. Hello, Tami, how are you, and thanks for joining us for this exclusive WLA12 interview."

"I'm very good thank you," replied Tami politely, sorely wishing she could air her grievances with Ben on the air.

"Tami, we are going to show a quick clip of you in action last Saturday at a dinner party in your honor, and afterwards, we would like to hear your interpretation of that encounter. Can you roll the tape please?"

The tape showed the confrontation with Alfonzo as the dinner party exited the foyer of Soirée's Restaurant. Culminating of course with Tami's knockout kick to the burly gentleman's chin.

"Tami, can you give us a little background to Saturday night's drama?"

"Certainly. We were disbursing after a gathering hosted by WBC at the lovely Soirée Restaurant last Saturday night, when our group was accosted by a man who apparently had an issue with another gentleman in our group. The man in question produced some false law enforcement identification and when he was confronted as to the validity of his identity by WBC's Chief of Security, he began to attack random members of our group. He was spraying people directly in their face and eyes with some type of strong propellent. I saw an opportunity to disrupt this attacker, and I reacted."

"Tami, this man was approximately twice your size, but you stepped up and instantly disabled him. How do you do what you do?"

"Candy, I am a dedicated runner." Etcetera, etcetera.

"This is the third supernatural incident to my knowledge, Tami, and all three are different. Saturday night you displayed extraordinary physical power. On the other two occasions, you were able to leap and bound thirty or forty feet at a time. Is this a part of the reflex action you speak of?"

"Yes, it is."

"You have stated that you are trained in Tae Kwon Do. Does this discipline help or assist your intuitive self-defense gifts?"

"Tae Kwon Do is a martial art that heightens one's self-esteem, one's mental and physical well-being, and one's self-defense mechanisms. I am blessed to have studied this art, but it is not the trigger to my power. It is merely one component of who I am."

"And who ultimately are you, Tami?"

"Please write this down or tape our chat for the permanent record, because it will never change. I would like everyone to know that I am first and foremost a mother to my four children. I am happily married to my husband, Scott, I am a dedicated runner, a CPA who practices yoga and Tae Kwon Do, and has been gifted with a skill that I will always use for the greater good."

"Tami, how do you manage to fit all your activities in. I mean you must be under an enormous amount of stress."

"Just the opposite, Candy. Running to begin the day relieves my stress and brings me peace and serenity. Yoga and martial arts enhance my life. In order to accomplish all that I do, I am extremely well organized from four-thirty or five o'clock in the morning on. My life can be compartmentalized into minute sectors. My kids help out and are committed to us keeping an orderly family weekday schedule. When the children were younger, I worked less, but now that they are all in school, I have taken a three-quarter time position in accounting here at WBC."

"Tami you are a remarkable woman, and I, and I'm sure our listening audience sincerely urge you to be safe and careful out there. We wish only good things for you."

"Thank you, Candy."

Interview over, the studio went to some commercial time while Candy and Tami took off their clip-on mics and shook hands. "Tami, I just want to say what a privilege it is to meet you and speak with you for a few minutes. You are a joy, and I wish you nothing but the best."

"Thank you, Candy, hey, you should come out and run with us sometime."

"I think I just might do that."

———————

Tami finally found the time to break away and took Scott out for a glass of wine on Wednesday night so she could discuss the subject of the Universal Games qualifying with him. Laid back Scott didn't feel like it would change their lifestyle that much, and in his own mind, thought it could be purgative for Tami right now. As a family who were adjusting to her newfound celebrity, and he liked Anne Marie's suggestion of Tami laying low and letting the family catch their collective breaths.

"I actually like the idea, Tam. It could be a healthy diversion for you from everything that's going on. It would be a life fulfilling dream for you to qualify, and you are in the prime of your running career right now. This would be the optimal time for you to go for it. I'll be happy to do more with the kids, Carrie has certainly been a big help lately. Anne Marie said she is willing to jump in around the house as well as co-train with you, she seems to have fit nicely into our family. Plus, you've already got your daily workout schedule set, so it doesn't really affect the rest of us. I say go do it; you may never have a better opportunity."

"Wow, all systems seem to be saying go here."

"Yep."

"My workout schedule won't change that much, if anything, I probably won't be running as many marathons. I rescheduled with Carl for ten to four hours Monday, Wednesday and Friday. Tuesday and Thursday I can work from home. That will cut down on the drive time commute. I won't take on any more personal clients, Anne Marie said she would help with the family dinner meals, what else is there to plan for?"

"Personal time with your husband."

"You will be thrilled with me; I will be in better shape than a high school cheerleader."

"As long as I won't have to make an appointment a week in advance."

"You can have an appointment every night if you want."

Scott leaned over and kissed her, and their deal was done.

"I've done some research, and I just don't want us to turn out like that guy who created the Wonder Woman series," said Tami.

"Who was he?"

"He was a brilliant man, a Harvard guy and psychologist by the name of William Marston. He and one of his wives invented an early protype of the lie detector test, and he also invented how to measure systolic blood pressure."

"One of his wives?"

"He was an instructor at Tufts University and lived under the same roof in a polyamorous relationship with two women. He had two children with each woman and led quite an interesting life and career.

His polyamorous lifestyle was said to have had a great influence on his creation of the Wonder Woman character."

"Was he Mormon?"

"No, just polyamorous."

"I think that's called a small harem."

"Not necessarily. There were relationships going on all over the place, but unlike a harem, they had a serious and permanent nature to them."

"You mean they were poly polyamorous?"

"Is that even a word?"

"I don't know. I do know I'm a mechanical engineer who has never written anything, and I am monogamously monogamous and boring. I think you are stuck with me."

"Boring, schmoring. You are my Prometheus."

Scott laughed and called for their check.

CHAPTER 15

Tami's interview ran again on the evening news spots with a great deal of interest in the Powers household. Scott and Tami agreed the older kids could watch it once, and Sadie would be distracted in the kitchen by Tami and Anne Marie. The news spots continued to astound Scott and Carrie who were still trying to process their sheer magnitude. Footage of Tami speaking on a studio set, cool and detached, was such a contrast to the clip the producers showed of Tami in action.

Charlie and Sonny thought Tami was the coolest mom in America. Although their parents said they could only watch it once, Charlie knew he could go to the station's web site and stream the video on his phone, and he would show Sonny how to do it. Then they would both have it for the playground when school started in a couple of weeks. The old adage of my dad can beat up your dad, had in their case had changed genders.

Carrie smiled at Tami with awe and admiration. Her mom also gave her a newly found sense of potential in herself. She was sure she would never have Tami's superpowers, but now she actually believed all the things her mom had told her about hard work, perseverance and setting big goals.

Scott's personal life hadn't changed. He got up and went to work every day, loved his family, loved driving his Porsche, really felt blessed to be living his California life, but now it had another dimension to it. He was along for the ride and faced new responsibilities. There were things to consider that had never existed before. He was going to embrace all these new adventures and as usual, go with the flow.

————

The dinner table that night was a mess. Charlie and Sonny were so excited they couldn't contain themselves. Sadie wanted to know what her brothers were raving about, Tami was in denial, until finally Anne Marie tried to explain to Sadie what was going on. It was kind of like trying to explain to a kid that her mom is bigger than Santa Claus right now.

Finally, Tami took Sadie into the master bedroom, ran a tape of the interview for her, sans the knockout scene, and said everyone was just excited about her being on television, and that she might be on now and then for a while. Sadie was surprised to see her mom on TV, but since the Powers home wasn't TV centric anyway, she seemed more concerned to find her doll and get back to her coloring book.

————

Tami, Anne Marie and Leona took off running at five-thirty on Tuesday morning. The sun was peeking out of the eastern sky, it was sunny and clear except for the L.A. haze. Tami was thrilled to be out of the house and on the road.

Anne Marie opened the morning conversation with some questions for Tami about the Universal Games and her qualifying routine.

"You know, AM, I have never been a technical runner; I just get up in the morning and run."

"I know that, but do you want to qualify or not?"

"Of course, I do.

"Well, you are going to have to add some technique to your training if you want to make it. We have already talked about this, and I have given it a lot of thought."

"That must have been so difficult."

"Shut it. We have already discussed Fartlek, and I would like to add some elevation by running in the San Gabriel Mountains starting this week."

"I want to do it. Let's get going."

Anne Marie turned right when the three women got to Arroyo Seco Drive and soon, they were at the Brown Mountain Dam trailhead, and climbing to the east, headed for Mount Lawlor.

Tami had never met a hill she didn't like. As a beginning runner, she hated them. But knowing they weren't going anywhere; she began to develop a taste for head-on assaults. Sure, they hurt, sure they burned, but in time they made you feel better, stronger, more confident. When she came to the twenty-second mile of a marathon, those hills gave her the gravel in her guts to dig deep and finish her race. Also, every hill has a downside, but as she was used to running hills from her past experiences in the Northwest, it was a different story for Anne Marie and Leona. They were panting and their chests were heaving, but as Tami led the way, no one quit; Tami wouldn't let them.

Tami and Anne Marie continued to work toward the fall months, alternating between AM's chosen styles of training. No one could say the three women were not in better shape. Leona younger, stronger and from a completely different discipline, was exponentially improving her running style and technique. Tami encouraged her to come run a marathon and Leona was wondering what the heck she had gotten herself into.

The girls began to chat about a fall race, and their conversation didn't get much farther than the New York City Marathon in November. Of course, without saying anything, Anne Marie had already sent in applications for herself and Tami.

Tami was mildly amused by this and accused Anne Marie of being a conniving biach. AM responded that she was merely fulfilling her duties as any good agent/manager would. "I think if I call Ben, I can get a spot for Leona," Tami said.

———

Friday morning arrived, again bright and sunny. The trio of runners entered the Angeles National Forest by the Spruce Grove trail and began to climb above northern LA sprawl. Spruce Grove was the polar opposite of north LA, and it couldn't have been more beautiful in the morning light. It helped to start lifting Tami's uneasy mood this morning.

The chaparral vegetation, mainly manzanita, wasn't as majestic as the heavily treed NW, but the women's low, bushy surroundings glowed almost biblically in the morning light. The diffused aura of daybreak resonating softly. An occasional jack rabbit would duck through the brush, or a coyote's mournful howl serenaded them, lamenting his lack of success in finding last night's dinner. The dusky, woodsy smells of the undulating parkland enveloped them.

Tami loved to get some air off of the bigger rocks along the trail and would do leg tuck inspired ski jumps along the way. Leona could do a standing jump from ground level up to almost forty inches from her former collegiate volleyball days. She would follow Tami and push off so high from the trailside boulders it startled Anne Marie.

Although they needed street running to prepare for the NY marathon, returning to Monrovia and Altadena's bland environment of unending suburbia was a drag. Typical street litter was everywhere, morning traffic, and the ennui of civilization welcomed them. Delivery box trucks drove past, and the drivers often honked flirtatious greetings to the runners. Ever-present grime and greasy streets only added to Tami's growing feelings of apprehension. Something wasn't right, and it seemed like she was developing a sixth sense when an incident was about to occur.

The trio of joggers progressed along Altadena Drive, and as if on cue, they saw an altercation in front of them. A young Asian woman had exited Din's Modern Chinese Restaurant in the middle of the block of small businesses.

She looked up and down the street and had taken three or four steps onto the sidewalk when two young Caucasian men jumped out of an old sedan parked in front of the restaurant and accosted her. They were probably thinking she had the previous night's restaurant's cash drop in her purse, as well as her phone and personal credit cards. They were grabbing at her, cursing and ended up knocking her down. But the smallish woman held onto her bag like a condemned man to his last cigarette.

The purse snatchers were probably not even aware that literally ninety to ninety five percent of all restaurant sales are now transacted electronically, so there was no cash drop in the purse. Local banks weren't even open to accept deposits yet anyway. The young woman was headed to LA's Farmers' Market aiming to get a jump on other produce buyers. Her intentions were excellent, unfortunately her timing sucked.

Seeing one of the punks draw his leg back to kick the woman was all Tami needed. In the split second before she began one of her trademark bounds, Leona managed to get her cell phone out. Tami leaped the block long distance between her and the attackers in two vaults, and in a nano second was behind the young thug. He never had the opportunity to strike his fallen victim.

Tami drew her own leg up and landed a solid roundhouse kick to the kidney area of the kid on her right. He doubled over in pain. The other dude turned in surprise and Tami stepped into him and gifted him with an open-handed uppercut with the heel of her hand to the underside of his chin. His head snapped backward, and he dropped immediately. When Tami reached into her waist band for her mace canister, the first guy turned to strike, but she hit him with a direct shot in the eyes. Now both miscreants were on the sidewalk groaning in pain, and Tami turned to attend the fallen woman.

Suddenly she was confronted by another half a dozen angry young thugs in dark hoodies and sunglasses. Two of them were carrying large, Bowie-style knives and another one brandished a pistol, and it was pointed directly at Tami.

———

Even though the action was spontaneous and happened in a matter of seconds, Leona was ready for her first professional photo op, and caught Tami on film leaping to, then forcibly subduing the attackers. Anne Marie was equally adept with her phone but called 911 instead of recording anything. Both women, as well as the fallen Asian women, immediately froze when the second wave of attackers emerged from a van parked streetside. They slowly surrounded Tami in a circle of menace while flashing their weapons.

"Put the gun down, son. There is no need for violence here," Tami said.

"Maybe there is you gook lover, and I'm not your son. I'm more like your daddy right now, and we don't like no gook lovers, do we boys?" The head punk raised his weapon and told Tami to "get down on your knees bitch!"

Time seemed to literally stop, as Anne Marie gazed at the scene in horror from half a block away, and Leona somehow continued to film with a trembling hand. The young Asian woman cowered and cringed on the ground, actually pulling her coat over her head in terror.

"I am asking you to please put the gun down and go on home, daddy," Tami replied.

"Ha-ha you dumb crack," Tami's tormentor said as he raised and cocked his weapon while pointing it at her head.

"Shoot 'er, Joe. Shoot the gook too," piped up one of the young thugs. "Shut her up for good."

———

But something incredible happened. A miracle occurred before their very eyes. One second Tami was there, physically standing in the midst of a violent street gang with a revolver pointed at her head. A nano second later her persona was gone. She had literally disappeared.

It was inexplicable, but she was now gone. The young punks looked sideways at each other in disbelief. In frustration Joe fired his weapon at the spot Tami had been standing, only to hit the banger across the circle from him in the chest with a direct shot. As the gunman gazed in shock at his fallen comrade, who had curled into the fetal position, gasping for air and was soaking his hoodie in blood, he suddenly felt Tami's left-hand crash down on the bridge of his nose. Her other hand then delivered a deadly chop to his throat. The pistol clattered harmlessly to the pavement while he gasped for oxygen, bent at the waist, covering his face with bloody hands from his broken nose.

As the other gang members stared in astonishment, an invisible hand picked up the weapon, fired a shot in the air, and a voice told the rest of the group to get down on the ground. They still stood and gaped senselessly at nothing, until she crouched down and fired an upward round that whizzed past the right ear of the biggest gang banger. Three of the remaining five dudes dropped immediately to the ground, and two smaller guys standing at the far edge of the group took off sprinting for their sorry lives.

While that was happening, and with six punks now lying prone before her, one of whom was seriously wounded, Tami transformed back into visible life and reached down to help her Asian friend up. Keeping the weapon trained on her subdued attackers. Anne Marie and Leona began to run to her, and welcome sirens could be heard rapidly approaching. The whole reversal sequence of her physical transformation had taken mere seconds.

A minute later three squad cars pulled up, screeched to synchronized stops, and six Altadena cops spilled out of their units, weapons draw, taking charge of the crime scene. It was quickly determined that this was not a simple purse snatching. Worse, it fit the profile of a series of crimes committed in the area. Hate crimes perpetuated by a local gang who had been tormenting the Asian community for some time.

The police officers, four men/two women, seemed appreciative of Tami's work, while confused at how she had managed to avoid serious injury in such a dire situation. They took control of the crime scene, called for an ambulance and EMTs, and began cuffing gang members and confiscating their weapons. Tami said as little as possible while standing to the side of the restaurant as the senior officer took her statement. A substantial crowd of neighborhood onlookers and press corps were gathering.

When Tami's interview was finished, the young Asian woman, whose name was Mei, was next. The officer grilled her as well as AM and Leona. Finally, Mei was able to take Tami's arm and guide her inside the restaurant's front door. Anne Marie and Leona followed closely behind, still shaking and breathing deeply.

———

Inside Din's Modern Restaurant, a jangled and emotional Mei went off to make tea, while the three amigas sat down in a large red, padded booth. Anne Marie and Leona were speechless, and having been a distance away from the action, were unsure of what they had actually seen. Leona's video wasn't much help, as it was just far enough away, and just jumpy and obscured enough to effectively blur the details.

Finally, Anne Marie observed with no small amount of irony, "all in a day's work, huh Tami?"

"Bummer actually, I was really enjoying our run this morning."

———

Leona made an executive decision. Rather than take her video straight back to the studio, she elected to do a live, on the spot interview. While not being studio quality, this would be much more intimate and timelier under the circumstances. She offered her services to Tami, who responded affirmatively.

When the tea service arrived with their hostess, and four small cups, laminated with the incongruous scenes from a lotus garden were set out, Leona asked if the lights could be turned up. She then directed Mei Chan to sit next to Tami, then Anne Marie and finally Leona directly faced Tami. Before she started her interview Tami took out her cell phone, called Scott, told him she was delayed, and asked him to see the kids off to school. Mei Chan poured her favorite recipe of green tea with a quivering hand, and they went live.

"Good morning, this is Leona Harris filming for WLA12 news. We are at Din's Modern Chinese Restaurant in Altadena this morning, and I'm here to report a serious crime and physical assault on one of the owners of the restaurant we are sitting in. Fortunately, three of us were out jogging, and one of the joggers was none other than our own Tami Powers. As you might expect, it turned out to be a spectacular T-Pow morning. Tami bounded into the scene of two young thugs attacking the restaurant's owner and subdued those two attackers of Mei Chan here.

Suddenly six more gangbangers, wanted by the law no less, who have been allegedly terrorizing the Asian community for some time, emerged out of nowhere. They began threatening Tami with deadly weapons. I'm talking large knives and a handgun.

Tami also subdued and held them captive until the police arrived. Yet again you intervened in a most harrowing and hazardous situation, Mrs. Powers. This seems to be becoming a habit with you."

"An undeserving woman was being viciously attacked. Wouldn't most anyone do the same thing as I did this morning?"

"The sad answer to that question, Tami, is no. Not only would few people intervene, but no one also has your physical abilities to help them achieve another successful outcome like you did today."

"Leona, I abhor violence, I detest physical harm, and racial discrimination of any kind is especially offensive to me. What kind of people would attack a single woman on the street like we saw today? Greedy, violent bullies, serial racists? I don't know. I'm just so glad I was here to help someone avoid serious injury and any personal losses. I would do it again in a nano second."

"Do you have any advice for the young men you apprehended today?"

"Yes, I do Leona. Guys, take a look at yourselves. What have you achieved but destruction and disfunction in not only your own lives, but also pain and fear in the lives of your victims. Young people out there, please do not go down this path. You only have one life to live. Make the most of it, go to school, study, become the person you dream of being. It will be difficult, nothing is easy in life, but make the effort. You will be so glad you did.

"Tami, those are such strong and inspiring words."

"I hope they are, and I pray they will help some of today's young people to take inventory of themselves. I understand there are different levels of advantage in society, but no matter where you come from or who you are, positive circumstances are out there for you. You only need to work hard and seek to achieve those opportunities. Crime is the easy way out, please don't take it."

"Ms. Chan how are you feeling, did you survive you your attack in one piece?"

"With Ms. Tami's help I did, thank you. Also, thanks to the policemen for responding so quickly. The Asian community has been trying to apprehend this gang for a long time. The attack on me was only the beginning of what could have happened here today. Other restaurants and businesses have been invaded and seriously damaged, sometimes senselessly trashed beyond repair. Tami not only saved me personally but also probably saved this family enterprise and many others from being ransacked and destroyed. I will never be able to thank you enough Tami."

"If you don't mind my asking Tami, what were you doing on the streets of Altadena at this hour of the morning?"

"I was finishing off my morning run when we encountered Mei Chan and her friends."

"Was there any hesitation on your part to intervene, to get involved this morning?"

"I always pause momentarily to assess the situation. This morning I felt like it was imperative to act, and act quickly."

"Tami, you are an inspiration to all of us, especially the women of America. Thank you, and do you have any further words for us today?"

"Just go out there, especially my women friends; dream big, work hard, and Be Happy. But do not try to do what I was able to do here today at home."

"Thank you, Tami, and thank you ladies and gentlemen for also being with us today. Live from Dim's Modern Chinese Restaurant in Altadena, California, this is Leona Harris for WLA12 news."

————

Leona shut her cell phone down, and Tami said, "Thanks Leona, you saved me a trip into the city today. By the way, how did my make up look for the interview?"

"Y'all look like the most beautiful woman in the world Tami."

"Thanks, shall we go?"

"Let's."

"Thank you, Mei, for the tea, it was most refreshing. Is there anything else we can do for you? Do you need to call anyone to come down and be with you?"

"No they will be here in a few minutes, but I would like to have a selfie with the four of us," and Mei pulled out her nearly stolen cell phone. The women posed together, hugged, said their goodbyes and Tami's crew headed for the exit door. "You please call me. Come back for dinner anytime," Ms. Chan said in parting.

As soon as the door opened, the women were greeted by a melee. The original crowd had remained and grown incrementally. Anne Marie's call to 911 had alerted the press, and there were now approximately one hundred people milling about in front of the restaurant. One third of whom were from media outlets or were independent paparazzi. It was all Tami, Anne Marie and Leona could do to jam the door shut again on a sea of extended arms and microphones. Thank God it opened in not out.

Mei led them around through the kitchen to the back door. There was a small, high ventilation window to the left of the door, and Leona grabbed a utility ladder that sat underneath and climbed up to do some recon. With only two or three reporters back there, the morning joggers felt like they could make an escape. They waited a few minutes, then burst out the back door, and took off sprinting down the trash can littered alleyway. The reporters with their cameras and microphone cables were no match for three Olympic quality runners as they dashed away.

Keeping to back roads, they got back to La Canada in one piece, but when they turned the corner onto her street, there was already a gathering of press in front of Tami's house. The three runners paused, took a deep breath, and willed themselves through the crowd and into Tami's front room. "No comment, no comment, no comment," was all they said. Tami was thankful and amazed the front door was open but scolded herself mentally for leaving it that way, or at Scott for not locking up when he left.

———

After getting inside the living room, the tired joggers collapsed on couches and took deep breaths. Tami and Anne Marie were getting used to interacting with the media, but this was a whole new level to deal with for Leona. And although she had given many post-game interviews back at CU, these press relations were a lot more phrenic and multifaceted than she was used to. As if to emphasize her feelings, the doorbell began ringing aggressively. It was ignored.

Leona went into the den to make some calls and forward her video to Carl at Headquarters. When she came back to the living room, Anne Marie had gone upstairs to freshen up, and Tami was still sitting on the couch staring at a photograph of smiling family members sitting on the mantle.

"Why is the world we live in so screwed up, Leona?"

"It just is."

"It's like we have the absolute best communication systems and technology in the annals of history, and it has only seemed to make things worse. Criminals are more sophisticated, and law enforcement is handcuffed much of the time. The legal system is broken, the country is floating in a sea of debt, people are living on the streets worse than they did in the great depression, and if there is a crime going on and someone steps up to help, everyone is shocked."

"Very few people help each other anymore."

"When did we lose our way? I don't think it used to be like this. Our country was pretty united when it came to helping destroy Fascism. Now all people care about is themselves."

"I know. That's why when someone like you comes along, it's refreshing. It's major news."

Anne Marie came back downstairs. "I am refreshed as a daisy, and I feel great after running with you two animals this morning. I'm also sorry the world is not a better place, so let's go eat some breakfast already. I'm starving."

Leona and Tami got up to go into the kitchen when Tami's cell phone rang. It was Carl Middleton, and Tami excused herself to take the call.

———

"Good morning, Carl, how are you?"

"Morning. I've just seen Leona's video, and it is powerful stuff, Tami. It is explosive! Are you okay?"

"Thank you for asking, Carl, I'm fine."

"After looking at the video, Ben will want to milk it for all it's worth."

"I'm sure he will."

"The video is a little blurry because of the distance Leona and Anne Marie were from you, however, there seems to be something even more remarkable about this sequence, Tami. I will have our technicians attempt to focus things up as best they can, and there could be a slight gap in Leona's clip. Do you have any additional comments or information about your confrontation with the gang members this morning?"

"No. No comments, other than if your guys blurred that segment or left it out entirely, I wouldn't mind."

"I'll see what I can do."

————

Tami went into her office, closed the door behind her, and called Scott.

"Hi baby, what's up? You all right?"

"I don't know, Scott, I really don't know."

"What do you mean?"

"Well, this morning got super serious. You know what you said about guns, and how I should be careful? Well, this morning things turned ugly when I went to the rescue of a woman who had been attacked by two guys. I took care of them, and suddenly I was surrounded by a whole gang with knives and a gun."

"Holy smokes, babe. I warned you, what happened?"

"Scott, I just evaporated. I disappeared, to where I was invisible, and I still had the physical strength and presence to subdue them."

"You're kidding me!"

"I wish I was."

"Did anyone film it?"

"Yes, Leona was there, but she wasn't too close, and the film is pretty indistinct."

"Does the newsroom have the video?"

"No, Leona agreed to send it to Carl instead of directly to them. I talked to him, and he said he would do what he could to be discrete. But we know what Ben will want to do, right?"

"Wow. The hell with Ben, are you all right? I mean do you feel differently now than you would normally?"

"I feel fine physically, that's the damnation of it. But it is certainly overwhelming mentally and emotionally to disappear and come back into your body at seven in the morning."

"I'll bet. Do you want me to come home?"

"No, I just wanted to talk to you, baby. When the video airs, it should be blurry enough that I can downplay anything. If it was up close and in focus it might be a problem."

"You sure you're, okay? I can be home in fifteen minutes."

"Nah, I'm good, and Anne Marie is here with me."

"Okay then. I'll see you this afternoon."

———

Carl called Ben on his private line, actually got through to the man, and related the events of the morning.

"She did what? You're telling me she subdued six gang members who were carrying guns and knives? This footage will explode, Carl."

"Yes sir, but the production people think we should edit out the scene where the head gang dude accidentally shoots one of his posse. The reason being it is too violent for live television. We will include all the footage of the guns and knives, etc."

"Just send me the finished edit ASAP. Actually, send me both versions."

"Yes sir."

———

Ben called Tami back an hour later and told her the news department would run the video in its entirety but blur out the fatal shooting scene due to its graphic content. Going forward, the network would retain the uncut video in its original form in their VIP Archives with the option of airing it at a future date.

"Mr. Benson actually agreed to compensate you for two separate incidents this morning. Wasn't that nice of him?"

Tami thanked Carl. She could care less about her double compensation but was happy to have allayed some of the infernal press coverage and intrusion into her life.

"I have been kicking an idea around for some time," she told Carl. "I'm thinking about taking the money from WBC for these interventions and creating a charitable trust to help kids in need. Give out some scholarships, host some athletic camps, donate books, equipment, housing money, help kids that need help and want to make something out of their lives. If Ben wants to match those funds and provide some airtime to help me raise more money, wouldn't that be great for everybody? I would appreciate that so much."

"I'll run it by him, Tami, that's a very generous thought. Will you be in the office tomorrow."

"Well, I'm scheduled."

"Okay. Take it easy and watch your step out there. Actually, take the day off if you want to."

"Yes sir."

CHAPTER
16

Carl called Ben in New York and relayed his conversation with Tami. "She's a piece of work, isn't she?" Ben commented.

"Yes sir, but in a good way. She just doesn't seem comfortable with the kind of exposure she is creating. She likes helping people but isn't happy to be considered a star in the global village yet."

"She'll get over it, we'll make sure of that. Let's promo her as the Power of Powers, Powers Cubed or something, run some heavy lead ups and social media releases prior to tonight's national spot. When she has her stuff together, we'll get her back on *Cheers! America*, where we can announce her foundation, and our network contributions. That would be an excellent vehicle for her to hit the public for more money, eh?"

"Absolutely, boss."

"How has she been doing in the office?"

"She does great when she's here, but every time there is one of her episodes, she's pretty much tapped out for a few days."

"Well, the more events she has, the more money we make."

"Yes sir, I'll talk to legal and find out what she has to do to create a foundation."

———

"Hi Tami, me again. I talked to Ben after our conversation, and he was excited about your idea of getting involved. He is willing to donate to the cause, and also schedule you back on CA to promo your foundation. I checked with legal, and you'll have some homework to do before going public. You'll need Articles of Incorporation to form an LLC, apply for tax exempt status, that takes a while, get a federal ID number, register with the state, define your mission and parameters, hire someone to manage your foundation, etc. There would be a lot to do before you could get this thing off the ground."

"Thanks, Carl. I will need to talk to my people and get back to you."

Tami walked into the kitchen and poured herself a cup of coffee, "Anne Marie will you please give Carl a follow up call and get a breakdown of everything we need to do to get our family foundation up and running?"

"Sure Tami, no problem. That will give me something to do when I'm not on the phone."

"Thank you."

———

Tami went back into her den/office to calm down after such an action-packed morning. She asked Anne Marie if she could distract Sadie later on while the rest of the family watched the evening news. The afternoon strolled by while both she and Anne Marie passed time working on their respective accounts. Scott called and they talked some more about Tami's morning. She assured him she had processed everything satisfactorily and was feeling fine.

"I want to watch the evening news with you and the family. Anne Marie is going to distract Sadie while we watch. I don't want her to see me kicking people around on television just yet."

"I get it. I'll be home around five-thirty; do you need anything out here in the world?"

"No, I'll order some pizza for dinner, and make a salad. See you soon."

———

Tami taped the national news so they could all watch it when they got together. At six o'clock the family, sans Sadie, sat down in the den.

Sadie and Anne Marie went to get some ice cream at the store for dessert. When everyone was settled in, Tami played the tape of national anchor Daryl Moore introducing her as the Powerful Tami Powers, which the boys' thought was hysterical.

"Hey mom, I guess I'm the Powerful Charlie Powers?" her oldest son wanted to know.

"You need to clean your room first, Mr. Powerful," Tami said.

The show went on. Leona's footage caught all of Tami's heroics, from bounding down the city street, to subduing the bad guys and then more bad guys. When the police showed up and put all the perps away, the boys stood up and cheered duly impressed by the sheer volume of thugs in Mom's newest intervention.

It was a lot of fun seeing their mom on television but was starting to be old hat. The boys had been behaving well, and both of them were smart kids, but there was an almost imperceptible divide between them and Tami now. It was as if their mom, in spite of all her protestations, had become a little otherworldly. A little larger than life.

After the show and the pizza pies, the family went on about their business, and Tami broached her idea about the foundation to Scott. He didn't care, she could do whatever she wanted, it was her money. But he wanted to know who would run the show. "You certainly don't have the time for anything like that."

"I know. Hey, how about Carrie getting involved? There would need to be an adult around, but wouldn't you be happy to see her doing something to help people, instead of working for that stupid network?"

"Tami, go ahead and get the ball rolling if you want to, but this thing is a lot bigger than I think you are aware of. You could launch the foundation on an initial basis, but ongoing funding would be necessary. You would absolutely need someone who knew what they were doing to manage the thing. WBC might help with some startup money, but how would you keep the money rolling in?"

"I don't know, maybe Oprah will adopt me."

"It might be easier just to find an existing organization that is working with kids and donate your money to them."

"We'll see."

————

The national news coverage was beginning to make itself felt in the Powers household. It's hard to live life as they once knew it when the press and paparazzi are constantly hanging around. The kids had to be closely supervised now. Their land line went away, and a security system was installed, and everyone had to be brought up to speed on how to punch in and out. Speaking of her growing celebrity status, Anne Marie's phone was ringing off the hook with offers, and Tami didn't know what she would do without her agent's help.

And then Malcolm Sparrow reared his ugly head once again.

————

Donovan Templeton had milked about all he could get out of the secondary market from Tami's video. He had some residual deals working with various media companies, and Tami was most obliging, as she kept herself in the limelight, but he knew it was time to get his black-market version of Malcolm's all but illegal interview to press.

It had been a week since Tami's intervention in the International District, accompanied by the ensuing publicity, when *Probe's* weekly tabloid hit the newsstands on a Friday morning. It screamed: PRIN-CESS of POWER on STEROIDS? along with a full page of Tami in her running gear.

Anne Marie had gone to the local market for a pound of coffee, and almost fainted as she checked out, and saw Tami's picture on the cover of the magazine and it's slanderous headline.

The written copy of the sleazy rag detailed Tami's conversation with an unidentified source, and also offered an audio link on their website so anyone could hear the interview live and in person. She bought a couple of copies and took them home with her. Better she found it first than Tami or one of the kids.

Tami was on the verge of tears after Anne Marie got back to the house, but then got mad instead. "Had to be that scumbag Malcolm Sparrow," she told Anne Marie. "Remember the little douchebag who was the director of the film where I took that independent contract to monitor their accounting back in Zion? That seems like ten years ago, but I do remember sitting down with him. He said the producers of the film wanted a post event interview after the film set was invaded. They needed it for insurance purposes."

"Sure, I remember him. He was in New York for *Cheers* and at Soirée for dinner."

"That's him. I need to talk with Ben, get the WBC lawyers on this right away."

————

At ten a.m. on Monday morning Tami was up on the seventh floor of the World offices in North Hollywood, looking at a TV monitor and Zooming with Ben Benson who was sitting in a similar room in New York. Ben had a couple of staff attorneys in the meeting room with him. Tami was sitting with Anne Marie and Carl Middleton.

"Good morning, everyone, these are two of our corporate attorneys from Human Resources with me," and Ben introduced them.

"Good morning."

"So, we have a problem, eh?"

"Looks like it boss," Carl replied.

"Tami," one of the corporate guys spoke up, "have you ever taken any performance enhancing drugs of any kind?"

"Of course not. Absolutely not. I am appalled at the implication. I am willing to go through any and all doper testing, lie detectors, anything."

"Who was the unidentified source?"

"It was a guy named Malcolm Sparrow. He was the director of the film being shot in Utah. I had agreed to a three-week temporary contract for a friend of a friend of mine to work on location. I was tasked with monitoring expenses for them while I was on the set. Manage payroll, overtime, payables, materials, take care of the caterers, tradesmen, that sort of thing. I went because I wanted to do some training and trail running around Zion National Park. Then we had the invasion on the set, and after the cops had come, and everything was over with, Malcolm asked me if he could interview me. He said the producers wanted a report from the principals in the incident for insurance purposes."

Ben Benson stirred slightly and sat up a little straighter.

"Tami, I am going to play you a recording of what is on *Probe's* website, and let it jog your memory," and the attorney hit play on a recording of the interview Tami and Anne Marie had already listened to a half a dozen times.

"Does this tape sound familiar, and is this the interview you participated in with Malcolm Sparrow?"

"Yes, yes it does. That is Malcolm I am talking to."

"Tami, do you have a copy off this interview in your files?"

"No, I do not."

"Did you ask for a copy?"

"No, I did not."

"May I ask why not?"

"Because I'm not a corporate lawyer who goes around suspecting everyone I come into contact with."

"Sorry, Tami, I meant no offense, but if you had retained an original copy of the interview, we could prove it was tampered with. We could shoot these slime bags out of the water."

"I agree, but unfortunately, I did not think to ask for a copy. I can assure you however that this tape has been tampered with."

"I agree Tami, but without any evidence to the contrary, your innocence might be hard to prove in a court of law."

"Look at the last sentence of the interview where Malcolm asks me if I ever took any steroids."

"Yes?"

"He asked me if I had ever taken any drugs. Of course, I answered a hard no. Then he probably asked me if I had ever been tested for any kind of substance use. Both of those sentences had to have been deleted and look at my response: Only if necessary. That is criminal. I have never uttered those words in that context in my life."

"Tami, we need to start our response by scheduling a performance enhancing drug test for you, and then the best lie detecting and psychological tests available. When you pass, that will be the defense's best and only premise at this time."

"That's fine, but when I pass your tests, I want the results run on your national news, and I also expect that our legal team will initiate a lawsuit against both *Probe* magazine and Malcolm Sparrow."

"On what grounds Tami?"

"Slander of course."

"As lead attorney for the network, Tami, I would suggest that you pass your tests which will validate your innocence. *Probe*'s article will dissipate in time, and the network will do everything in its power to promote you in the positive manner which it has already been doing. With a couple more heroic episodes, and the ensuing publicity, you will have completely exonerated yourself. People forget about rags like *Probe* pretty quickly, Tami."

"That's easy for you to say. This is my reputation we're talking about, and my character that has been assassinated on a national forum for nothing other than profit and greed. I feel like these scumbags should be held accountable and my character absolved. At least we should try and prevent them from attacking other innocent people."

"Tami, I sympathize with you wholeheartedly, but remember, if you sued *Probe* Magazine for libel your case would be tried in the national media. Trials can take time and the discovery phase alone could easily run up to six months. In the meantime, you would be constantly castigated and manipulated by *Probe* magazine on a national stage. A lawsuit would do nothing more than arm them with more fodder to defame you. You would have paparazzi all over you and your family. Are you willing to endure these kinds of hardships to pursue this course of action?"

"Couldn't you file, and have a gag order put on them or something?"

"Tami, the constitution of this country is pretty specific about freedom of the press. If the processes of a lawsuit filed by this office were transacted in a public forum, which they would certainly be, anyone would be free to publish anything they wanted. Including *Probe* magazine and WBC news. Also, as Malcolm Sparrow is a resident of Great Britain, it would be difficult to file a case against him. You would basically be suing *Probe* magazine."

Ben Benson interjected himself into the meeting at this point in time and suggested that Carl Middleton go ahead and select the finest testing facilities in the district of Los Angeles County.

"Once the test results are in, and they are conclusive of your innocence, we will chart a course of action acceptable to everyone." And the Zoom meeting was adjourned.

Tami and Anne Marie walked out of the building, and Tami was steaming mad. "Those guys don't care about me or my reputation," she growled.

"I think they were just trying to define the process of what proceeding with a lawsuit would be like, Tami. And I'm not agreeing with them at all, I only think it's important to know what you would be getting yourself and your family into."

"For sure. Thanks for being there with me today. Don't forget I also have the option of pursuing a case on my own, just to say screw you to those bastards. And if I take on a personal injury case, aren't any proceeds realized shared on a percentage basis with my representation?"

"If there are any proceeds, Tami. I think the lawyer today was try-ing to tell us that it would be difficult to litigate successfully without proof of tampering by the *Probe* people."

"Still, here I am with my face plastered all over the cover of one of the sleaziest rags in the country. Everything I stand for and have worked all my life for has been thrown in the mud and stepped on."

"I know, I know. Let's get the testing over with, talk to Scott and weigh our options."

"That just upsets me even more. I'm the one who has done nothing wrong, and yet I'm the one who has to go pee in a damn cup. Why isn't *Probe* being probed here?"

"Sorry, girlfriend, unfortunately things don't work that way."

———

The technician from HR shut the zoom meeting down. Ben Benson dismissed her, and turned to the lawyers. "What are our options, gentlemen?

"Ben, your suggestion to complete the testing before any decisions were made was spot on. If she wants to proceed, I can only tell you that a positive verdict would be difficult if not impossible to achieve. She has no tangible proof that any of *Probe's* allegations are unsubstanti-ated. Not to mention that proceeding would be both expensive, time consuming and again, a verdict in our favor would be elusive."

"That's true, Councilor. But don't forget that she is an extremely hot commodity right now. Whenever she is programmed on either the national or local side of our news casts, ratings double. Seriously, they double. And when ratings double, our ad revenues spike considerably. Maybe a long-drawn-out trial would be a best-case scenario for the network. It would keep her in the news. Besides, you are on retainer anyway, what difference would it make to you?"

"Keep in mind, Ben, that my position as counsel with the network has a provision excluding any trial work. My fees to litigate are five hundred dollars an hour. Calculate what your ad revenues might be, and we can analyze them against legal fees. The costs of going to trial would be in the six-to-eight-hundred-thousand-dollar neighborhood. With absolutely no assurance of a successful outcome. Let me know what you decide."

"Totally. Going through testing will give us time to decide."

CHAPTER 17

After the kids were bedded down on Monday evening, Tami corralled Scott and they discussed the day's events. Tami was visibly upset and still feeling intimately violated. Which weighed heavily on Scott.

"It's the crappy part of being famous, hon," he said finally.

"You know I never really asked for any of this, but here I am. What if Charlie and some of his friends stopped off at the market for a snack or something and saw the magazine sitting there slandering his mom. How would he feel?"

"Well, we better have a chat with the boys, explain to them what happened so they are forewarned."

"And tell him about unpleasant things like this just fading away? That you can say terrible lies about anyone, and in time, they're just gone?"

"Tami, you are very emotional right now, and I would give it a couple of days to let yourself cool off. I hope you realize that *Probe* magazine is the farthest thing from any of your kid's minds. When you are done testing, WBC will certainly publicize the results. That will go a long way to exonerating you, and you can ask for some airtime to refute everything that was published about you. Nobody with a lick of sense pays attention to those rags anyway. People know they just print rubbish."

"This is not anyone, Scott, this is me."

"I know baby, let's be a little patient and see how things develop."

Tami went to bed with a heavy heart. Things were not right, and she was feeling crushed by outside circumstances controlling her life.

She tossed and turned all night and woke up sad, depressed and with her eyes red and baggy. When she was on the road with her two running partners, she took her frustrations out on the trail and almost ran the legs off of Anne Marie and Leona.

Back at the house she began getting the kids organized for the day and told her boys and Carrie they she wanted to meet them around three. "This is important guys, please come straight home."

When the kids were out of the house, Anne Marie was next on the agenda, and Tami told her she wanted to fight back and take this thing as far as she could. She wanted to stick it in *Probe*'s ear.

"Tami, you have the opportunity to make a big positive out of a negative here. I have every talk show in the country calling me—Oprah, Ellen, Kelly, The Watch, Jimmy K. You go pass your tests, which you will do with flying colors, and you will make money while you vindicate yourself before national TV audiences. Who has more credibility Tami, Oprah and Ellen, or *Probe* magazine? Think about it. And also know that many big-time celebrities have gone through something like this in their own lives, they will be able to relate. Not to mention WBC will back you all the way."

"Maybe you're right and thank you for your perspective. I'll call Carl and have him arrange the tests as soon as possible."

———

Tami called and learned that she was already scheduled for this week, tomorrow as a matter of fact and with expedited results which would be ready by the end of the week.

"Thank you so much, sir, I really appreciate it."

"Tami, please call me Carl, and I am happy to do anything I can to help you."

"There was something else I wanted to ask. Is it possible I could work from home for a while? There is so much going on right now, it is really hard to commute in, leave my home unguarded so to speak, and be away from my kids. I would just have to talk to my department head and have her forward the spread sheets to me. It's nothing I couldn't do from here."

"Absolutely, Tami. I will put a bug in her ear, but I can tell you it won't be any kind of a problem."

"Thank you, Carl."

———

At three o'clock Tami went and picked Charlie and Sonny up from the YMCA. She brought them home, and they sat down and had a chat about the magazine article. Both boys were startled to hear anyone accuse their mom of foul play, told her not to worry, they loved her and would fight to the death for her.

Tami also chatted with Carrie later that afternoon and was relieved to find out that she thought the magazine article was a joke. "Let it pass, Mom," Carrie said. "No one will even remember this in a few months."

———

Early Tuesday morning Tami was scheduled for her substance testing. Anne Marie went along to the lab in Pasadena, and they both filed into the monitoring facility. Anne Marie waited in the reception area while Tami went back into the exam rooms. Her blood test came first and was painless. The nurse was very smooth and professional. Next up was the urine test which Tami was not looking forward to.

Testing standards and regulations have seriously advanced since the beginning of these evaluations. Due the extent and thoroughness of Tami's testing—blood, urine, hair, nail panel—she would be under-going testing for parent drugs as well as metabolite testing, which was much more definitive and time sensitive. This meant, among other things, Tami had to have a monitor watch her urinate so there was no possibility of contamination or manipulation of the test—i.e., substitu-tion of a urine specimen, which had been attempted before by a very small percentage of amateur and/or professional athletes.

Tami felt humiliated by the testing she was undergoing, especially having some stranger watch her complete such an intimate function. Her attitude got much worse while she was taking her test and she accidentally missed the cup and peed on her hand. Even though she was wearing a latex glove, she felt exposed and debased.

"Don't worry, Mrs. Powers, that's the worst of it," her nurse told her. "Thank you."

Hair and nail sampling were nothing and Tami was done in another twenty minutes. After signing out, the lab tech told her the outcomes would be done by the next day. They had prearranged for the test results to be sent directly to Carl at the World offices. In addition to all of the poking and prodding, Tami had missed a running session which cranked her off even worse.

"If it wasn't so early in the morning, I would take you to Houston's and buy shots of tequila," she told Anne Marie.

———

Wednesday's polygraph test began at ten a.m. and was much smoother than her substance session although more mentally rigorous. Once she was seated in a padded chair with arm rests, four sensors were attached directly to the skin of her chest area and two to the tip of each index finger. She felt absolutely stress free and answered all of the questions from her male examiner quickly and with confidence. Since it was again a definitive version, the test took almost four hours.

After a snack break, Tami was asked to step into what looked like a tutoring room and was seated at a desk in front of a laptop computer. It was explained to her that she would now take the second part of her exam, an EyeDetect Test.

EyeDetect is an animated polygraph test and measures ocularmotor deception. The test only takes half an hour and combined with the results of the traditional polygraph provides a ninety-seven to ninety nine percent accuracy rate result. Test results are available in about an hour and the rest of the testing went smoothly.

Tami left the lab after her four-hour ordeal and was again annoyed at having her time and patience invaded. She was alone and this time she did stop at Houston's, the venerable restaurant/watering hole in downtown Pasadena, and enjoyed a glass of Rombauer Chardonnay. The smooth, oaky wine in the dimly lit padded atmosphere was delightful and refreshing to her. While the testing was physically finalized, it would remain acutely vivid in her mind for some time. After her pit stop, she headed back to La Canada and decided it would be nice to take the family and get out of town for a long weekend.

———

The boys beat Tami home, and Anne Marie had picked Sadie up. Tami was in a better mood after her glass at Houston's and stopped by the grocery store and bought three dozen lamb chops with salad fixings and yellow potatoes for dinner. She was busy in the kitchen when Scott rolled in. He pecked her on the cheek and went out to the patio to turn on the BBQ grill. Tami already had the chops marinating, but Scott picked some more fresh rosemary sprigs from the herb garden to throw on the fire. When he started cooking, the smokey aromas almost instantly had the boys nosing around. This made Tami happy because she knew she and her spouse were creating a family favorite.

At the table, Tami threw out her idea of leaving for the weekend. Since nothing else was on the calendar, and summer was rapidly slipping away, her idea was well received. Scott could take a vacation day, Tami would get ahead of her work schedule on Thursday, and it would be a nice getaway before school restarted later in the month. They debated where to go. Santa Barbara, Ojai, Lake Arrowhead, Mexico, the Grand Canyon?

The vote came in five to one, with Sadie abstaining, for the Grand Canyon. Departure time for the drive to Flagstaff was scheduled for eight a.m. on Friday morning. They would stay overnight at the Courtyard by Marriott, Tami and Anne Marie would get up early on Saturday so they could run the Flagstaff marathon course, letting them leave for the Canyon later in the morning. Then they would all do some day hiking and eat lunch out on the trail. Tami was especially looking forward to getting out of LA and into the cool air of the San Francisco Mountains.

Scott told all three older kids to google the Grand Canyon on their phones, write him a short summary of what they expected to see, and give him some history of how the canyon was formed. He knew there was no greater physical demonstration of our place in time by measuring it against the millions of years of layered strata that comprise the canyon walls. He only wished they could really get down into the canyon's depths and experience the magnificence of the mighty Colorado River blasting through the lower channels. Winding majestically mile after mile through the centuries old crevasse.

————

Leona came by at five-thirty on Thursday, and the trio of runners took off to run some mountain trails in the San Gabriels. Tami was frisky to get going as she had missed a day's training yesterday. So, she set a brisk pace and Leona and Anne Marie were straining to keep up. They looped out to the east for about ten miles then back to their western trailhead, having gained about two thousand feet of altitude in the bargain.

Back home Tami and Anne Marie got the kids up with Tami driving Sadie to summer day school. Both women jumped into their respective professional duties when the kids were settled. Tami to catch up on a project for WBC, Anne Marie was working on a couple of marketing proposals. Tami was anxious to take a break after her testing was complete. Anne Marie was eager to see the Grand Canyon. She was equally anticipating getting back to Pasadena and looking to capitalize on some of the offers she was receiving as Tami's Registered Agent.

Thursday evening was the time to get packed up, and as self-reliant as the Powers kids were, it didn't take long. Carrie made a half-hearted petition to stay home alone and take care of the house. She felt a little like the odd person out when her mom and her friend went off running, then she was left with Dad, two dorky boys, and Sadie. That plan was quickly shot down by her parents. No problem, she knew she could score some points by taking care of her little sister on the trip.

CHAPTER
18

Tami called and gave Leona the day off, so she and Anne Marie could run a quick ten miles and call it a day. They were both excited to challenge the Flagstaff Marathon course the next morning. Getting back home at quarter to seven, they roused the troops, started packing the Suburban and hit the road on time.

Scott took the 210 freeway to Interstate 10 and continued east. I-10 is not the most scenic route in the world by a long shot, but after they had cleared the sprawl of the east LA basin, the Suburban stopped in Indio and Dad bought all the kids a date shake. The I-10 across the Mojave Desert is also no bargain unless you love rustic backwaters like Blythe, California and Quartzsite, Arizona.

Two and a half hours into Arizona, they hit Highway Seventeen north, and started climbing toward Flagstaff. Having made great travel time Tami suggested they detour through Sedona and give Anne Marie, the East Coast city girl, a preview of red rock country. They pulled into the Tlaquepaque small businesses center for a late lunch and enjoyed some fantastic Mexican food Arizona style. After lunch, the Information Center had all the info they needed to get up to speed on day hikes in the area.

Once in Flagstaff, the first stop was a drive through the campus of Northern Arizona University. Followed by a tour of South San Francisco Street where they saw an older, more colorful sector of town and local talent. Longhair students, Chicanos, Native Americans, Black residents all mingled around bookstores, bars, winos, an antique LP and CD store, college-style restaurants, and more bars in old buildings with steel grilles bolted over their windows.

Heading further north they crossed the Santa Fe Railroad tracks and rolled over the legendary Route 66 Highway. Route 66 is lined with even more low rent bars and roadside diners heading off in both western and eastern directions. Thus, Mom and Dad continued the children's unintentional education of sleazy roadside watering holes.

Driving north through downtown Flagstaff they all observed the antique well-worn feel of the historic little mountain town. After checking into two suites at the Marriott, with Anne Marie, Carrie and Sadie in one, and Scott, Tami and the boys in the other, they sent the kids down to the indoor pool under Carrie's supervision. Soon enough everyone was at the pool, the adults mostly reading, the kids mostly splashing.

Tami's alarm went off at five-thirty; she gathered Anne Marie, and they headed north some eighteen miles to the trailhead for the Flagstaff Marathon layout. Flagstaff, through the auspices of the Northern Arizona University Athletic Department, has developed into a premier high altitude training center. Both ladies were excited to run a course utilized by so many world class runners.

The track winds in a northeasterly loop through the Coconino National Forest, and meanders over technical trails at nine thousand feet of altitude. Both women approached this run as more of a recreational outing, although the altitude work they had been doing in the San Gabriels would certainly give them a leg up on a flatland runner. The goal was to finish in under three hours, fifteen minutes. This would necessitate a pace of around seven minutes a mile which they both thought doable.

Three hours and ten minutes later, two tired runners jogged over the finish line, having been taxed to the max by the altitude. They sucked for air with only a few other hardcore distance runners straggling into a large trailhead with no finish line and no one cheering for them. But Tami and Anne Marie didn't need any of that. They were both happy to experience a new course in such a beautiful, high dessert pine tree forest.

Back at the hotel, the runners grabbed a shower, snack, some fruit, and everyone packed up to leave for the Canyon. The hour and a half drive north jogs back west through the little roadside town of Williams, made famous by really no one. They stopped at a local market and picked up sandwiches, snacks and bottles of water, then pressed on. After heading north, the highway meanders through some more beautifully wooded country until the terrain flattens out, and half an hour later they pulled into Grand Canyon Village.

Scott insisted they stop and check out the venerable El Tovar Hotel, founded in 1905, and is the epitome of a historic landmark. The dark, wooded interior with huge deer and elk heads hanging prominently, a grand fireplace, and wood burning stove was a Western history lesson for the kids in and of itself.

Talking to the concierge secured Tami a current walking guide, and the group selected the Yavapai Trail for their day outing. It was close to the canyon rim, had a more gradual slope which Sadie could manage going downhill. Scott or Charlie would have to carry her on their shoulders most of the way back up. The trail meanders for three miles just under the Canyon rim, has gorgeous views, and numerous vista points complete with water refill stations.

The Powers family clan dropped onto the trail just before one o'clock. As their group edged below the Canyon rim, the temperature warmed to a hot but tolerable eighty degrees. The excitement of being out in the elements together on a family outing, not to mention the spectacular views, exhilarated everyone.

The canyon is a huge kaleidoscope in that its perspective changes as one progresses down trail. New peaks and crags emerge, different geological formations present themselves constantly. The light diffuses in interesting ways as the day lengthens.

The farther one travels; the more humbling is the experience. To realize the Canyon averages approximately thirty-five million years of age (different sections vary in age from six to seventy million years) and was carved out of solid rock over eons of time by erosion and the raging Colorado River is stupefying. When you juxtapose yourself in the middle of this environment, you realize you are just a flea on the enormous flank of time and space.

The Powers kids probably didn't fully appreciate the profundity of their afternoon hike, but they certainly enjoyed galloping about on the trail. The boys made numerous stops to throw rocks toward the distant canyon floor.

Anne Marie was someone who did appreciate the grandeur before her, especially as she had seen nothing like this ever before. Her canyons consisted of Times Square and downtown Boston. Scott suggested they stop at a vista point about three miles out, and the group settled down in the shade to eat a late lunch and relax. The sun was hot and life giving, the air was crystal clear. After an hour, our day hikers broke camp, and started back. They wanted to watch the evening's dusk settle over the Canyon from the upper rim.

———

Billie and Jessie were also out of the city for the weekend. They lived in southeast Phoenix, which resembles Los Angeles for suburban sprawl but on a smaller, hotter scale. A trip north to Flagstaff or Sedona in the late summer got them out of the blazing Valley heat. Billie worked at the regional Walmart warehouse six miles from his parent's house, and Jessie was a part-time barista. They both lived at home, but were saving, mostly Billie, to get their own apartment someday.

Billie was twenty-one and not quite six foot tall, but sturdy and sported a blonde buzz cut. Jessie, soon to turn twenty, was slightly built, had longish brown hair, hazel eyes, wore bell bottomed pants and was a Leo. They had graduated high school one year apart and as the typical dispersal after school ended, they both, especially Jessie, spent hours on her cell phone interacting on social media. This weekend would not only be a fun get away, but they were actually going to the Grand Canyon instead of just to Cottonwood to see her cousin. The Canyon would offer some great selfie ops, and to celebrate the day, Billie pulled out his new brass pipe, and packed a bowl of BC bud for them.

They smoked up as Billie drove north from Williams. The initial buzz from the potent marijuana infiltrated his mind while he body rushed, but Jessie put on a Tom Petty CD, and they both mellowed out and started to enjoy their high. Mellowed out and arriving at the canyon, Billie found a parking spot open in the back of the public lot. He toyed with the idea of jumping in the bed he had made in the back of his van with Jessie for a while. But then he thought they had all night for that, so it was probably better to get out and enjoy the Canyon while the light was still strong. He knew Jessie was itching to get going and start shooting selfies.

The two kids, still feeling euphoric, tripped across Village Loop Drive and headed towards the El Tovar. Billie went in and bought a Mountain Dew for them to share. They took some pictures standing on a concrete bench that wrapped around the ancient Lodge.

Jessie hopped down and they started walking on a trail to the east along the edge of the Canyon's Rim. After about a half a mile she told Billie she wanted to get a selfie of them looking out over the Canyon. He was happy to just be looking out at the scenery, but Jessie was the adventurous one. And she was most anxious to post something spectacular on Instagram.

"Let's get as close to the edge as we can," she told him. "It will make a dope pic."

Jessie loved to pose, Billie was the shooter, and he took a couple of selfies with Jessie's phone. "These are okay," she said. "But let's get closer to the edge and we can get more of the Canyon in."

"I'm not afraid of heights or anything," he told her "but we are pretty close to the edge."

"You big puss," she said. "You stand there, and I'll back up while you shoot. Then we'll have some bitchen shots." Billie shot gunned the cell phone's camera, taking about a dozen photos.

They stepped away from the rim, while Jessie looked the batch over. "These are good. Let's try it one more time," and she stepped backwards while Billie flipped the camera around to adjust the focus.

As Jessie, who was already dangerously inside the chalked caution line, took one more step backwards, her heel caught a shrubbery root, and she lurched for her balance as her foot slipped out from underneath her. Billie looked through the lens of the cell phone camera after having fine-tuning his focus function, all he could see was Jessie's face contorted in terror as she began to fall backwards over the South Rim of the Grand Canyon. In his confusion he had pressed the selection button on the phone. It had shifted into video mode, and the camera lens was half filled with Jessie's mouth, open and covering her face, as she began to emit the loudest, blood curdling scream he had ever heard. Helplessly, she continued her backwards tumble.

Billie stood there shocked to the marrow of his bones, dumbly looking through the lens until Jesse disappeared. He could still hear her screaming and screaming, although the screams were getting fainter and had an echo like quality to them. He wasn't about to get any closer to the rim to look over and see what was happening.

———

Fortunately, he wasn't the only one to hear a scream. Three hundred feet below the rim as the Powers family hiked back to the trailhead, Tami froze. She looked up towards the terrifying/terrified shrieks and was able to make out a free-falling form fifty feet behind where they were standing. The body was plunging grotesquely half the way down the canyon face. Jessie's body mass, one hundred one pounds, would calculate to fall about sixteen feet per second, and in a little over nine seconds, she would crash land to her death on the rocky canyon trail. She was extremely lucky to be falling from above Yavapai Trail.

It took Tami only two leaps and two seconds to position herself on the other side of Jessie and with her third leap, which reached almost twenty feet in the air, Tami intercepted Jessie's fall. She wrapped her arms around the petit, quaking body and they began to descend together. Fortunately, Jessie's body was in an upright position and as Tami wrapped her arms tightly around Jessie's torso, her forward motion and superior weight directed their tandem flight onto a gradually descendant plane. As they landed back on solid ground, Tami's legs were churning forward. She absorbed both their weights when they touched down and she continued running another fifty feet up trail until her momentum slowed.

She ran directly by her astonished family still holding Jessie while they quickly scrambled out of the way, then scurried to catch up with her. Scott, who had been carrying Sadie on his shoulders, gently handed her to Carrie, and reaching Tami, he took a still hysterical Jessie out of Tami's arms and set her wobbly legs on the ground. She looked around with wide, incredulous eyes, then started to sob uncontrollably. Tami took her back into her arms and Anne Marie stopped filming the episode and called 911. Carrie put Sadie down and came over to join her mother in consoling Jessie. Soon enough there were two Park Rangers running down the trail towards them. The sound of sirens could be heard above from approaching aid cars.

Billie saw where the aid cars parked, and with fear and dread in his heart, he had the good sense to follow them to the trailhead and came running. As people arrived at the scene, they encountered more confusion than anything else. The Rangers were stupefied by the description they received from Anne Marie as to what had happened. Billie arrived panting for breath and could not believe his eyes. The EMTs ran down the trail carrying a stretcher, which they soon found to be superfluous. Jessie was now walking under her own power, and ran to Billie, still crying hysterically. Billie, as only a twenty-one-year-old could, awkwardly tried to comfort his shell-shocked girlfriend.

The Rangers were attempting to fill out an incident report, but only one of them had heard of Tami, and the other one was still having trouble grasping what had happened. Anne Marie showed them her video, and they both decided that about all they could say was a flying woman had saved a girl who had fallen from the Canyon's rim.

When they interviewed Billie, he showed them his own cell phone footage, and the Rangers could easily see the kids had been far too dangerously close to the rim. One Ranger pulled out his citation book and wrote Billie and Jessie up. Anne Marie asked if she could watch Billie's video, and after seeing it, inquired if he would mind forwarding it to her.

"Hell, no, I don't mind. Y'all saved my girlfriends life."

The EMTs, who had also seen the film clip, checked to make sure everyone was all right, then conducted an in-depth interview with Jessie and Tami. Although still traumatized, Jessie's crying had reduced to a sniffle and after a preemptory physical exam she seemed to be cognizant and had sustained no injuries. The EMTs recommended a visit to the local hospital and offered her a ride. But as she was feeling no pain and had no health insurance, she declined their offer. Tami also declined an offer of secondary medical care, assuring the medics that she was feeling fine.

Before they let anyone leave, the Rangers again warned the group to conduct themselves with caution in and around the Canyon. Then they turned and began hiking up the mild grade and off the trail. The Powers also slowly reorganized and started back up with Billie and Jessie walking in the middle of them. It was as if the Powers were literally and figuratively a live safety net for the two shaken kids.

When the group got up to the rim and out of the Canyon there was a reporter from WKNX TV, another WBC affiliate, waiting for them. This one was from Flagstaff but covered the Grand Canyon in the summertime. She chatted with Tami and Anne Marie for a spell, the women described the daring rescue, answered some questions and then moved on. Anne Marie had full footage of the whole scene on her phone but wasn't about to share it with some small station from out in the boonies. She had her own video, and now she had Billie's, which graphically portrayed Jessie as she began her terrifying fall backwards.

If you wanted a live image of normal life, suddenly confronted by eminent death, Anne Marie had it for you. Not only was Jessie's face cramped and contorted in terror, but her mouth was also agape in an angst-ridden scream, her eyes protruded with ghostlike intensity, and the last image you saw as she dropped out of sight was her scraggy brown hair flying askew, and the underside of her arms flailing. They glared back at the camera, pale, white and helpless.

Billie and Jessie hurried off, jumped in the rear of the van and huddled in a viselike embrace on Billie's little platform bed. They were both shaking in the aftershock, especially Jessie, and they held each other for what seemed like an hour. Finally, Jessie asked if they could just, please get out of there. Had she been raised in a religious home and family; her thoughts would have been running to convent life.

The Powers hiked on back to the Lodge sans Anne Marie who stayed outside to forward her videos to Carl in LA. They continued on into the coffee shop and ordered some treats for the kids. Everyone was quiet, still overwhelmed by all they had just experienced. It had been an awesome day especially as the Yavapai Vista Point was one of the best for appreciating the grandeur of the Canyon. But watching their mom fly by and snatch a body out of the air, much like an American Eagle might swoop down and grab a fat salmon out of the Columbia River was still processing with them.

Finally, Charlie broke the ice and said, "That was freaking awesome, Mom."

"Yeah Mom, and it all happened so fast. That girl almost died, and you flew up there and saved her," chimed in Sonny. "How do you do that, Mom?"

"I don't know kids, that's what is so amazing about it to me too. I just react, that's all I can say."

This was Carrie's second rodeo with her mom's superhero events, and she was still concerned for her safety. "Mom, you could really hurt yourself one of these days. I wish you would stop saving everybody all the time."

"Carrie, please don't even think like that. When someone needs help, I just react. It's a feeling so strong and I have such a powerful surge of energy enveloping my body, it doesn't seem like anything could hurt me. Would you rather I didn't do anything, and that poor girl just fell to her death right in front of us?"

"No, but . . ."

"You are like Peter Pan, Mom," Sadie said. "You can fly everywhere."

Tami pulled Sadie onto her lap, hugged her, and said, "that's exactly how I want you to think of me sweetie."

———

Scott got up and went over to the hostess stand by the exit door to pay the bill. Everyone else filed out. Scott wanted them to watch the start of sunset before they left for Sedona. There was plenty of room in the rocking chairs on the back porch of the Lodge, so they all sat down and started checking out the sky as it turned a scarlet pink and the Canyon walls morphed into a deep mauvy purple.

"We should come back here someday," Scott said, "and go on a raft trip down the Colorado. The river runs for a couple hundred miles right through the bottom walls of the Canyon and has lots of Class A rapids."

CHAPTER 19

Scott drove back to Williams and the family stopped at a funky-looking, Western-style café for dinner. The evening's special was home-made meatloaf which was fine for the guys. The three older females ordered salads with protein and Sadie nibbled off their plates.

It took another hour or so to get to the Poco Diablo Resort in the heart of Sedona. Scott was going to sign up for adjoining rooms, but Tami told him to rent separate rooms for the adults so everyone could have a little privacy.

Scott and Tami relaxed, channel surfed, and at ten o'clock the local news came on. They were watching the same channel as the young woman reporter they had talked with earlier in the day. But as WKNXV was the WBC affiliate for Phoenix, they now got to watch Tami's heroics in the Canyon.

"It is almost unworldly watching that video after the fact and on live television, isn't it Scott?" And now she knew why her cell had received half a dozen calls from Carl Middleton.

———

Tami was sure Carl wanted to speak urgently, because he had left his personal cell phone number, so she finally called him after her morning run with Anne Marie. The women took off at six-thirty and ran only eight miles because it was Sunday, upon returning to their rooms, they were both glad no red rock boulders had fallen from the sky at them. Tami called her boss after she got out of the shower, about eight-thirty.

"Good morning, Carl, this is Tami."

"Morning, Tami. I'm so glad you called, how are you doing, how are you feeling?"

"I'm feeling just fine, thank you for asking. How are you doing?"

"Tami, I couldn't be better. The clips Anne Marie sent us yesterday were some of the most dramatic footages ever seen on American television. New York is going crazy; Ben wants you to do an interview on Monday for the national broadcast with Daryl Moore. Then he wants you on the *Cheers* show next Friday afternoon. I think he is going to keep you pretty busy for the next week or two."

"Gee, Carl. That won't leave me much time for cost analysis."

"That's a joke, right? Don't even think about CA right now."

"Well, you will have to speak with Anne Marie, she handles the business side of things."

"Are you still in Arizona?"

"Yep. We're in Sedona and are going hiking in the red rocks today. I'll be home late."

"Great. Do you mind if I call you first thing in the morning?"

"Carl, I'm up by four-thirty every morning."

"To go running?"

"Of course."

"Let's talk tomorrow around nine, and I will send a Limo for you. Oh, and by the way, your test results came in, and you passed them all with flying colors."

"Great, can Carrie come along with me and Anne Marie?"

"Bring whoever you would like."

"Oh, and one more thing, could you please call security and make sure our house isn't inundated with reporters when we get back?"

"Done, Tami. Have a great day with your family."

———

The Powers hit the Resort's coffee shop for a country breakfast. They were all pretty hungry and still buzzed after yesterday's action and all the fresh mountain air. Tami ordered sandwiches, and some fruit for lunch on the trail, plus a case of bottled water. She sat next to Anne Marie, and they were able to chat a bit. AM had already spoken to Carl and remarked to Tami that WBC seemed to be in a pretty urgent frame of mind.

"They want you to do the national news tomorrow night, and then *Cheers* next Friday."

"Yeah, I spoke with him this morning. I'm okay with appearances, as long as *Cheers* is a remote feed, I don't want to fly back to New York this week. After what we all went through yesterday, I need to spend all the time I can with my kids. He is sending a limo for us tomorrow. I told him it would be us and Carrie, but now I think she'll be better staying home with Sadie."

"Why can't you to go to New York?"

"I just don't think it's a good idea. My family needs me now and I want to be here for them. School is starting soon, and we have lots to do."

"They'll probably make you an offer to go back there."

"We can do a live feed from here for them. That is almost as good as me being there anyway."

"Tami, you should know I have been getting calls from sponsors and programmers who want to book you at substantial rates. It's going to be really intense when we get back. I think you should think about doing a couple of spots, maybe not with WBC's direct competitors, but do something, just to let them know they don't completely own you."

"Whatever you think is best. Let's talk about it some more tomorrow on our run. I'm really looking forward to our family hike today."

———

Scott opted for the Cathedral Rock Trail. It was a little steep in places but was only one point two miles long each way, which was good for Sadie. They got to the top of the trail and the view was awesome. You could see for miles and enjoy some of the most spectacular geological monuments in the Southwest. They stopped and had their picnic lunch and enjoyed the hot, but otherwise beautiful weather. Anne Marie hiked with the guys up and through some natural rock formations. They amazed her. After another hour frolicking, and suntanning, they headed back and loaded up for the drive home. Anne Marie sat in the front with Scott so Tami could be in the back with the kids.

"What did you guys' thing of the Canyon Country?" Tami asked.

"Pretty cool Mom."

———

The Powers left Sedona around two and started home on the seven-hour drive. When they finally arrived after numerous pitstops including a dinner break, there was only a limited amount of movement on the street. A security van from the station was parked in the driveway. That and the lack of activity around the house all weekend had discouraged the media circus. The van backed out for them, and after pulling into the drive, everyone grabbed their bags and went into the house.

"Let's hit the hay, kids," Tami told them. "You've got a full day tomorrow.

———

Tami was ready to sleep as soon as she got in bed, but she wanted to chat with Scott for a few minutes. "Thanks for a great trip, hon."

"Yeah, that was one of our best. Even without all of the theatrics with that girl."

"It would have been perfect without that. At least the kids saw me do something good without having to knock anybody out."

"Well, you definitely saved her life, and the kids still seem to be handling things pretty well."

"Yeah, they've been great. Anne Marie says this is going to be an intense week. They want me to do a couple of national spots, and I'm sure there is going to be media jumping all over our front yard. Want to be on the Jimmy Kameron Show with me?"

"They'd probably throw me out the side door and roll out a red carpet for you."

"No way, Jose." They kissed goodnight and turned the lights out.

————

Tami and Anne Marie had decided to get out of the house by four-thirty the next morning to avoid any early bird press members. Leona met them out front and Tami accepted her congratulations on the Grand Canyon rescue. They ran for eighteen miles and by the time they got home, the paparazzi were gathering. No one can stop someone from taking pictures on public property, but Tami and Anne Marie just brushed past them and into the house. It was still early, so they had a cup of coffee, and started getting breakfast for the fam.

"Tell Carl to send the limo for us at ten will you please, Anne Marie? I've got some stuff to clean up in my office."

"That should give you plenty of time to process once you get there."

————

The limo arrived in North Hollywood around ten forty-five, and Carl Middleton rushed out of his office to greet them as soon as the elevator hit the sixth floor. He ushered them into an executive meeting room and called a hostess for refreshments. Anne Marie and Carl ordered coffees; Tami had a guess what.

After talking about their weekend for a few minutes, Carl, who was still in awe of her efforts, finally had to break up the visit and send Tami off to wardrobe and makeup. She will be taping her interview with Edward Johnson, WLA12's lead anchor at noon. Then their chat would be fed back to New York and introduced on the national broadcast by Daryl Moore.

Tami didn't spend much time in wardrobe, a department she had little interest in. Makeup was entirely different. She received a fifteen-minute neck, scalp, and facial massage upon arriving. Then sat with her favorite technician and was made up and airbrushed. When the crew was through working on her, she was off to the guest set with her beautiful green eyes sparkling and interview ready.

"Hello Tami, I'm Ed Johnson, so nice to meet you."

"Likewise. Do you have any special questions for me?"

"Yes Tami, I was hoping you could help me learn how to fly. No, just kidding. I would like you to share your feelings from this weekend. Dial us in on where you were, what you were doing when your extraordinary experience occurred. I assume from what I have heard that your family was with you, and how are they coping with your sudden talents and fame? That sort of thing."

"How long do we have here, Ed?"

"Only a two-and-a-half-minute segment, Tami. The network wants to share a personal moment with you and our audience, then we will promo a much more in-depth session on *Cheers* this coming Friday."

"Okay, I'll try to keep this short and sweet."

———

An Irish Mystic once said: no matter how big of a house you have, no matter how expensive your car, no matter how many jewels your wife wears, we all end up in a box about the same size when we die. So, Stay Humble. This axiom could have been authored by Tami. She deferentially related her weekend experience, albeit giving some insight into how it felt to be flying through the air with another person's life in her hands.

"To be honest with you, Edward, I was as surprised as anyone to be where I was in space and time. These incidents tend to occur quickly, and they are over in an instant. Even though time seems to decelerate to what feels like super slow motion for me, Saturday I was able to enjoy the ride so to speak. Flying with Jessie in my arms, was like flying through time itself in that incredible, majestic canyon. When you consider it has evolved over so many millions of years, and here you are, doing what only birds and later flying machines have done for so long. It is uniquely beautiful, emotionally moving and felt inspiring and humbling at the same time."

"Tami, thank you for sharing your experience with us in such a personal and eloquent manner. With that, we are going to say goodbye for now, please be with us again this Friday afternoon for our exclusive, live interview with Tami Powers. An original Tami Powers presentation, right here on WBC TV's *Cheers! America* show."

———

"Tami, it was so great being able to meet you. You are an amazing person; I wish you the very best and please take care out there. In the news business we relate tragedy after disaster every night, and I want you to know what a pleasure it is to be able to report your events. They are always upbeat, uplifting and positive. So, keep the good work coming at us, but please, I beg you to stay out of harm's way."

"Thanks Edward. Wouldn't it be some kind of wonderful where you could report on positives and people working together. People helping each other, nations bringing peace to earth instead of war and murder. I guess that's pretty naïve, huh?"

"I believe that would be called Paradise."

———

Tami proceeded to the executive dining room where Anne Marie was having a pleasant chat with Carl. She sat down in a padded leather dinner chair and the starched waiter immediately brought her favorite beverage. "How'd it go in there, tiger?" Anne Marie asked. "By the way, I have contacted the Coca-Cola offices in Atlanta. They want to set you up as a spokesperson for one of their products."

"You should. I know a lot of people think it's crazy that a serious marathon runner like me drinks as many Diet Cokes as I do, but I love 'em. The taste, the temperature, it has just the right amount of caffeine for me. I completely love everything about 'em."

"How did your interview with Edward go?"

"It went well. He's a total pro and very easy to work with."

"Carl and I were talking about scheduling, Tami. Ben wants you to be in New York for a live interview on *Cheers* this Friday. We were also looking at options for the Jimmy Kameron Show. Later on, down the road, we could sync our trip back to the NYC Marathon with another visit to *Cheers! America.* Look at the New York as a qualifier for the games?"

"Can Scott come with me to Jimmy K's show?'

"Front row seats for him, Tami. You would be on stage with Jimmy."

'That would be fun. And about Friday, we'll need to do a live feed to *Cheers,* because I don't feel comfortable leaving my family this week."

"Why not, Tami? You know Ben will bring out the red carpet for you back there."

"I know he would; I just feel really strongly about staying home right now. School is starting soon and getting the kids ready for that is a full-time job for me."

"I'll tell him, but I don't think he'll be so happy about your decision."

"While you're on the phone with him, and now that I've passed my testing with flying colors, please ask him how soon legal is going to file my libel suit against *Probe* magazine. You know Carl, no amount of performance enhancing drugs could enable anyone to do what I was able to accomplish this past weekend."

"Tami, I'm very sorry to tell you this, but Ben and the legal department have expressed no interest in pursuing a case of this nature in a court of law. They feel your testing results offer ninety-nine-point nine percent proof positive that you have NEVER taken any performance enhancing drugs. To expose you to a lengthy, negative and high-profile trial would merely continue to drag this unpleasant issue through the press indefinitely is a no go. It could be damaging to you personally and to your career. Not to mention the fact that there isn't a smoking gun.

It would simply be your word against theirs that you didn't say what they have on an actual tape recording. Ben said the network will provide maximum coverage of your test results on the network as a means of compensation for you."

"So, you are saying that my word against those sleaze balls would have no gravitas? And doesn't legal realize that tape recordings can be altered?"

"That's not at all what I'm saying, Tami. What's at issue here is what concrete, admissible evidence in a court of law would convince a jury of your innocence."

"Well, I guess we'll see about that, huh?"

"But what about your career, Tami?"

"My friend Carl, let me tell you that I don't consider any of this 'my career.' My career is my family, my running, my personal clients and the wellbeing of all of those things."

"We understand that Tami, and perhaps career was a bad choice of words. I think Ben is concerned what effect this process would have on you and your family. Every sleazy tabloid rag, podcast, cable TV show, social media, etc. will have the opportunity to potshot you. The way the courts work now this thing could drag on for at least a year. Is that what you want?"

"What I want is to have my name cleared and my reputation returned to me."

"Tami, in the spectrum of life in the entertainment business, *Probe* magazine is a gnat looking for a dust bunny to call home. They are nothing, and I assure you that this very minor storm will fade away as quickly as it blew in. WBC will do everything we can to uphold your image and support you in every way possible."

"I appreciate WBC's support, but how can you sit there and say to me that this situation will have no effect on myself or my family? I feel like they have opened a dark door, and if I don't protect myself, anyone out there can say whatever they want, whenever they want. Please tell

Mr. Benson if he does not wish to proceed with a lawsuit, I will initiate legal action on my own dime."

"I don't think he will appreciate that, Tami, but I will relay your sentiments."

"Thank you, Carl. We better take off Anne Marie, when would you like me to start taping for Friday?'

"No, if you don't go back there, this would be a live feed, so you would need to be here by nineish on Friday morning."

———

Anne Marie was quiet while exiting the studio, but when they got back in the limo, she started laughing. "You are one independent son of a gun, you know that?"

"It is what it is."

"Well, I know some good lawyers in the city who would love to get their hands on a high-profile case like this."

"This will be pretty ironic, huh? A lawyer suing someone on a morality charge."

———

They got back to La Canada to find the kids were fooling around in their rooms. Carrie had driven her mom's car that day and was able to deal with Sadie. So, life would hopefully move on in a normal fashion for the Powers until Tami had to return to headquarters on Friday morning for another appearance.

"How was your day?" Carrie asked her.

"It was fun. They sent a limo for Annie and me to go into town. I did some taping for the national news show tonight. I'm going on Jimmy Kameron sometime soon. You want to come with Dad and me?"

"No mom, I think I better stay home and clean my room. Are you kidding me? Of course, I might be able to fit you into my schedule."

"You're so funny," Tami said and gave her a hug.

Watching mom on the news was getting to be a non-event anymore for the kids. But the adults watched the show, and then went into the dining room to eat dinner.

As it wound down, Scott said "So kids, ask your mother what it feels like to be flying through the air and saving someone's life."

"Did it feel like you were Spider Man, mom?" Charlie asked.

"No, she's Peter Pan," Sadie interrupted.

"It felt incredible kids," Tami replied. "It was like a condor might feel. It is so different flying rather than it felt like walking along the trail with you all. Not that I flew all that far or anything, but there is a magical feeling to it."

"If you were birds," Scott asked, "What kind of a bird would you want to be?"

"I would want to be a butterfly," Sadie said jumping into the conversation.

"That's not a bird," Charlie smirked at her.

"I'm a pelican. Then I could hang at the beach all the time, and dive through the air like a bullet for fish," Sonny said.

"I want to be a swan," said Carrie. "They are so beautiful."

"Let me be a swallow," was Anne Marie's choice. "They are able to travel so far and are so small but strong. Imagine all the things they can see while they are migrating."

"I think I would be a road runner," Tami mused. "They can fly if they need to, but they are so fast, unique and graceful on the ground."

"Charlie?"

"Maybe a parrot or toucan. They can fly, but they can also talk. What if a bird that could already fly, could be like mom? She's human but has developed special new talents. If I was a toucan, I would develop the ability to have deep conversations with people. Talk on TV, give lectures on bird life at universities, maybe be a psychologist. Stuff like that."

"That's very creative, son," Scott said. "Well, no one took the Bald Eagle, our national symbol of strength and beauty. No one took the falcon or hawk, who are very incredible predators. But maybe I'd be a crane. They are also chill and very beautiful. They wade around in the water all day catching fish, then fly gracefully away to their nests at night. "Isn't ornithology amazing, it is so diverse," Scott opined.

"What does that mean, Daddy?" Sadie asked.

"That's the study and knowledge of bird life sweetie," Scott replied.

"Well, I would also like to be a lovebird, and then be able to fly around like Mom and save lots of peoples," Sadie said and crawled up into her mom's lap.

CHAPTER 20

Carl dreaded calling Ben Benson the next morning, but he manned up, and relayed Tami's reluctance to fly back to New York, which didn't sit well. Then he had to tell him about Tami's decision to proceed with a lawsuit on her own. That blew Ben's cork out of the bottle.

"That pisses me off, Middleton. What in the hell is going on out there? Do you have the slightest idea how to manage this woman?"

"She's very independent, sir. She has a real idea of how she wants to do things."

"Well, so do I. You are back down to your office on the fourth floor. I'm assigning Dick Cannon to handle her from now on."

"Yes sir." Carl hung up and thought, *Good luck with that, Mr. V.P.*

———

While Carl and Ben were chatting, Anne Marie called her contact at Reinvaan, Mills and Katz. She asked for Katherine Katz, and when they connected said, "KK, how are you?"

"Anne Marie, is that you?"

"Sure is, and I have a plum of a case for you."

"Really, what've you got?"

"You've heard of Tami Powers, I'm sure?"

"Are you kidding me? Power Woman?"

"Yep, none other. I'm here in California with her now, I'm her personal representative, and she wants to initiate a lawsuit against *Probe* magazine. She is very upset with their recent allegations of her drug use."

"Heck yes, girl, I don't blame her. Sign me up. When do we start?"

"Right now. She's here beside me, say hello."

"Well, what a pleasant surprise, Mrs. Powers, hello."

"Hello, Katherine. Anne Marie says you are one of the best."

"I try, Mrs. Powers. How may I help you?"

"I want to sue *Probe* magazine, which has made some audacious accusations, character assassination really, and I want to sue their fannies off. They say they have a tape recording of me admitting to taking performance enhancing drugs "if necessary," but that tape was tampered with. I have just passed extensive blood, urine, and psychological testing with flying colors. That, and my personal character and track record should count for something, shouldn't it?"

"How did this tape originate, Mrs. Powers?"

"It originated after the first rescue episode I had out in Utah on the film set where I was employed. The film's director is an English guy named Malcolm Sparrow. I believe he is currently back residing in London, but he requested I interview with him for insurance reasons to protect the film's producers. This happened right after our film set invasion. I did converse with him for his interview, and I doubt if the producers have ever even seen or heard the tape. Then this slime ball must have sold it to *Probe*. And please, call me Tami."

"I would certainly be interested in representing you, Tami. Will WBC be involved with this case at all?"

"No, they feel that the case has no merit, so I am proceeding on my own."

"Very well, Tami. I will need a retainer of fifty thousand dollars, and then any compensation we should recover would be split fifty/fifty between you and our law firm."

"That's acceptable to me, Katherine."

"Do you have a copy of this tape, Tami?"

"No, that's the problem. But the tape is so incongruous with my values and personal conduct. That has to have some validity, doesn't it?"

The three women chatted for another twenty minutes, and Tami told her they would wire funds either this afternoon or tomorrow morning.

"Finally, Tami, it appears because of the diverse nature of this case, i.e., you, as the plaintiff living in California, the defendant whose offices are in New Jersey, codefendant in London, and the fact that they disseminated false information nationally indicate we should file in U.S. District Court here in New York City. Since these types of defamatory cases often settle, I would suggest a significant request for damages. Also, as this tape recording is secondhand material, we may also have to file against your director friend in absentia. I want to also assure you I will proceed in the most expeditious manner and attempt to move our action along as quickly as possible. I know this will not be the most pleasant experience for you and your family."

"Thank you. Speaking with you is exceeding my expectations."

"Well then ladies, let me get to work. I look forward to meeting you in person, Tami, and in the meantime, I will be in touch. Nice to speak with you again, Anne Marie, thank you for the referral, and I will be in touch with you for all the related information I will need."

———

And just that easily, Tami had started her legal process. "Thanks, Anne Marie, that was just what I was hoping for. Have we been receiving the one hundred-thousand-dollar checks on schedule?"

"Oh yes. Immediately after an incident occurs, I am on the phone with Carl. He direct deposits the money into your checking account. After deducting my ten percent, the money is transferred into an interest-bearing account until you decide what you want to do long term. I will send a wire to Katherine this afternoon if the Beamer is available to me."

"Sure, go now before I need to pick up the kids. And Anne Marie, I can't thank you enough for all your help. You are becoming a sister to me and everyone in our family loves you."

"Thank you."

———————

Tami's phone rang again. She looked, and when her caller ID said it was from the WBC's switchboard, she answered. A strange man's voice was on the line, and he said, "Hello Tami?"

"Yes, this is Tami Powers."

"Tami, my name is Dick Cannon. I will be handling your affairs from now on, and I need to meet with you today. Will two o'clock give you sufficient time to get over here to headquarters?"

"What happened to Carl? He was assigned by Ben Benson to work with me."

"There has been a realignment, Tami. You will be working with me from now on. Again, I would like to meet with you at two p.m. today."

"Oh, that won't be necessary, what was your name again?"

"Dick Cannon."

"Goodbye now," and Tami hung up her cell phone.

———————

"WBC New York City, this is Gianna in Mr. Benson's office, how may I help you?"

"Hi Gianna, this Tami Powers, is Ben available?"

"For you, I believe I can find him. Would you mind holding a moment?"

"Not at all."

Several minutes later, Tami heard a familiar voice, and she said, "Hello Ben."

"Well, hello Tami. How may I help you?"

"Ben, I just received a very strange call from someone named Dick Cannon. He said I was working with him now. What's up with that?"

"Oh, nothing serious Tami. Carl is very busy in the accounting offices, and we thought Dick would have more time to devote to your file."

"Well, Mr. Benson, I'm not a file, I'm a real person, and I have enjoyed my time working with Carl. We connect well and have begun to develop a comfortable working relationship. I hope I can continue working within that context."

"Tami, that is not possible right now, which is why we have assigned one of our top young executives to work with you."

"Ben, I don't want to disrupt corporate planning or anything, but I feel certain Carl could continue finding time for me. I hope we understand each other here?"

"Well, if you put it that way, Mrs. Powers, I will see what I can do. Goodbye."

———

Ben Benson, not a man to be trifled with, called Carl back and informed him he was back on the Tami account, and also to polish up his resume, because when Tami went, he would be going with her.

Carl smiled. He was proud of Tami for standing up to Ben, and doing something he himself did not have the starch to do.

———

The calendar moved on to September and it turned out to be a relatively quiet month for Team Tami. Thankfully, after all the chaos involved in getting the kids prepped for school. It enabled Anne Marie to ramp up their training routine in preparation for the New York City marathon. Katherine Katz had filed their Institution of Suit, summons had been served, and the defense statement had been received. KK's senior partner at the firm suggested ten million dollars as an appropriate amount for the filing. Tami and Anne Marie concurred.

In their statement, *Probe* magazine produced a copy of Malcolm's recorded interview as defense exhibit number one, albeit the altered version, and swore to its veracity. They claimed that Tami's suit was frivolous, and although they benefited from the recurring exposure and notoriety from the suit, they were also desirous of a speedy resolution to the case.

When the plaintiffs responded to the defense with arguments of Tami's impeccable character, and her near perfect passage of the polygraph and bodily specimen testing she had been subjected to, the entertainment channels had a field day. They debated the merits of Tami's virtue versus *Probe*'s questionable record and reputation. However, it was widely agreed that the existence of physical evidence carried more weight than circumstantial evidence.

Probe was milking the headlines of their sleazy rag just as Ben Benson and legal had advised they would. And while Ben was publicly lying low on Tami's position, secretly he hoped for her comeuppance. He also took the opportunity to lambast Carl Middleton every time an opportunity presented itself. Criticizing his judgment in handling Tami's account, demanding extra reports and financial analysis on short notice, undermining him at executive staff meetings, etc.

Carl knew Benson was out to get him and was forced to suffer the indignity of weekly abuse and being nitpicked to death by a senior VP. It was humbling, stressful, and unsettling to have one's nerves skewered and grilled on a regular basis. But Carl was hanging in there. He had been a collegiate wrestler at Iowa State University and therefore was no stranger to hand-to-hand combat.

While Carl was suffering his occupational torment, Benson would, of course, loved to have received his resignation. As is so often the case in corporate culture, when an entity such as Tami is protected, a superior has little choice but to attack a weaker link, re Carl.

And Tami wasn't helping much, as the only positive publicity she had produced during the month was rescuing some dufus college kid who was jaywalking while on his cell phone. This was back page stuff which barely made the local news. But Carl happily wrote out another check to Tami which annoyed Benson even more. Carl was hesitant to point out that it was Benson who had driven the construction of

Tami's contract, so he wisely held his council and continued writing the checks.

While she cared for Carl, all of the corporate kerfuffle was out of her sphere of attention. Not that it overly concerned her anyway. She and Anne Marie were getting in some of the best training of their time together, and she was hoping to drop her all-time best number by a significant amount.

———

On the first Friday night of October at six p.m. the phone at Luca's West-Side Italian restaurant rang. The hostess answered the call and transferred it back to the bar. On the fourth ring, Mick answered the phone, and heard a voice ask for Alfonzo.

Alfonzo and his wife had just made their semimonthly stop for drinks about twenty minutes ago. They had cocktails in front of them, and Alfie was surprised to get a call on the house phone in such a public place.

"Allo," he said.

"Hello scumbag, I want me money and me phone back."

Alfonzo, of course, recognized the voice immediately, but played it cool. "Who is this?"

"You know damn well who it is, and you heard what I said."

"You must be mistaken, sir, I have no idea what you are talking about." Alfonzo's beautiful wife looked at him and raised her left eyebrow quizzically.

"Let me tell you what I'm going to do. I'm going to give you one week to return my money, or you will have the Interpol authorities to deal with. See how you like having an international law enforcement agency up your sorry ass. You can keep one hundred K for a commission, and I will call Luca's back next Friday night at this same time to make some arrangements. You better have your shit together my friend, or else."

————

Malcolm's reach out to the Italian gentleman was a grave error on two fronts. To call a made man in a social situation, one in which his wife could be present was his first error. Then to give him an ultimatum was close to suicidal. Alfonzo and Geo had been extremely cautious with their windfall. They had driven to Vegas dumped the car, stayed at Caesar's Palace for one night, where Alfonzo cashed only one cheque, gambled a bit, but largely laid low, and cashed out basically what he had put in. Geo went down the street to the Mirage and did the same thing. Then they flew right back to New York the next morning under their aliases.

When they got back on the street, Alfonzo paid off Uncle Carlo with two of the certified checks, and he and Geo each FedExed the rest of the checks to the Bahamas and into their new offshore accounts. They also agreed to put the majority of the one hundred K they cashed at the casinos into safe deposit boxes, and therefore maintained an identical lifestyle to the one they led prior their trip out West.

————

Perhaps Malcolm was aware how difficult it is to retrieve money from the Cosa Nostra, and that's why it took him so long to make the attempt. Maybe he was resigned to taking a stab at getting something back, no matter how futile it might be. Maybe, even though he was still in London and working on a consulting project there, this lawsuit thing with Tami and *Probe* made him nervous, who knows? He was sure if Tami's suit was somehow successful, *Probe* and Donovan Templeton would turn on him.

————

Alfonzo and his wife were meeting friends for dinner at Luca's that Friday night. When their friends arrived, they went into the dining room and were seated at a back corner table. As they left the bar, Alfonzo, who would call Geo the next morning, tipped Mick a hundred-dollar bill.

"If that guy calls ever calls back for me, tell him I can meet him at his mother's house any time."

"Yeah, sure, Mr. DeNardo. And thanks."

CHAPTER
21

Halloween had been a blast for Team Powers. Carrie hung out with her older friends while the boys helped relocate large sacks of candy from the neighborhood back to their bedrooms. Scott and Tami had walked Sadie around for some early trick or treating, then returned home and passed out candy for two more hours.

———

Now Anne Marie and Tami were focused on the NYC Marathon. After prepping for almost three months, they were both anxious to get back to the City, and the runners felt like they were in top condition. The plan was for Anne Marie to set a fast pace for the first half of the race, then Tami would take it from there.

The NYC, like all races, had qualifiers seeded appropriately, and our two women were near the middle of the first group due to their excellent recorded times. This would minimize the dodging and jostling toward the rear of these huge races.

Tami had been disinvited to the Jimmy Kameron Show due to her little tiff with Ben Benson, but she had been paid another reward for rescuing the jaywalker. When *Cheers* got a discreet message from within the organization, that she was running in the NYC marathon, they promptly sent her an invitation. Which to Ben's chagrin, contained all the perks of a VIP guest to their show.

Tami and Anne Marie were scheduled to arrive in NYC on Tuesday afternoon. They would be staying at the Plaza in Tami's room, compliments of the variety show. Also scheduled was a meeting with Katherine Katz on Wednesday for lunch. As far as running was concerned, the only agenda scheduled were some light workouts in Central Park to stay tuned-up.

———

Marea Italian Bistro is a four-minute walk west of the Plaza. As Tami enjoyed strolling about in the city, she and Anne Marie left the hotel half an hour before their luncheon reservation. The mid-November crowds and activity on the street helped Tami feel anonymous again. Not a famous person who was on national television frequently, or someone who was embroiled in an ugly lawsuit with a national sleaze rag. Not a person who was seeing disgusting headlines in the airport like: CHEATER to RUN in NYC MARATHON, or WHAT'S POWERING POWERS TODAY?

As Tami had been advised, the resultant bad publicity and social gossip was any number of degrees worse than the initial ambush. But there was little she could do about any of it besides soldier on. The worst part of the harassment was that it was now filtering down to her kids. Carrie was old enough to stay above the fray. But Charlie and Sonny had already gotten into fights at school defending their mom's honor. Tami was determined to focus on the upcoming marathon, and take her frustrations out on the course.

Anne Marie led the way into Marea through the highly polished, brass trimmed revolving glass doors. Katherine was waiting for them in the foyer of the elegant Restaurant. She was a statuesque woman Anne Marie's age. They had actually met at NYU. Attired in a smartly tailored grey twill business suit, with a complimentary black, high neck silk blouse, her hennaed brown locks were worn just above shoulder length. Her plump cheeks were rouged perfectly, and her hazel eyes dissected you.

"So nice to meet you in person Tami, I feel like we have known each other for years," she and Anne Marie hugged as the tuxedoed maître d' approached to seat them. They would be dining in a coveted corner booth; Katherine immediately ordered a bottle of chilled Pouilly Fume.

The ladies small talked, ordered, and continued to chat. Katherine was deliberately steering them away from any discussion of legal matters. The elephant in the room. Anne Marie ordered a bowl of spaghetti, Tami, trying to avoid rich food, ordered the thirty-seven-dollar house salad with crostini. Katherine was more interested in drinking than eating, but she ordered some fusilli and waved her fork at it once in a while.

After luncheon, three cappuccinos materialized, and Katherine finally opened a conversation about the elephant.

"Ladies, we reached the judgment phase of our case last Friday, and all I can say is the matter is in the hands of the Honorable Anthony Waters. He is an old-school type of Senior Judge, a no-nonsense guy, and I would be remiss if I didn't tell you that there are some concerns. He is possibly the worst Jurist we might have drawn. Although his decision could go either way, my feeling is his allegiances and track record suggest he could lean toward the defense. Waters is a juror who likes concrete, physical evidence and that is why I feel we may be at a disadvantage."

"Thank you so much for expediting this thing as quickly as you have Katherine. Is there anything else we can do?" asked Tami.

"I'm afraid we've already presented everything we can. If you have any miracles up your sleeve, now would be the time to pull them out."

"Are you saying that all my testing was for nothing? That I'm facing the possibility of living with a false accusation of cheating for the rest of my life? Losing this case would be even worse than the original accusations."

"Tami, anyone who knows you, and is familiar with your character would know that to be preposterous. However, a court of law is like a football game. Once the game starts, there is a winner and a loser, there may be differing degrees of both, but the Judge will not evaluate the case based on emotion. We fought like hell in there. We brought in the leading experts in the country to testify on your behalf. They affirmed that the results of your intensive testing by the best laboratories in the country precluded any possible doping. We showed your Grand Canyon video. The experts attested that no matter how many performance enhancing drugs a person took, they could never do what you were able to do.

Now, I am just reiterating that the case is in the judge's hands. I only want you to be aware of where we stand, and not be shocked at an arbitrary decision. And don't forget, we can always appeal if the decision goes against us and you should decide to continue the battle. Judge Waters may even find for the plaintiffs, but only award a dollar, which is really a de facto decision in your favor."

Tami would be ecstatic with a favorable decision, and she would frame an award of one dollar, but this whole conversation was a difficult pill for her to swallow. Here she and Anne Marie sat with Katherine as she wore her thousand-dollar business suit, her buying this ultra-expensive client luncheon and everything. But essentially, she didn't have any skin in the game. Yes, she could miss out on half of a sizeable settlement, but otherwise, she would dab the corners of her mouth with her linen napkin after lunch, touch up her lip gloss, and walk out of this tony restaurant. She would be back in her elevated corner office, where she would order a latte from some gofer and start to work on her next high-profile case.

"Tami, and what I can tell you is this; your case is not over by a long shot. It may be adjudged in our favor; Judge Waters may impose conditions, adjust the proposed damages, there are all kinds of possibilities. Right now, we have as good a chance as *Probe* to win this thing. During closing arguments, I will continue to stress your testing, your character, your incredible acts of heroic bravery. The obvious hardships visited on yourself, your family and your career, so keep your chin up. In the meantime, I will be at the finish line in Central Park on Sunday morning cheering you both on. Let's all hang tough, eh?"

"When can we expect Judge Waters decision?" Tami asked.

"That's hard to say exactly. I would think his decree would/could/ should come down no later than the end of next week." Katherine put her platinum American Express card down and did in fact dab the edges of her ample lips. She briefly checked her reflection in a discrete compact mirror, ran her tongue over her teeth, and the principal plaintiff, her advisor and her attorney all slid out of the booth. KK left a generous tip at the Maître D's stand and retrieved her credit card. Then they were all back on Fifth avenue, standing in a chilly wind, they hugged and parted ways.

Anne Marie was at wits end to cheer Tami up after their ritzy luncheon. She was Tami's best friend, running partner, business rep, and roommate, but she had never seen Tami so down. They walked the streets aimlessly for an hour, until Anne Marie took out her phone and made a call.

"Hey, girlfriend, we are going to the Comedy Club on East 24th tonight. Let's head back to the hotel, get some rest or read a book and go out to a local joint for a slice and then go have a few laughs. It'll work wonders."

"Whatever," Tami mumbled, and they headed back to the Plaza.

———

The very same afternoon Geo and Alfonzo met at a diner in the Meatpacking District. In his earlier call to Geo, he outlined his conversation with Malcolm last Friday evening. Once they were together, he emphatically described his irritation with Malcolm's attempt to threaten or intimidate him.

"We need to lose that little geek for good," he told Geo. "I mean we have his mom and sister's addresses over there. Does he think we won't get after them if we need to?"

"Relax Alfonzo, there is no way the little puke has anything on us. That paper was like holding cash, negotiable and untraceable."

"Plus, he gave it to us, right?"

"Right, I think he really wanted us to have that money. We even gave the stinking watch back to him. We shoudda kept that too."

"Alfonzo, I have been following this Sparrow dude, and there is some stuff going on. I have an idea I think will put the final nail in his coffin and might make us some dough in the bargain."

"Whatta ya got, Geo?"

"You trust me, right?"

"Sure."

"We done everything right on this little job, huh?"

"Sure, we have. Even Uncle Carlo says we done good. And he's hard to please."

"Okay then, I know what's going on. I been readin' the papers; I know just what to do."

"What?"

"Better only one of us knows. And I guarantee you, we ain't never gonna hear from the little assbite again." Their meatball sandwiches arrived, and the conversation turned to the NY Rangers and hockey season."

———

After lunch Geo went over to Brooklyn, turned the combination on his locker in the men's club dressing room and put on a suit and tie. He grabbed a fedora, some sunglasses and a covid mask. Drove to the Brooklyn Bank, paid a quick visit to his safe deposit box, and headed back over to Manhattan.

He pulled into valet parking and rolled down the passenger-side window. "I'll only be a couple of minutes," he said to the attendant, and gave him a twenty-dollar bill. He put on his oversized sunglasses and face mask, topped it with the fedora, got out and walked into the lobby of the Plaza Hotel. As he was making his way, all he could think about was how ironical it was to encourage someone like him to wear a mask and walk into a business. But right now, he was a good citizen, well within his rights, and he was on a mission.

Geo entered the posh hotel's gilded lobby and approached the front desk. He palmed a fifty-dollar bill into the surprised desk clerk's right hand and asked if she would please ring Tami Power's room. Anne Marie answered on the third ring, and the clerk announced that it was the front desk calling, and could she please hold for a moment.

"Of course," AM replied.

"Do you have a message for her, sir?"

"Yes ma'am. Could you please tell her I have something she will find very, very valuable. I will wait for five minutes here in the lobby, and if she wants my present, she should come down."

The desk clerk delivered the message, and Anne Marie said she would be down in a minute. Geo discretely slipped the clerk another fifty and went and sat down on a settee facing the elevators. Anne Marie pulled on some yoga pants, slipped a tee shirt over her head, and headed for the elevator. When the lift touched down on floor level, Anne Marie was excited but apprehensive, and looked towards the front desk. The young lady pointed with her chin in Geo's direction, and Anne Marie approached cautiously.

"Hello sir, can I help you?"

"You're not Tami Powers," Geo said as he stood to his full six-foot two height.

"No, I am her personal representative. My name is Anne Marie Stein, what can I do for you?"

Geo stood up and looked closely at Anne Marie. He stuck out his hand, which Anne Marie reluctantly shook, and finally he handed her a purple Crown Royal sack. "There is something most valuable to you in here. Examine it carefully, and you will be elated that I came to visit you today." Then he turned abruptly and strode out of the ornate lobby.

Anne Marie watched him go, wondering where she might have seen him before, then turned and walked briskly to the elevator bank.

CHAPTER
22

Should Anne Marie have run up the stairwell in her excitement, the elevator would have come in a distant second. The door to their suite burst open, and she jumped on top of Tami, who was lying on one of the queen beds reading and brooding.

"What's happening?"

Anne Marie rolled off and held up the Crown Royal sack. "There's something in this bag, and a guy downstairs said it will be very valuable to you."

"What is it?"

"I think it's a phone."

"Get out of here! It's probably a bomb."

"Not a chance. A dude just gave it to me in the lobby, I'm sure it's a phone, come on let's take a look."

"Who was he?"

"I don't have a clue, but he said we should check it out very carefully."

Anne Marie opened the drawstring on the sack and shook out the contents. Sure enough, there sat an iPhone on the bed, with a password taped to its back on a small Post-it note. Anne Marie plugged in the phone, they waited a few minutes, and turned it on. In several seconds up popped a picture on the home page of Malcolm Sparrow in a tuxedo holding some kind of award hardware.

"Oh my God," Tami said.

AM keyed in the password, Tami's hands were shaking too badly to function, and the phone opened promptly. Excitement wasn't an adequate word for the two women scrolling through that phone. There was nothing of note in the contacts. They checked texts and by now the latest emails had almost loaded but offered nothing of any interest. Anne Marie started scanning the home screen and noticed a Voice Memos App. She opened it, looked down through the menu file and there it was, pretty as a baby's smile. *Tami Interview, September.*

"Could this be it, Anne Marie, the original interview?"

They began playing the tape, got into the second half of it and heard the beautiful lines:

"Have you ever taken any anabolic steroids, or any other performance enhancing drugs?

Absolutely not.

Would you be willing to take a lie detector test to that effect?

Only if necessary. Etc."

Tears of joy came streaming down Tami's face. Anne Marie grabbed her, and they began dancing around the room. They were both crying happy tears now, hugged, and couldn't stop jumping up and down for joy.

"It's my miracle," Tami shouted.

Anne Marie came back to her senses, picked up her cell phone and called Katherine Katz. She was still in the office, and Anne Marie told her the miracle she requested had just come in. They had Malcolm Sparrow's cell phone in their possession, and the original interview was intact and still stored on the phone, and yes it had been altered substantially.

"Get that beautiful ass of yours over to Judge Waters' chambers and file an injunction or something."

"I will call his office right now and request a stay until the new evidence can be submitted. You two get over here ASAP. I need to hear that tape, I need to make copies of it, and I need to get one of those over to the judge's chambers today. So, hustle it."

Tami threw on clothes, it didn't matter what they were, and they dashed out their hotel door. It was quarter to four. When they got out on the street, there was so much traffic, Anne Marie simply took off running to Rockefeller Center.

Once inside, a secretary ushered them into Katherine's office suite and Anne Marie played the taped conversation. "There is a God, Tami, and he loves you," the expensive New York attorney gushed. "Let me make a call and then we can run off copies of the tape and get ready for submittal."

Katherine reached Judge Water's clerk. "Ma'am," she explained, "I have newly acquired evidence in my possession that is highly conclusive and could conceivably alter the disposition of our case."

"When did this new evidence materialize," the clerk inquired.

"It came into my possession literally minutes ago." The clerk dialed the judge to inform him of some new developments. After waiting ten minutes, Katherine agreed to be at chambers promptly by nine a.m. the following morning.

KK called a senior technician into her office and asked him to make three independent copies of the interview, without disturbing the original in any possible way. She opined that supplying the original recording might help a lab prove that *Probe*'s tape was a bogus forgery.

'Tami, it may be more effective to submit Malcolm's original recording, I don't know. Maybe we should submit the whole phone." It was decided that Tami, Anne Marie and the phone would accompany Katherine to the courthouse tomorrow morning.

"I am going to secure Sparrow's cell in our office safe for now, I will bring it with me in the morning. Tomorrow, I want you both to dress conservatively and conduct yourselves with contrition. Be humble and act injured. Express nothing but gratitude that the tape found its way into your possession. Anne Marie will be there to confirm the method of delivery.

If I am not mistaken, this will overwhelmingly confirm your innocence and terminate our case. It will also give the *Probe* people an out. I'm sure they will maintain the tape recording they received from Sparrow was already altered, and they will most likely proceed against him to help defer their assessed damages. Congratulations ladies let's go out and have a celebratory cocktail. St. Pat's B&G is just three blocks down. You would think they would have a damn wine bar or something here in the Center, wouldn't you?"

Tami wanted a few minutes to make some calls, and Katherine led her down the hall to a conference room. She called Scott and was in tears telling him the good news. He was beside himself with excitement, and told her how happy he was for her, and yes, everything is just fine here. The older kids will be so excited to hear the news. "You can go now and run the race of a lifetime, babe."

Next, she called Carl Middleton and excitedly gave him the update. "Gee, if the judge resolves everything by tomorrow, you can break the news on *Cheers*. Wouldn't that be incredible?"

"You better believe it. And please give Mr. Benson my regards, won't you?"

"Oh, rest assured of that. Maybe you can stop into headquarters and say hello yourself."

"We'll see." She was so excited, she decided to talk to her kids personally, and called Carrie and asked her to gather the troops. She spent ten minutes laughing and crying on the phone with them. Finally, Anne Marie gently knocked on the door and let Tami know they were about to lock up the offices for the evening.

The three colleagues marched out of the building and in less than fifteen minutes were in front of St. Patrick's. Tami wasn't sure whether to cross the street and go into the magnificent Cathedral to offer a prayer of thanks or go in the bar and have a drink. Katherine made the decision for her, and she followed her companions who sat down at a table in the lounge. Katherine ordered a bottle of Santa Margarita Pinot Grigio.

The attorney opened the conversation and said, "This is one of the biggest turnarounds I have ever been involved with, or I have even witnessed. Maybe someone besides Christ rose from the dead sometime, somewhere or something, but for now this one is the cat's pajamas."

"There had to be something good come of this," Tami said. "It's not just me, but everyone in my family has had to go through so much crap over these jerks. Thank you so much Katherine for keeping the faith. I just kept hanging in there hoping against hope for justice to prevail. Thank you too Anne Marie, not only for sticking by me throughout this ordeal, but also for recommending Katherine."

The three celebrants sipped through a glass of wine, then Katherine announced she had an engagement for the evening. Tami wanted to go back to the hotel and rest up anyway. She couldn't wait to get up and go out in the morning and run her tail off.

Tami and Anne Marie ordered a light supper from room service, and Tami called Scott again and talked to him for half an hour. By nine o'clock Anne Marie set her alarm for five AM and turned out the lights. Tami slept as soundly as she had in months.

———

Next morning the two close friends and running partners took off into Central Park again. Tami was chomping at the bit to overdo it, but Anne Marie reined them in at the eight-mile mark. Their morning run was completed without the need for Tami's lifesaving efforts of their last jaunt through Central Park.

Getting back to the Plaza, they went into the dining room for breakfast. Tami high fived a few fans along the way, then they hustled upstairs to get ready to meet Katherine. She texted and told them she would meet them at the United States District Court, 500 Pearl St. Tami and AM took the subway down Lafayette to Wall Street and hiked back up to Pearl.

They entered the austere building, and it seemed in many respects more like a church to them than a courthouse. At least a place of serious reflection. Katherine was waiting for them in the foyer, handed Malcolm's phone to Tami, and guided them up to the third floor and Judge Water's courtroom. Tami and Anne Marie waited in the front of the gallery, while Katherine approached the court clerk, who smiled, picked up her phone and chatted for a moment with the judge. She then stood and told the attorney and the two nervous women she would escort them back to his chambers.

"Good morning your honor, how are you today?" Katherine asked.

"I'm fine, thank you, come in." He motioned to three chairs sitting in front of his desk. "And why don't you introduce me to your friends, Ms. Katz."

"Your honor, this is Tami Powers and her personal representative Anne Marie Stein."

"Pleased to meet you ladies, particularly you Mrs. Powers. I have enjoyed seeing some of your remarkable talents on television over the last few months."

"The pleasure is mine your honor."

"What can I do for you today Ms. Katz. My clerk tells me you have some new evidence to submit?"

"Yes, your honor."

"You are aware that it is highly irregular to introduce new evidence at this late juncture of my trial?"

"Yes, your honor. However, this new evidence only came into our possession late yesterday afternoon. If you would take a moment to review it, I'm sure you'll agree that it is most compelling."

"What is your evidence, Ms. Katz."

"Your honor, I have here in my possession the cell phone of one Malcolm Sparrow. He was the director of the film where Tami Power's first rescue occurred. He is the originator of the interview which the plaintiff maintains has been tampered with, and the defense argues is in its original state. Our newly acquired evidence is the original copy of that initial conversation and will prove the defense has a flawed copy of such."

"You are aware that it is illegal to present evidence without the permission of the owner of the property in question, do you not Ms. Katz?" Tami squirmed.

"Your honor, I believe it is permissible to submit for review if there are extenuating circumstances."

"And what would be the circumstances in question, Ms. Katz?"

"Your honor, the court has previously consented to submission of a tape recording from *Probe* magazine, which the plaintiff contends has been tampered with. Our evidence is merely a rebuttal to that submitted evidence."

"Ms. Katz, federal law clearly states that a one-party conversation may be recorded without the other person's knowledge or consent. And also, there is the ownership issue."

"Yes, your honor, but this was not a one-party conversation. Mrs. Powers was cognizant of her conversation and was merely responding to questions imposed on her by her former employer. This cannot be considered a normal conversation, merely a forced sequence of responses by my client who was under her employer's supervision and direction and therefor a recording with proper consent by both parties. Also, your honor, I maintain the relevance of the defense's evidence is tainted because the original interview with Mrs. Powers was demanded by Mr. Sparrow under the auspices of a legitimate request by Sparrow's superiors. He said that he was instructed to gather evidence to confirm the lack of any negligence on the part of said producers due to the violent confrontation on the film's set and the absence of any prearranged security.

I spoke with one of the producers of Mr. Sparrow's film last evening, and they had no knowledge of, nor did they request Mr. Sparrow to conduct any such interview. I will be happy to produce an affidavit to corroborate my findings, if necessary. And therefore, one can only conclude Mr. Sparrow proceeded to unlawfully procure this interview with my client on completely fraudulent premises. He coerced Mrs. Powers to testify for the sole purpose of selling his illegal recording at a later date. He knew this would impart severe distress upon Mrs. Powers and severely damage her professional reputation. Worse yet, he may be the guilty party who himself altered the tape recording."

"You have made your point, Ms. Katz. Will you please play the recording for me?"

Tami, trying not to be too obvious, breathed a sigh of relief, and Katherine obsequiously flashed Malcolm's picture on the home screen of his cell, and played the tape for Judge Waters from Sparrow's own phone. She was happy, upon the request of Judge Waters, to replay the portion of the tape which differed substantially from the altered version.

"Ms. Katz, I am going to allow your recorded evidence for submission. The fraudulent intent in this case overrides proprietary considerations. I am going to send the recording to Audio Forensics for testing of its veracity, and I will also have my clerk call the defendants and inform them of this turn of events. I'm sure you have made a copy of the tape for your files?"

"Yes sir."

"Do you have one of those copies with you?"

"Yes sir."

"Ms. Katz, I request your copy of that recording, and I am going to take that copy of the conversation and enter it into evidence. I may introduce the recording at a later date in my courtroom if necessary. If the lab will confirm the tone and diction of Mrs. Powers voice is an authentic match to the defense's copy, and the recording has in no way been tampered with, I will award my verdict to the plaintiffs. I must warn you that if the lab should find any inconsistencies in your copy, the verdict will be the diametric opposite. Do you understand that ladies?"

Judge Waters heard a chorus of yes sirs.

"And you are willing to proceed under those conditions?"

Another affirmative chorus.

"Very well, in consideration of these late developments, I am delaying my decision until I have conferred with the defense. My clerk will be in communication with you, Ms. Katz. Good day ladies."

———

Tami departed the courthouse with dampened underarms, but a joyous heart. "Wow, you did it, Katherine," she said.

"Negative on that. Your mystery man couldn't have materialized at a better time."

Anne Marie said, "Come on ladies, let's go to the Fulton Fish Market for an early lunch."

––––––––

Judge Water's court clerk connected him to *Probe* magazine's lawyer. The judge explained what had just transpired in his chambers and gave *Probe*'s attorney an option.

"Mr. Davidson, I want you to speak to your client as soon as I terminate this call. You tell them the defendants have somehow come into possession of Mr. Sparrow's cellular phone. Explain to them that said cellular phone contains the original version of his interview with Mrs. Powers, and it is significantly different from the recording of the interview which is the basis of your defense. Mrs. Powers maintains this version is indeed the original recording. I have sent the Sparrow tape to our forensics people for authentication. I will give your client until three o'clock this afternoon to consider a decision.

If the tape recording in question comes back to me and verifies that it is the original and your version has been tampered with, I will have no other option than to uphold Mrs. Powers civil suit against your magazine. I will then apply additional penalties such as research and witness costs, legal fees, travel expenses, etc. However, if your client should wish to abrogate their claim of authenticity, and vacate their defense, I will take that into consideration, and be inclined to look more leniently upon the damages due Mrs. Powers. Do you have any questions, Councilor?"

"May I inquire how this late piece of evidence suddenly appeared, your honor?"

"Council for Mrs. Powers avers that the cellular phone in question was delivered unsolicited to the plaintiff yesterday at the Plaza Hotel. They maintain the identity of the individual who delivered the evidence to their hotel is unknown to them."

"Thank you, your honor. If I may say, this is a most unusual development, but I will deliver your message to my client. If I should be unable to contact the principals, or they are unable to reach a timely decision, I may need to request an extension of your three o'clock deadline, sir."

"The conditions of my offer remain the same, Councilor. I suggest you make every effort to contact your clients at your earliest convenience."

"Yes, sir."

————

Councilor Davidson called Donovan Templeton at *Probe*, explained the situation to him, and listened while he cursed, swore and uttered some more profanities.

"If I may offer a suggestion Donovan, get your CEO and let's have a conference call right now."

"He is out of the office."

"Well, you get in touch with him immediately. Tell him his councilor recommends he vacate this case. Waters has already seen the original tape on Sparrow's phone. We can claim that the evidence we obtained, upon which we released our magazine's expose, was already tampered with by Sparrow and that we are victims here. This will give us a better settlement, and then we can go after Sparrow to recoup some or all of our damages."

"Dammit Davidson, you said these cases always turned out to be inconclusive."

"It's too late for that, Donovan. This new evidence changes everything."

"Crap, how did that broad ever get hold of Sparrow's phone?"

"The judge said it was anonymously delivered to their hotel yesterday."

"Where are they staying?"

"The Plaza, I believe."

"I want to see the security footage of that hotel lobby for the date in question."

"I can send someone over there this morning. You talk to Myron and explain to him the urgency of reaching a decision here. Even though I recommend vacating, this is as good a possible scenario as we could ask for. We salvage our integrity, lower the damages, libel insurance pays off, and we create an adversary with culpability. Don't forget, Waters wants an answer by three p.m."

"Can't we extend that?"

"I already asked, and got a hard no."

————

Donovan called Davidson back just after noon and told him to go ahead and vacate. Davidson called Judge Water's clerk, was told that he was out of the office, so he went ahead and vacated their defense and asked for a call back from the judge.

Judge Waters clerk called him in his chambers and relayed her conversation with defense's council.

"Mr. Davidson requested a call back from you. I told him you were unavailable."

"Thank you. Looks like we have wrapped up another one, Marlene."

"Yes, sir."

————

After he finished eating his sandwich, and looked though some files, Judge Waters instructed his law clerk to return Councilor Davidson's call.

"Mr. Davidson, I have Judge Waters on the line, please hold."

"Yes, Mr. Davidson, Waters here. I understand you wish to vacate, is that correct?"

"Yes sir, however my client wishes me to convey to you that we are the victims here. The information we received from Malcolm Sparrow was entirely erroneous and had already been altered when it came into our possession. That information was the sole basis for our published articles which we believed to be based on fact. I am respectfully requesting you take these extenuating circumstances into consideration, and I also petition the court for these reasons to eliminate any damages imposed on my client. *Probe* magazine also offers to publish a complete retraction of all material related to Mrs. Powers, which alleges any and all wrongdoing by her. We will frontpage the retraction in our next edition."

"Very generous of you and your clients, Councilor. However, I need you in this courtroom within the hour, and you will sign my Order to Vacate. This case is over, except for my assignment of damages which I will deliver to the litigants by this time next week."

"Yes, sir."

————

Judge Waters directed his clerk to call Katherine Katz and inform her that the defense team would be in his office within the hour to sign an Order to Vacate, which effectively ends litigation in this trial. Ms. Katz, your presence is also requested for signage, the judge is deliberating damages, and will disclose his ruling within a week's time.

————

Katherine called Anne Marie and relayed her conversation with Judge Water's law clerk and asked to speak with Tami. "Tami, it's over. We won, you won, and you are completely exonerated. I am going over to the courthouse now to sign the final papers, part of which include a complete retraction by *Probe* magazine. When I'm finished, I'll call you."

"Thank you, Katherine. As you might expect, I am overcome with emotion and elation. I couldn't be happier with the results of your hard work."

"I'll call you back later. Gotta go."

And Marie and Tami again went into their victory dance. Finally, they calmed down, and Tami sat on the settee to gather herself. "I feel like Camus' boulder has just rolled off my back, my family's back. Finally, good things are starting to happen."

"For sure, partner. And could the timing on this be any better? You can break the news tomorrow afternoon on *Cheers*. Let the world know justice has been served."

"No kidding. I'm going to call Scott, then Carl Middleton."

Scott was delighted to receive her call. "Congratulations, baby. You did it. I wish you were here to celebrate with us."

"I'll be home on Sunday night, and we will light it up."

———

"Hey Carl, we just won our case."

"No way! What happened?"

"We visited the judge's chambers this morning, and he heard the tape. He apparently communicated with the defense about the new evidence, and all I know is that my attorney got a call that the case has been vacated. The ruling on damages will come down next week."

"I am speechless and couldn't be happier for you. This is just between you and me, but Benson tried to block you from being on *Cheers* on the grounds that you were tainted by the damaging lawsuit still pending in court. But *Cheers* fought him on the grounds that you were innocent until proven guilty and we should stand by our own. Congratulations again, Tami, you took these lowlifes on all by yourself, when our own senior management wouldn't help you, so one more time, huzzahs. Your vindication will also vindicate *Cheers'* loyalty for sticking by you. Enjoy your time on the show tomorrow afternoon."

"Well, you stuck with me too Carl, and I appreciate that so much."

"You're welcome, partner."

———

It is not often an executive manager gets to thumb their nose at a senior counterpart. But after Carl's call to update him on Tami's gutsy victory and having made an unsolicited comment about what a courageous young woman she was, Benson was wise enough to go with the flow. Now he had to try and salvage some credibility out of the situation.

Maybe even harvest some political cache in the bargain. He called the corporate florist and ordered three dozen long stem red roses to be delivered to the *Cheers* Times Square studios. Then he called the studio and explained to a production assistant he wanted them placed in Tami's lap when she was introduced on air tomorrow afternoon. After which he sent her a text of congratulations and wished her a healthy settlement.

––––––––––

Tami and Anne Marie went out for a celebratory dinner, and even though Tami was in line to receive a handsome settlement within the week, they chose a less ostentatious venue than Madea. Anne Marie knew a quiet neighborhood restaurant, and they toasted by splitting a .375-liter bottle of prosecco. The *Cheers* limo was coming for them tomorrow morning so it would be an early night. Anne Marie was happy to see her friend back on the nationally syndicated show, no one deserved it more than her.

On the way home, Tami said, "Can you please call Katherine and invite her to the show tomorrow?"

"Yes, of course," Anne Marie replied.

CHAPTER
23

Tami was so excited the next morning getting ready for the show, she put on new running shoes. She also wore black yoga pants, a silk, black and dark green scoop neck camo top, and contacts, which brought out the emerald color in her eyes. That was all she had to do; makeup would take care of everything else. Anne Marie wore black slacks with a bright pink jacket top.

————

The staff at *Cheers! America* was cordial as ever and whisked her past production and into makeup. She was professionally primped and preened over, the women French braided her hair, and she came out beaming and looking like a cover girl.

Anne Marie led her into the green room, where Tami enjoyed an energy bar and asked for a Diet Coke.

————

After twenty minutes of national news and weather updates, some breaking local events, a hostess came for Tami and Anne Marie, except Anne Marie stood backstage. Tami was ushered onto the more informal of the *Cheers* sets to a standing ovation and welcome. She and Tobin, Mara and Michelle all hugged, and after she was seated in a director's style chair, Mara struck up a conversation. Finally, Tami was able to interject and break the news of the victory in her lawsuit.

"Everyone, I have some very exciting and wonderful news to share with you. Tobin, Michelle, Lisa, Mara all the guests in the audience and our television viewers. My lawsuit against *Probe* magazine was officially terminated yesterday afternoon. *Probe* vacated their defense of my lawsuit when critical evidence surfaced of the original recording of an ancient interview I had taped back in Utah. The evidence proved that *Probe*'s allegations of my taking performance enhancing drugs was false, frivolous, fraudulent, invalid and soon to be forgotten."

The audience stood and roared in approval. Her *Cheers* hosts gathered around and hugged her. There were some pertinent questions, and Tami voiced her appreciation to the anonymous gentleman who had intervened at such a crucial time in the trial.

Tami explained that her immediate supervisor at the site of her first intervention had insisted she sit with him and recap the events of the day for executive management. She had not requested or received a copy of the original interview, and a tampered copy of the original had apparently been sold to *Probe*. Or maybe *Probe* itself did he tampering, I don't know. But without a copy of the original, I had no defense other than the testing I volunteered to undergo. Miraculously, the original showed up at such a critical time.

They chatted about the trial, and George innocently asked if it was *Cheers'* attorneys who had defended her honor and reputation. "No, we decided it was best for me to go it alone. Which I was able to do with the support of my family, my supervisor at WBCLA Mr. Carl Middleton, my best friend Anne Marie Stein, my attorney Ms. Katherine Katz, and so many faithful supporters from far and wide." Then Tami called Anne Marie out from backstage, hugged her, and made Katherine stand up in the audience.

Anne Marie related how the mysterious gentleman had appeared virtually out of nowhere, gave her one of those classic purple Crown Royal sacks and told her to check the sack for evidence. When they did, voila, there it was.

After some more trial chit chat, Tobin asked Tami what else was going on, and they yacked some about the family, the trip to the Grand Canyon, that intervention, school, work, etc.

"Would you like to share some words in parting with us?"

"Thank you so much everyone," Tami said. "What a wonderful day it has been. There is no place in the world I would rather be to share my positive news of the trial than here on this sound stage. Thank you, *Cheers! America,* for giving me this opportunity. I was advised by some very important people to let it go, that all of the evil allegations against myself would just blow away in time. That I didn't have enough solid evidence to exonerate myself in a court of law. But I didn't want these individuals to get away so easily with slandering not just myself and my family, but possibly any one of you out there. Then, through perseverance, the help and support of my family, some key people in my life and a little magic dust, we won. That means the world to us.

"I also wish to say today that none of my interventions would have been possible without my running habit. I owe so much to running to help get my feet back on solid ground when I was a lost and overwhelmed mom to four small children. Running brought me health, happiness, a sense of fulfillment, and the physical ability to be able to do good things for people. I urge all of you out there to give it a try. If you can't run for whatever reason, get some exercise by walking or riding a bicycle. Do something. Start as slowly as you need to. Consult with your physician but do it. It will help you be healthier, happier, and feel better.

"I would also like to announce at this time that we are starting to organize a Powers Family Foundation, offering aid and scholarships to deserving youth in our communities. More on that later, and thank you, everyone, especially the best show on television, *Cheers! America.*"

Tobin stood and closed the show by wishing everyone a great weekend, and then said, "That'll do it for today. Goodbye all, and good luck in the race on Sunday, Tami." As Beyonce's "Break My Soul" came on the sound system, everyone on stage stood and waited in line to hug Tami and Anne Marie.

———————

AM and Tami tried to rent the Plaza's town car Sunday morning, but the hotel concierge would have none of that. The black Lincoln sedan was ready for them, dropped the two runners at the southern tip of Manhattan. They would board the Whitehall ferry over to Staten Island, then grab a shuttle bus to the starting line. The first wave of racers was scheduled off at nine-fifteen a.m.

Both women were feeling rested and relaxed. Anne Marie had been able to check on her subleased apartment, conduct a couple of business meetings in person, and enjoyed an early dinner with her mom and some family friends last night. She felt like a yearling racehorse and couldn't wait to compete in her hometown marathon.

Tami was so amped to run her toes itched. Like Anne Marie, she was rested, in optimum physical condition, and now her mind was singularly focused on a spectacular race. Her best marathon time was 2:51, and she was determined to not only beat that time, but also knew she had a shot to qualify for the Universal Games.

Anne Marie was going to set as close to a six-minute-mile pace as she could across the Verrazzano-Narrows Bridge and north through Brooklyn and Queens to the Greensboro bridge. Tami would take it from there and be on her own to continue north through the Bronx and then loop south to the finish line. About eleven and a half miles were left in the race when they parted company, but it was Tami's favorite of finishing layouts. Harlem was colorful and historic, and as soon as she hit the north end of Central Park, she felt like she was running downhill.

At the appointed time, Tami pulled steadily away from her running partner, and at the twenty-two-mile mark, finally started to hit the wall. Throughout her racing career, this was her moment of truth. It required digging deep into her mind and body, and simply continuing to run on courage and stamina. But somehow being next to Central Park buoyed her spirits. It inspired her to keep grinding until she rounded the corner of the Park at 59th Street, where there were only one-point-two miles left. Any inspiration is a bonus, today she had the added incentive of having won her trial and being a free woman.

———

Running twenty-six-point-two timed miles is probably surpassed in exertion and stamina by only the Ironman Races. Maybe Olympic level rowing championships. When Tami hit the wall, her steely resolve was all that sustained her. Random inspirational thoughts might visit her; Katherine Switzer, the first woman to complete the Boston Marathon in 1967, giving birth four times, the love for her family, her conviction that running was part of her destiny, etc. Today her victory at trial was a huge motivator, and then came that right turn. The home stretch and she bore down like never before.

Tami had run hard and kept close to the pace Anne Marie had set. When she got near the finish, she could hear the crowd screaming loudly, but she was now in the place only marathon runners go. Utterly exhausted, both physically and mentally, she was sustained only by the knowledge that the race was over. As she drug herself in a tortured sprint over the line, her finishing time read 2:31. She had not only taken twenty-six seconds off of her best time ever but had also qualified. Someone draped a blanket over her shoulders in the recovery area, and she continued to walk off her momentum and slow her heart rate. She dropped onto a massage table for a quick rubdown. Her right leg had cramped as soon as she had crossed the finish line. It was as if she had willed it to perform, but only for twenty-six point two miles. Now, it was cranky, and that was okay.

———

Marathon running requires an incredible amount of dedication. There is no money in it except for the elite few who win consistently and train fanatically. In 2023 there is a $100,000. purse going to the men's and women's winners in New York, with lesser monies being paid to the lower place finishers. 47,839 total participants ran in the race, and over 47,800 of those finishers ran for the pure joy of running. The Super Six Star races, Boston, New York, Chicago, London, Berlin and Tokyo are among the highest paying events, but still only a gifted, miniscule minority are rewarded financially.

If you factor in the cost of flying to New York or Boston, not to mention Tokyo, meals and lodging, miscellaneous necessities, it costs people major money just to run in these road races. The payoff comes from the satisfaction of completing such a grueling event in one of the world's greatest cities. There may also be the thrill and addictive nature of running in the same race as someone who might set or break a record, but for eons of time people have simply run. To survive attack by man or beast, to hunt for food, for physical exercise and development, and from the time of the Greeks in athletic competitions. To this day we continue taking part in one of our ancestors' most basic legacies.

Any year now an elite runner will break the two-hour marathon barrier, just like Roger Banister broke the four-minute mile barrier back in 1945. But runners like Tami and Anne Marie don't run to break any major barriers or set any records. Running came along at a strategic time in her life to help define Tami. It became her elixir, her personal brio. And now it had even given her special superhuman powers. Space, time and acceleration powers that are beginning to defy the Laws of Physics.

CHAPTER
24

After the long flight home, Tami settled into her routine. Everyone she came into contact with was thrilled about the outcome of her lawsuit. The final judgment was to come down this week, but Tami seemed unconcerned about it. She was just happy to be back in LA, able to run again in the mornings with Leona. She loved competing in the big-city marathons, but her own environment, on her trails and in the foothills of the San Gabriel mountains, was where she belonged.

Anne Marie was going to stay a while longer in New York. Her mother was ailing, and she still had her marketing business back there. She would continue to act as Tami's personal rep and monitor her commercial calls, even though she would be off of the West Coast for a while. Tami's finances were taken care of. The 100K bonuses she had been accruing, less Anne Marie's percentage, were split between stock and bond funds. As far as ongoing business, New Balance Shoes wanted her, as well as Adidas, Diet Coke, Etsy, Macy's, etc.

———

Ben Benson was in a bit of a quandary. Tami was becoming a national heroine, and he felt he was being judged rather harshly in the corporate culture he loved so dearly. There was some blowback from the Board that Tami's comments about having had to go it alone with her lawsuit, on his own national television station yet, was reflecting badly on WBC's management team. Being the Senior Vice-President in Charge of Operations and Scheduling, this directly affected him. He would need to book a West Coast trip soon.

Mid-week of Tami's return from the New York Marathon, and as Thanksgiving approached, Sadie's first grade teacher had asked her young students what they were most thankful for. Sadie, of course, answered she was most thankful for her mom who a is superhero. After Sadie told the class how she had seen her mom fly through the air to save a girl from dying in the Grand Canyon, her teacher asked if Sadie's mom might be willing to come and visit their class. She sent an invitation for Tami attached to Sadie's shirt that day. Sadie's job was to get the precious note home intact, and she guarded the piece of paper pinned to the front of her shirt like it was spun gold. Tami was only too happy to go to Sadie's classroom on Friday morning.

Anne Marie called Wednesday evening, and they discussed Judge Waters looming decree on damages, although the payout would probably not be eminent, there still needed to be a plan in place about handling the money when it came in. Anne Marie suggested that T Bonds or Munis might be the safest option for her. Tami wanted to check with she and Scott's financial advisor.

Friday morning dawned on Tami and Leona running up past the Rose Bowl stadium and headed for the foothills. It was a beautiful California fall day, and the two women were running freely while Tami filled Leona in on New York. Tami mentioned that she was going to Sadie's school this morning and invited Leona to come along. Now that Anne Marie was staying in New York, Tami and Leona would be spending more time together.

Arriving home at the usual time, Tami went inside to rouse the troops. Sadie jumped quickly out of bed; she was so proud that her mom would be going to her school today. Carrie had a friend picking her up, and the boys wanted to ride the bus, so Tami had a lighter load this morning. Leona ran home and hit the shower. She got back to the Power's place a minute before Tami and Sadie were ready to leave and jumped in the Beamer with them.

Ten minutes later they pulled into the elementary school parking lot and drove through the visitor's area. It was full. Tami pulled out of the main entrance, and turned left onto the boulevard which fronted the school. A block down the street she found a parking spot and paralleled in. They got out, locked the car, crossed the street, and Tami started walking down the sidewalk, holding Sadie's hand, Leona bringing up the rear.

As they approached the expanse of lawn which fronted the school, kids and parents were arriving, and Tami noticed two young men on the sidewalk, walking towards them. They were fooling around with what looked like a pit bull who was not on a leash. The guys were rough housing with the dog, who was snarling and jumping at them. All in good fun, Tami hoped, although it was somewhat disconcerting to the parents of the school bound children who were giving them a wide berth.

Tami's trio was almost directly in front of the wide perpendicular sidewalk which led to the school's double entrance doors, as the two dog owners approached from the opposite direction. These guys were ragged and sported unkempt hair, greasy and overgrown. They wore holey jeans, dirty hoodies and they seemed to be taking pleasure in annoying everyone. The pit bull bounded back towards his owners/ tormenters growling, and one the hoodie boys kicked the dog solidly on its back left haunch.

It was a hard kick with a construction boot, not meant to be fun, and infuriated the dog. It spun to its right, still growling, ran across some twenty yards of lawn and grabbed a mouthful of the skirt of a tiny kindergartener who was walking toward the school with her mom.

The pit bull started shaking the little girl like a ragdoll. The mother, the daughter, everyone present halted, gasping in shock.

While personnel began to emerge from the front offices of the school to see what was going on, the enraged dog continued shaking the terrified, screaming child. Tami gently pushed Sadie over to Leona, then stepped in front of the angry dog and tapped it solidly on the head. The dog looked up and she rapped it firmly again. The terrified child dropped like rock from the mutt's mouth, and she scrambled back into her mother's arms. Now the pit bull turned and snarled viciously at Tami.

Tami looked the pit bull straight in the eye. They stared at each other for thirty seconds, and Tami pointed her right index finger in his face and said "No." The dog stared and continued to snarl, although not as aggressively. Spittle frothed in the corner of his mouth. Tami pointed again and said firmly "no, no, no!"

The dog sat back on its haunches and looked at Tami with his head cocked to one side. It had stopped growling. Tami said, "good boy, stay," and squatted in front of the dog, who was still eyeing her curiously. She extended her hand, palm down, for the dog to sniff, when one of the punks reached out with his foot to push her down and away from the dog.

Tami spun, grabbed his ankle, stood, and twisted his leg while jerking it straight upwards. She could feel his groin muscles tear as she pushed him over backwards and looked at the other guy. He started to make a move, and she told him "you don't want to do that." He stopped in his tracks. Leona had filmed the entire episode, but now there were more phones out and 911 had been called.

One of the administrators brought a length of rope outside with her. Tami reached down and patted the dog on his head. She held him until the woman arrived, then looped the rope through the dog's collar. She tied it off and led him away from the school's entrance over to a small sycamore tree and tied him to it. The dog sat down passively and panted while his tongue lolled out of his mouth.

Tami patted him on the head one more time and walked back to Sadie and Leona while the admin lady went to get the dog some water. Sirens could be heard in the distance, and the second guy helped his buddy up. He threw his arm around his waist, and they hopped away from the rapidly approaching cops. Retracing their steps back around the corner before two patrol cars pulled up. By now people began to realize who Tami was and started cheering for her.

The policemen wrote out a report, complete with a description of the two would be thugs. While Tami made her statement, one of the officers spun his patrol car around and sped off to the corner looking for the dudes. Tami finished with the cops, and Leona hurried her and Sadie into the schoolhouse just as a couple of reporters arrived on the scene.

———

Sadie's teacher had been an observer to the incident and walked over to greet Tami. She picked Sadie up and gave her a hug while introducing herself to Leona. They walked slowly back to her classroom and sat talking as other children filed in to stow lunches and take their seats. Several of the children had observed the trouble outside and looked at Tami in awe. Everyone was very quiet. Tami sat with Sadie who seemed prouder than scared by her mom's confrontation. She knew her mom could do almost anything.

School was able to start on time for most of the teachers and students. Once the dog had been subdued, things quieted down pretty quickly. When they had gathered all the information they needed, and the other officer returned without the suspects, animal control arrived, untied the dog, and led him into the back of their vehicle. Of course, the little girl the pit bull had terrorized was still in shock and had been excused for the day. Her mom wouldn't leave the school offices until she was able to personally thank Tami for stepping in so bravely. They hugged, and then Mrs. Cleveland called her class to order.

After taking attendance and doing whatever elementary school teachers do to start the day, she introduced their guest, and the kids pulled their little chairs into a circle. Tami smiled and thanked the class for inviting her to join them. She tried to talk about how important school was, but one of the boys was in front of the building this morning and started asking questions. Soon enough another kid asked if she could fly, and things veered off of the lesson plan.

Tami did her best to explain her special talents to the kids. They talked for almost an hour about some of her episodes, what it meant to help people, and how special it felt to be a good person. Like by helping your mom and dad, your brothers and sisters, your teacher. She finally got in a plug about the value of being able to go to school and how important that was. Then it was time to go, and Mrs. Cleveland called the Principal's office for someone to come escort Tami and Leona out of the building.

Tami hugged Sadie, kissed her goodbye, and waved adios to the children. As she got up to leave a feeling of apprehension again enveloped her. Walking down the corridor towards the entrance/exit, the school principal was profuse in her thanks for Tami's intervention this morning. She asked if Tami would be interested in coming back sometime and speaking to the entire school population in an assembly. It was an easy decision, because Tami was basically all about kids. She agreed immediately.

As the three women approached the entrance doors, a parent was leaving, and before the heavy door could reclose, suddenly it slammed back open, and three angry young men burst into the foyer. The two losers from the dog incident this morning were back, and now they had a friend with them. Two of the punks were carrying machetes. The third didn't seem to be carrying a weapon, although he was limping badly from the defensive move Tami had introduced him to earlier.

"That's her," the unhurt guy from earlier said. He pointed at Tami.

"Where's my dog, bitch?" snarled the new guy. Sounding not unlike his dog this morning, he looked to be the ringleader of the motley crew. Then he took a menacing step towards the three women.

Leona and the principal stepped backward; Tami stepped forward. "Animal control took your dog to their facilities." The principal tried to edge toward her office and was warned not to move.

Again, "you bitch," he said and looked straight at Tami, "I want my dog back." Some of the admin staff were peeking around doors and through windows, and realized they had another situation on their hands.

"Your dog is at animal control. Why don't you get out of here and go get him, before you get into serious trouble."

"You're going to come with me and go in and bail him out, you and your friend there," he nodded at Leona who was busy filming. "Come over here now."

"Listen to me, sir. We are not going anywhere with anyone. Please get out of here now."

All that did was set him off, and he lunged at Tami, swinging the machete in a wide forehand swath. Tami two-stepped backward, and as soon as the large grey blade had passed by her body, she jumped forward, planted her left foot on top of her attacker's left foot so he was immobilized and with the four fingers of her right hand extended firmly away from her thumb, she delivered a compact chop directly into his larynx. As he began to choke, she followed that move with another strike. This one with her right knee to his groin.

He groaned and began to slump. Tami's peripheral vision glimpsed the other machete pulling back to strike her backhanded from her left side. She again sidestepped and the machete connected instead with the abdominal area of the already damaged gang leader. Blood started to soak his Raiders jersey and he moaned in pain before hitting the ground.

Tami's latest attacker almost dropped his large knife in surprise, it didn't matter. As his momentum spun him to the side, Tami turned and delivered a high kick and caught him flush on his right ear. He grabbed his head before another kick to his thorax removed all the air from his lungs. He joined his buddy on the ground.

She looked at her torn groin pal from this morning, who was starting to reach into one of the pockets of his baggy cargo pants. Tami stretched over, grabbed his free arm, and spun him around in a circle. This made him stride in excruciating pain on his torn adductor muscles. Being flung around in one cycle was all it took to have him join his buddies on the floor. Tami patted his pocket and found what would prove to be a loaded handgun.

The police had been called for the second time today to Oakville Elementary School. However, a school invasion is much, much more serious than an aggravated dog situation. In reality, the innocent dog was far better behaved than his owners when he wasn't being provoked. But by now, sirens were screaming, and half a dozen squad cars had descended on the entrance to the elementary school.

The principal stepped outside to tell the officers everything was under control. They told her to stand down and entered the schoolhouse two abreast with weapons drawn in full combat gear. The press was already gathering on the other side of the area being cordoned off with bright yellow police tape.

As Oakville went into lockdown, the cure was proving worse than the ailment. Exercising extreme caution, the officers took control of the three perpetrators in the foyer. They turned the bleeding leader of the gang over to the EMTs but continued to insist on securing the entire building. Parent notification had begun, and the scene turned into the mayhem that naturally follows a school invasion.

An hour later, the police had secured the building, and it was declared safe. The three dudes and their weapons had been hauled away. The chief was there interviewing the Principal, Leona and Tami in the office. The remaining patrolmen had gone outside and were doing everything possible to calm an anxious crowd of parents. Leona had discretely put her phone away for fear the police would confiscate it. They could make all the copies of her video they wanted once World News was through with it.

After his aide had compiled the statements of the three women, the chief allowed them to go. But not before he thanked Tami for her help, and again advised her to steer clear of police jurisdictions. The decision to dismiss school for the rest of the day was going smoothly, and relieved parents were reuniting with their kids. Everyone breathed sighs of relief. Leona told Tami she should probably speak with the press on their way out. "Let me hold Sadie," she said.

That took half an hour and was chaotic. People were picking up kids, school buses were pulling up, there were media trucks parked on the street, cop cars were everywhere. Tami was glad they hadn't parked in the school's lot this morning. It would have taken them forever to get out of there.

People were recognizing Tami and were hanging around to see if they could hear part or all of her interviews, maybe get in some background screen time. Now that everyone was assured the day's trauma was over, and thankfully the damage was minimal, they were relaxing and slowly dispersing.

Tami spoke cautiously to the half dozen microphones that were shoved towards her face. Yes, there had been a confrontation, no, no one from the school had been injured. In light of the tragic number of school invasions of late, she was so thankful this one was more of an isolated incident that had been contained by our local law enforcement. The confrontation had been confined to the entry of the school, and yes, she had been able to help subdue the invaders. Etc. She continued to answer questions pleasantly and patiently.

Finally, everyone was satisfied that the story had been exhausted, and by now there were fewer people left on the scene. For the public's safety, the police chief left a couple of officers at Oakville on security duty. The principal and office staff were still working, and they came out to crowd around Tami and bid her a very sincere farewell. Tami and Leona were holding hands with Sadie as they skipped off back to the car.

"What happened today?" Sadie asked.

"Oh, nothing really, sweetheart. Just a little more trouble with those same guys who were mean to the dog this morning. And because of them, we get to take you home from school early."

———

Leona's second video of the day was emailed to Carl at the office. He passed the latest on to the news division and put in a call to Ben. "Lively day here boss, Tami has been involved in two episodes already."

"You're kidding me."

"Nope," and Carl proceeded to describe the events of the day.

"Anne Marie get everything of film?"

"Oh, Anne Marie is still in New York. She stayed in the city to take care of some business. Leona has been doing all of the camera work."

"Well, I guess it was a pretty good move of mine to put her on Tami's team."

"Yep, they seem to get along famously." That gave Ben an idea, and he asked Carl to get Anne Marie's cell phone number for him.

"Oh, I've got it right here."

———

When Tami got home, she, Leona and Sadie had a bite of lunch. Leona suggested they call in so Carl could schedule a follow up. Carl said Ben wanted to profile sixty seconds of Leona's live coverage on national news, and then they could do an interview with Edward for local WLA12 and a more in depth look at the day's events. He was sending two techs' out to Tami's house for a live feed. While Tami waited for them, she called Scott and gave him a brief update. He told her he was glad everyone was safe, and they could talk more later on. She thanked Leona, who took off and headed back to headquarters.

Next, she got Anne Marie on the phone. But before she could say a word, Anne Marie told her "I've just come back come from the Federal Courthouse." Tami said nothing.

"Six million bucks."

"You mean he made his decision?"

"Yes ma'am, you are now a wealthy woman."

"Were you in the courtroom?"

"Yep, I was there with Katherine."

"What did the judge say?"

"He just said the late evidence had swayed the case, and because of that the defense had vacated with cause."

"Katherine said the judge released the plaintiff's evidence to her which consisted solely of Malcolm's cell phone. She felt the award was a decent one. Sometimes a lower amount is easier to collect than an award at the higher end, where someone will appeal if nothing else to forestall payment. He also stipulated that the award was to be retired within thirty days, unless an appeal was filed. If not, it would begin to accrue interest at the rate of ten percent monthly. That would increase the amount of the award by $60,000. a month, so that was definitely in our favor."

"What's she going to do with the phone?"

"She going to FedEx it to you. You had better put it in a safe deposit box or somewhere secure. Somebody is going to want that phone back who knows when."

"I can't believe all this happened so quickly. When the money comes, make sure you take your ten percent out first."

"Thanks Tami, you are a sweetheart, but this award is actually not within the scope on my employment contract."

"Take your ten percent out and quit arguing with me."

"Yes, ma'am."

"I've gotta go, there are some techs' here to film a live feed for WBC."

"Of what?"

"There was a double incident this morning at Sadie's school. Watch the news tonight." And Tami hung up.

———

The tech people were set for her. Tami and Edward spoke for twenty minutes. After their chat he congratulated her on another successful caper, two actually, and wished her a quiet afternoon.

CHAPTER
25

Scott arrived home around six-thirty after an hour at the gym, and by then Tami had the kids fed and the champagne chilled, and had shooed everyone upstairs so she and her husband could have some quality time. He strolled, smiling, into the kitchen with a dozen red roses, and they embraced. Tami pulled a couple of chilled champagne glasses out of the freezer, grabbed the fancy bottle of bubbles by its neck, and they retired to the living room.

"Well, congratulations, baby—you did it. And on a day when you also saved Oakville Elementary from disaster."

"Oakville was minor league stuff. Anne Mari thinks *Probe* will pay off soon. I spoke with Carl, and he is going to talk to the legal department about setting up a foundation for us. We can start a scholarship for a kid or two in need."

"How much did you get?"

"Three million minus Anne Marie's ten percent. I'll need to do some research on the federal tax liabilities, which are probably going to be a pretty good chunk since these are punitive damages. We will probably net around two."

"I think one million for the kids education in some kind of conservative investment account, and one mil for your foundation. Wouldn't the mil for the foundation be tax exempt?"

"Like I said, I'll have to check out some tax codes. What if we just took the money and moved back to Gig Harbor or Idaho or something?"

"Hey, I love my job, and the kids are all established in school and doing well."

"I know. I'm just getting tired of all the BS. It's like we're living under a microscope. Every time something happens, someone is there to film it, and then the merry-go-round starts spinning again. I had to spend an hour on a live feed with Edward today. Two minutes on WLA12 tonight, and forty-five seconds on national. To make matters worse, I am starting to get premonitions. I knew something was going to happen today at Oakville. Even worse, those guys saw me walk up with Sadie. They know who she is. What if they get out on bail, and come back to the school and try to hurt her to get even with me?"

"We could take her out and homeschool her."

"I know that. But she loves Mrs. Cleveland, and she loves going there. I will just have to be extra careful and walk her in and out every day. I can talk to the principal; she'll be willing to help, I'm sure. And then if I have a premonition, she will stay home that day."

"We could take some of your foundation money and donate it to Oakville so they can beef up security."

"That's an excellent idea if it's possible to make a direct contribution like that."

"Maybe we should get away for winter break. Go up to Schweitzer Mountain and have a nice 'ski-cation.' Lose the city for a week. Unless a lot of ski bandits show up and need to have their asses kicked."

"Ha, ha, ha. That's a good idea, the kids all love it up there."

"Let's do it."

A week later, Tami received a registered letter from Katherine containing a certified check for two point seven million dollars. Katherine had been asked to deduct Anne Marie's percentage. The rest of the money was deposited in several accounts while Tami did her research.

She had been running every day with Leona and was otherwise lying low, except for carefully taking Sadie to and from school. Scott bought Carrie a used, late model Jeep Cherokee and now she was a big help with the commuting duties. Otherwise, Tami's body was feeling strong, and less stressed from her other commitments. The Universal trials were coming up in the spring, and Anne Marie was coming back from New York in January to start training again.

———

A. M.'s business was all caught up back east. She had been running in and around Central Park during her time in New York, but it was getting cold. She had also been casually seeing Ben Benson, who had called and invited her to dinner. Rather than bother Tami, he had expressed his regrets at not being more supportive of her lawsuit directly to Anne Marie. She was pretty sure it was easier for him to go through her to get to Tami, but she didn't care. Their relationship was totally casual and consisted of dinner out occasionally.

———

Around the middle of December *Probe* magazine filed suit against Malcolm Sparrow in the same U.S. Circuit Court. Judge Waters recused himself from the list of possible adjudicators, and the Honorable Ms. Clarise Morten was appointed to sit for the case.

Donovan Templeton had been wise enough to wear a wire to his meeting with Malcolm Sparrow and his thugs back in September. He was sure *Probe* could manipulate that tape to their advantage, and their attorneys could successfully litigate against Sparrow; however, he was unsure if Sparrow had six million dollars to cover the damages. Maybe two million and garnishment of future income would have to do. *Probe* should be able to gain some additional revenue and valuable exposure from their coverage of the case.

———

Then Geo called Alfonzo for a lunch meeting in mid-December to discuss a piece of business.

"I been following the news about the broad, and she collected a nice chunk of dough."

"How much?"

"She should clear three million after she splits with her mouth."

"That's a lot of ching."

"Especially since she might not have got any of it without our help."

"What're are you thinking?"

"What I'm thinking is, maybe we is due a commission. You know, like a sales commission."

"How much?"

"I don't know, maybe half a rock. How about six hundred, three hundred grand apiece?"

"She ain't gonna want to pay, you know that."

"Ah, they never do, but she got kids, four of them. Yeah, I done lots of research on her husband, her four kids and the broad who is still here in New York.

"Kids are always helpful in persuading people who don't like to share things."

"Yep."

"You really think we should move on something like this? Don't forget they got my mugshot, not yours, on file back there, and Malcolm already got in touch with Luca's in the city asking questions, leaving messages. They can track me, man."

"Well, the only way they could really track us is through Malcolm, and I made him a call. Plus, youse don't have to be anywhere near what I am going to suggest."

"Yeah?"

"Yeah. You know those *Probe* people just sued him for the six mill. But if he had his phone, they wouldn't have nothing on him. Capiche? I told him he don't know nothing, and he gets his cell back. He said okay. He ain't stupid."

"Why don't he just call runner broad and ask for his phone direct from her?"

"I'm not sure she actually knows where his phone is. Also, there's a cousin of mine from Marseilles, he happens to be in London working on a project. He could speak to Malcolm or one of his family members if we need him to. He can be very persuasive."

"So, you get in touch with Malcolm, convince him to clam up. You get in touch with LA, and make a deal with the broad for six hundred Gs and that includes the phone?"

"That's right. We get our six hundred, Malcolm gets his phone back, everybody's happy. In the first place, you is laying low, they never even seen you. They don't know me; I deal with the broad. If she goes to the Feds, she's asking for trouble."

"The Feds is trouble, all right."

"Sure, they are. But if we make it easy for her, she will play along."

"Easy how?"

"Well, she got four kids. We ask her nice. If we have to, we grab a kid and take 'em to the safe house, you think she won't play along?"

"Well, that brings Uncle Carlo back into the deal."

"Jesus Christ. We already paid him two hundred Gs. He won't just let us use his place for a couple of days?"

"I can ask, but isn't that broad pretty stubborn? Didn't I read that she went out on her own to sue *Probe*?"

"Yeah, she did. But I don't think *Probe* ever grabbed one of her kids and axed her real nice to drop her lawsuit either."

———

The Powers were getting ready for their trip to northern Idaho. Vacation time had been arranged. Winter break was here, and flights to Spokane were booked. A Suburban was reserved, and they were going to head north up the Idaho Panhandle and stay for three days in the very cool little town of Sandpoint and ski Schweitzer Mountain. Then it was south to Coeur d'Alene for a day of R&R at the gorgeous Hagadone Resort and maybe do some cross-country skiing or snow shoeing. Then they would proceed farther south to Moscow, Idaho, tour the University of Idaho, cross the border back into Washington, and take a look at Washington State University.

Carrie thought this was a total waste of time. She was going to be a communications major at UCLA, and was sure her 3.9 GPA was good enough to get her in. Maybe one of her brothers was interested in these smaller northern schools. Not her. Finally, it was a two-and-a-half-hour drive southwest on US Route-95 to McCall, Idaho for another two days of winter fun. Then they would head south to Boise and fly home.

A grand time no doubt, and the family was excited, but Tami had been experiencing uneasiness since she started planning the trip. Usually, her morning runs could dispel negative thoughts, but these anxious feelings hung on and would not leave her.

––––––––

One morning in mid-November, Anne Marie received a phone call. She didn't recognize the number, but she was always getting business calls from unknowns, so she hit the green button on her cell.

"Hello, is this Anne Marie Stein?"

"Yes, it is. Who's calling please?" Anne Marie asked and switched her phone onto speaker.

"This is your friend from the lobby of the Plaza Hotel."

"How did you get this number?" Anne Marie asked and switched her phone onto her Voice Memos app.

"Oh, that ain't important. What is important is that it's time to renew our friendship."

"I was unaware we had a friendship."

"Well, where I come from, friends take care of friends. And since Mrs. Powers made out so well in her trial, thanks in large part to my present to you, I think it would be friendly if you were willing to share a portion of those proceeds with me."

"Who are you? Who is 'me'?"

"Again, Ms. Stein, names are not so important as you and Mrs. Powers considering us part of the family now. You, us, Sadie, Carrie, the boys, Scott—we're all in this together, and we think six hundred thousand dollars in six cashier's checks might make us feel more welcome into the fam."

"Maybe you would like to also welcome the FBI into your family?"

"See, now I don't feel no welcome at all. Which is too bad, because we want this transaction to go smoothly and quietly. We would hate to have to mail Sadie back to Mom and Dad in a box, wouldn't we?"

"What the fuck? You asshole."

"Now you stop that kind of talk. Just ask Mrs. P nicely and get the money arranged and you won't need to ever speak to me again. Otherwise, we can hurt anyone of you we choose. Whenever we want to."

"I'm not even sure she has gotten the money yet."

"Don't play games with me. I've got connections in the court system and have already verified those things."

"I'll try to talk to her, but she is on vacation somewhere, and I don't know what she will say or do."

"Great, you girls talk, and I'll call back in a day or two," and Geo hung up.

———

Anne Marie shut her phone down, and immediately sank back into her new beige settee.

She picked up her phone and started dialing. "Hi Mom, how's it going? Good, hey I'm sorry, something has come up, and I won't be able to come over tonight."

"Okay dear, I'll be all right tonight, but be sure and call tomorrow, I have a doctor's appointment in the morning."

"I will, don't worry, I can take you."

She hung up and called Ben Benson's private cell phone number. "You won't believe this," she said when he answered.

"What?"

"I just got a call from the guy that dropped the phone off to me at the Plaza."

"What did he want?"

"Oh, about six hundred thousand dollars."

"You're kidding me. Did you tell him to fuck off?"

"I tried to, but he knew everything about Tami, Scott and the kids. He even knew the kids by name. He threatened to hurt any one of them. Whoever/whenever they wanted to."

"This is serious stuff, Anne Marie. I'm coming over right now, and we are going to call the FBI."

"No, please don't come over here. Send a car for me and I'll come down to your office."

"Okay, it's on the way. You at home now?"

"Yes. I'll stay downstairs inside the lobby until the car comes, and I can caution the doorman and his staff to be careful."

"Great, I'll wait for you there. I am going to call a friend in the Bureau and get ahold of someone ASAP."

"Okay. I made a voice tape of our conversation. Maybe that'll help."

———————

Anne Marie jumped in the shower, put on slacks and a sweater, grabbed a topcoat, and took the elevator down to the lobby. She spoke to the doorman and asked him to alert the other shifts that her apartment was now on lockdown. "Hold all deliveries here, and I will pick them up. No one goes up there but me."

"Understood, Ms. Stein."

Turning, she walked into the lobby, sat in a padded chair and stared vacantly out at the street. Twenty minutes later the town car pulled up, and she stepped outside as the doorman opened the door. She cautiously looked both ways before walking over and sliding onto the polished leather seat of the luxury sedan.

In another twenty minutes they rolled into Times Square at WBC Headquarters, and she was escorted by the driver into the marble lobby. Ben was waiting in his office and speaking with a grey suit, who he introduced as Gerald Dixon FBI agent with the NYC offices.

"Pleased to meet you ma'am, did you bring your recording with you?"

Gerald Dixon fit the part of an FBI agent to a tee. Grey suit, black brogans, white dress shirt, muted necktie. His hair was high up on the sides, military style. Brown eyes, brown skin, his face was clean shaven and athletic looking. Anyone who called Anne Marie ma'am was already in trouble, and did he really think she would leave her cell phone at home? But she held her New York tongue.

"Yes, of course," and she retrieved the cell out of her handbag and pulled up the Voice Memo app.

Geo's conversation was replayed in its entirety. Ben was shocked at what he was hearing. Gerald recognized that this was possibly the start of something big. He asked if Ben could make a copy of the conversation, and Ben beeped for a technician. Gerald said he would have to inform his station chief right away, as soon as he could get a copy of the tape and get back to his office. He assured her the FBI would be on high alert. Did she have any idea who her mystery caller was?

"No, not really, other than the time he contacted me in the foyer of the Plaza Hotel."

Ben interjected, "Anne Marie, don't you think this has to be somehow connected to the disturbance we had at the Soirée dinner three months ago?"

"You're right, Ben. Malcolm was there, and the guy who brought me Malcolm's phone was the same type of guy who confronted us in there. Big, burly, had an accent. The lobby cam might give us something. Also, I can get Malcolm's contact info from Tami, and see if he maybe knows anything, or how his phone went missing."

"You need to call Mrs. Powers first and inform her of your conversation. Give us her location, and the Bureau will provide security and surveillance for her and the family."

"She's on vacation."

"Where are they?"

"Somewhere in Idaho skiing."

"Just call her and alert her to the situation. Tell her to take extreme caution until we can catch up and get a detail on her. I'm going to leave now and will call you and Ben as soon as I get back to the office and talk with my boss. If you could possibly stay here in this building until I am back in touch, I would appreciate it."

Gerald left and Anne Marie picked up Ben's desk phone, punched in an outside line and dialed Tami's number. It was almost six in New York, so it would be around three in the afternoon on the West Coast. Tami didn't answer, neither did Scott. She grabbed her cell and texted Carrie. "Call me now," it said, and ten seconds later her phone rang.

"Where are you?" Anne Marie asked.

"Some place in Idaho called Tamarack Resort, we're all skiing. I'm in the lodge with Sadie, everyone else is on the mountain. The resort is in the town of McCall."

"Please Carrie, this is very important; have your mom call me as soon as she comes in, please."

"I will, Anne Marie."

CHAPTER
26

Dixon and his bureau chief called back. The chief's name was Jensen, and he told Anne Marie and Ben to remain vigilant, and that they would immediately notify both the Crime Division of their SoCal FBI counterparts, and the Los Angeles police and sheriff authorities. They will discuss putting the Powers family under 24/7 protection. But things wouldn't intensify until the official demands had been communicated for the cash transfer.

As far as New York, Jensen congratulated Anne Marie for having the presence of mind to record the call. He further stated he wanted her to continue her role as the contact person. The FBI, however, wanted to tap her cell phone. Her caller was surely using a burner phone; however, they might be able to pick up a signal locator if the call came from the metro area.

The agents concluded the conversation, and Ben suggested that perhaps WBC could just pay six hundred thousand to alleviate the problem.

"Ben, Tami probably won't go for anything like that. I bet she will want to confront these people and take things to the bitter end."

"Even if her family is in eminent danger?"

"That woman does not, will not, scare easily, or back down from anyone or anything."

"I agree with you on that, she has a mind of her own, but I am going to call Soirée, and get a copy of their lobby monitor's film. I think we need to review that. When we first looked at it, we were primarily focused on Tami and the assailant."

"Couldn't hurt," Anne Marie agreed. "Let's call right now see if we can have them email us a copy, call the Plaza as well." Then her phone rang, and while Ben was calling Soirée, Anne Marie had to explain what was happening to an unamused Tami Powers.

"I am so sorry to bother you on your vacation, something big just came in. We need to warn you of something right away."

"Thank you, Annie. Don't you think we will be safe here in Idaho, and I can connect with the FBI when we get back to LA?"

"Probably. I doubt if some New York thug is going to go after you at an isolated Northwest ski resort. But please fax me your arrival time so the FBI can meet you at LAX."

"I will."

"Tami, please be careful. The guy who called me knew all about you, he knows a lot about your family, and even mentioned the kids by name. This is some serious stuff."

"We will be careful, and thanks for the call. I guess it was too good to be true that some guy would just waltz in and give us Malcolm's cell phone. I wonder how he got it in the first place?"

"I am with Ben at his headquarters office. He is sending Carl over to Soirée to get a copy of the security feed from our party there. Ben feels like that night has something to do with Malcolm and the phone. Do you have a contact number for him? Plus, Ben has already volunteered for the corporation to pay the extortion money for you."

"Thank him, but that won't be necessary."

"I'll thank him, but you should at least talk to Scott and think about it Tami. It's a very generous gesture by Ben and the network and would save everyone a lot of grief."

"I will discuss the issues with my husband, but I don't think we will need to take Ben up on his offer. Thank him, and we will also be careful."

————

Geo was correct in assuming Malcolm would want the same cell number as his original phone, and Malcolm's voice mail answered and requested a message and a call back number. Geo's message was short and sweet,

"Mr. Sparrow, this is an old friend of yours. I have a deal for you. Please be at this number at seven p.m. your time tonight and I will call you back."

Being a savvy businessman, Geo called back at six o'clock instead of seven so no one would be properly set up to try and intercept the call. Malcolm answered, and Geo immediately cut to the chase.

"Mr. Sparrow, I have something in my possession which is of great value to you. If you would like your cellular phone returned intact, meet me at the North London Tavern on Kilburn High Road tonight at nine p.m. Come alone, and do not share this conversation with anyone, or we will destroy the phone. We will be watching you; do you understand me?"

"Yes, yes I do."

"Don't be late," and Geo hung up.

Malcolm was, of course, elated at the thought of getting his phone back.

————

That evening Geo's associate from Marseilles, whose name was Lucien, met Malcolm on the street as he was approaching the tavern and directed him to keep walking. They continued north a few blocks to Golder's Hill Park and Lucien told Malcolm to have a seat on a nearby park bench.

"Have you been followed?"

"Nope. Who are you?"

"Say no sir when you speak to me, and I am a dear friend of the friend who called you tonight."

"Whatever."

Lucien rose and began to walk away. "Whoa there, no sir."

Lucien turned and gave Malcolm a severe look. 'Don't play games with me, little man. Do you want your phone back or not?"

"Yes sir, of course I do."

"Here's what you must do to get your phone back."

"Is it untampered with?"

"Yes, it is."

"My associates have the phone. They can have it in my hands in the next couple of days. You must speak to absolutely no one from America under any circumstances. Do you understand me? No one. If you co-operate with us, you'll get your phone very soon, and you can get the *Probe* people off your back. Does that sound good to you?"

"That sounds perfectly fine. I rarely speak to the states now anyway."

"Say, how is you mum doing these days?" Lucien pulled a recent snapshot out of his inside leather jacket pocket and showed it to Malcolm.

He blanched noticeably. "Where did you get that?"

"One of my friends lives in the neighborhood. He chats with your mum all the time. Loves her."

"You stay away from her."

"Don't be naïve, Malcolm. She could be with us right now it we wanted to harm her, or your sister, or her kids, or you could have had a fire at your flat, or a bomb under your coach. All kinds of bad things could have happened to you. But none of us want anything like that, do we?"

"No sir."

"And what is your part of the bargain?"

"Keep my mouth shut."

"Even if you get a call from someone in New York?"

"Keep my mouth shut."

"Do you know how badly the *Probe* people want this phone?"

"I'm sure they do."

"But we like you Malcolm, we know you like your life, and we want to do business with you. Only you."

"Thank you."

"Thank you what?"

"Thank you, sir."

"Oui, so I think we understand each other. But if you talk, we will know, and you can watch us kill your mum and your sis. That would leave you to care for your niece and nephew, only you wouldn't have any arms to do it with. Does anything like that sound appealing to you?"

"No, sir."

"Good job, Malcolm. You can go now. Remember, we will be watching you and your family very closely. Your troubles could be over in just a couple more days if you clam up. And the best part of all this is you don't need to do anything at all. Just keep quiet and your phone will be here tres vite."

———

Malcolm walked back to the North London Tavern and stepped inside to have a pint of Watney's and collect himself. He sat down and looked at the antique, polished old mahogany back bar, and waited for a barman. When he had been served, he took a sip and the wheels of his mind started turning.

Of course, he wanted his phone back, but could he possibly trust the crooks who had already stolen one million dollars from him? Could his phone have been returned to Tami by the court after the trial? He also assumed correctly that Geo, although he didn't know him by name, had given his phone or a tape to Tami's lawyer in time for her to enter it into evidence, and that was what had turned the case for her. In order to get the *Probe* lawsuit dismissed, he had to have that phone back, or he could never work or travel in the states again.

He didn't have the scruples to care how he got the phone back, he just needed to have it back in his hands. If he called Tami directly or called Interpol or the FBI, he would possibly put himself or his family in grave danger. If he didn't call her, could these miserable thugs actually deliver the goods? He continued to ponder the situation. The two Italians must be trying to extort money from Tami after she had won her court case, and the only way they could shut him up was to threaten his family and promise to return his phone. If he contacted the FBI and told them what had happened to him, all they had to do was take Alfonzo's mug shot to Luca's Bar and try to get a positive ID. At least one of them would be getting some heat.

But it wasn't the New Yorkers who had contacted him here in London. They had him pinned. Even if someone got arrested in New York, he could still be in trouble over here. He decided he needed to call his attorney in New York and have him delay the *Probe* case as long as possible. Then for the short term he would play dumb and wait to see what happened.

––––––––––

Tami and Scott sent for pizza, left Carrie and the TV in charge, and huddled over cups of coffee in the resort bar to create a game plan. They agreed the family's safety was tantamount. Scott suggested they just let Ben Benson pay the blood money; Tami wouldn't hear of it. Nor would she budge on just paying the money themselves.

"They are threatening our family, Scott, they are threatening our children. Who knows where that might lead?"

"Sweetheart, this is all found money anyway, why don't we just pay them the six hundred grand. You might not even have it if they hadn't gifted the phone to you."

"Found money? You call me sweating my ass off as every sleazy rag in the country dragged my name through the mud while I tried to defend myself found money?"

"I didn't mean it that way."

"Well, it is yet again the principle of the thing to me. I stood up for my rights. If they wanted to waltz in and hand over a critical piece of evidence, that was their business. Now, they want in on the action. Not a chance in hell."

"Well, what are we going to do then?"

"I think we go on home and when we get there the FBI will meet us and give us a security detail until we nail these jerks."

"I don't know if that's a good idea. You'll want to confront them, and these are not people to mess with."

"I wish they were in this bar right now, and I could mess with them."

"That's just the point, Tami. These guys aren't going to attack you frontally. They will try and compromise one of our children to get what they want. These kinds of guys don't fight fairly. You have confronted any number of situations and bad guys. But it scares me to think you might face someone who is carrying a gun again. Who knows if you can defy the physical world and pull off another miracle? And you just have to know these guys will be heavily armed and dangerous."

"I am aware of all that, and I promise never to put any one of us in danger. But I am also not about to cave into these kinds of threats. Can we just wait until we get back to LA and see what the FBI has to say?"

"Thank you, I think that is the best approach."

———

Geo and Alfonzo met again that night, this time at Donatello's, another Upper West-Side watering hole. Geo told his pal that if this scam was going to work, they needed to get busy. "We have made our demands, we have covered ourselves with the little man, and now we need to make it work while they are still scrambling."

"You have to make it work. You're the front man, so if you are ready, go do it."

"I'm the front man for sure, but you still have to help me heist da broad."

––––––––––

Ben and Anne Marie went out for a quick bite to eat, and by the time they got back to his office Carl had sent them a copy of the Soirée footage. But it was a copy of a copy that he had gotten from the Beverly Hills PD. Soirée was so busy when he called, they wouldn't even talk to him.

Anne Marie and Ben began to pour over it closely. The doors of the private room had opened that night and they all started filing into the foyer. The confrontation began, and they watched frame by frame as Tami stepped up and faced off with their assailant. Towards the end of Tami's heroics, they observed Malcolm slip towards the exit doors, but when he went outside, he was lost from view.

"Damn it," Ben muttered. He felt some measure of guilt because he had seen Soirée's video of the WBC dinner party filing out of the restaurant, replete with the unedited shot of Tami's license plate, which had been aired by his station. But no one else knew that, and the problem was, the video only filmed the western side of the covered driveway. Once outside Malcolm exited to the east. "We need Soirée's film from the valet area, Anne Marie." He picked up his phone and called the restaurant.

Finally, on the third attempt, Ben got in touch with his buddy the GM, and was promised a copy in the morning. "You might get lucky, that footage only scrolls for ninety days before it deletes. I bet you are pretty close to that right time frame right now."

––––––––––

Malcolm phoned his sister to give her a warning to be careful, and explained that his phone had been stolen, and some criminal types were causing him some problems.

"What kind of problems?"

"Well, you might know I am being sued about a tape recording I sold to a magazine in the states. They altered it, got sued, lost, and now are trying to say I sold them bogus material. I need my phone back which has the original recording on it to defend myself."

"Okay, but some guys stole your phone?"

"Yeah, they are trying to extort money from me for the phone. They even threatened mum if I didn't pay them."

"They have a picture of her and everything, so they know where she lives, probably you, too."

"Malcolm, Malcolm. How do you get involved in this kind of shady crap."

"Hey, anyone can lose their phone."

"Especially when they are schnokered."

"You know, Ellie, I just called to ask you to be careful. I would never forgive myself if something ever happened to you or mum."

"If you care so much, you should drop round once in a while. Mum is always askin' for you, and your nephews too."

"I've been awful busy sissy; I'll try to call more often."

"And come by?"

"This weekend. Please don't say anything to mum. I don't think these guys would do anything, I just wanted to warn you is all."

"Thank you for the warning, we'll see you this Sunday for dinner then?"

"Definitely. I'll be there."

———

Anne Marie got up the next morning, showered, dressed and walked the four blocks to her mom's apartment. She called for an Uber, and the two women left for a chiropractor's appointment. Her appointment took an hour, then they stopped at a deli for a bite of lunch.

"We might as well stop in at Macy's as long we are so close," she said.

When her mom started to tire, they walked outside, and rather than recall for their Uber driver, Anne Marie hailed the first cab she saw. The driver started back north for the Upper East Side, fighting traffic as soon as they departed. She did not notice the Kawasaki motorcycle that followed them. When they got to Mom's place, Anne Marie released the cab and walked her mom inside the building to her apartment.

"I'm going for a run. You rest up and I'll cook a nice dinner for us."

"Okay, dear."

She changed into jogging gear, and hip-hopped down the two flights of stairs to the lobby. Did her usual right turn and headed north, made it a couple of blocks, and paused when she came to the corner of eighty third and Madison before crossing the street. Seemingly out of nowhere, a black Escalade turned in front of her. But the SUV stopped, the back door opened, and a man with a camo balaclava mask on, pointed a handgun at her and ordered her into the car. It happened so quickly she didn't have time to scream or resist. The next thing she knew, they took her cell phone, there was a pillowcase over her head, and she was pushed down onto the floorboard between the seats. The car kept going east on 83rd until it felt like they were passing over Queensboro Bridge. *These crafty bastards*, she thought.

Tami had texted their arrival time in LAX to Anne Marie, but after they had deplaned and cleared the baggage area, there were no FBI agents there to greet them. *Weird,* Tami thought. She tried to call Anne Marie, but there was no answer.

Ben had also called her several times to no avail. The Bureau had called, as Chief Jensen was to have received an ETA for the Powers from Anne Marie. Finally, Ben got a call from Tami and when they compared notes and realized that no one, including Anne Marie's distraught mom, had had any contact with her, they started to worry. Ben called the FBI office and told Agent Jensen the Powers were on the ground. He told Ben to tell them to hang tight, a staff Suburban was on the way with two agents in it.

————

The sinister Escalade continued on, and finally pulled into a driveway in southeast Brooklyn. The garage door of a smallish, unkempt house opened and closed behind them. Anne Marie was led into a back bedroom with her head still covered. She heard the door lock behind her and removed the pillowcase. There was one window which appeared to have been boarded up from the outside, a dumpy single bed with no bedding on it, a scuzzy looking pillow, a chair, and a small bathroom. That was it. *Gorgeous place*, she thought. They had, of course, kept her phone and ID, having been careful to turn her phone off as soon as they had kidnapped her.

————

Tami didn't need the FBI to tell her Anne Marie was in trouble. Her antennae were receiving distress signals from her close friend, she also knew the signal was beaming from far away. The FBI arrived in good time, loaded team Powers up, and cut across surface roads until they caught the 110 freeway north to Pasadena. When they were about halfway there, Tami's phone rang. She looked at the caller ID, and although didn't recognize the number, she answered immediately. She could sense the presence of her friend.

"Hello, Anne Marie?"

"No," said a muffled male voice. "This is a friend calling. Anne Marie is unavailable right now. She wanted me to tell you to get the money together quickly. She is all right, and we won't hurt her as long as you perform. By the way, we need eight hundred thousand now, our costs have gone up. And I also want my phone back."

"What phone?" Scott was giving her inquisitive looks.

"Malcolm's and don't play dumb broad with me. Get back home, and I'll call in the morning." The line went dead.

"Who was that?" he asked.

"Those guys. They've got Anne Marie."

"Oh shit. Excuse me, gentlemen," Tami said to the agents in the front seat, "can you please pull off the freeway for a moment?"

"What's going on?"

"Get off at the next exit and stop. We need to make a call to the FBI in New York."

"Yes ma'am." Everybody in the car got quiet.

CHAPTER
27

When they connected with Agent Dixon, Tami delivered the bad news. They chatted for a few moments, he asked Tami who her phone carrier was and told her the chief would be tapping the line. The Powers finally got home in one piece, the kids dispersed, and Tami sat down on the living room sofa, deep in thought. Scott joined her, put his arm around his wife, and told her everything was going to be all right. "The FBI will have this cleaned up in no time," he said.

"I have to go back there, she needs me."

"Tami, that's not a good idea. Why can't you let the FBI take care of things?"

"I'll let them do the heavy lifting, I just won't feel right if I'm not there for her."

"How about you are here with our family for her?"

"Scott, if nothing else, I can help her mom, and you aren't in any trouble out here."

"I'm sure there are people who can help her mom."

"Scott, I love you, and I don't want to fight about it, but I feel a strong urge to go back there."

"Who is going to help us out here?"

"I can call Leona. She will come over in the mornings and get the kids off to school, pick them up, and start dinner for everyone."

"You are incorrigible."

"I love you too, and I won't be gone that long."

———

Tami made one of everyone's favorite dinners, Mac and cheese with shrimp. She told the kids she was going to be gone for a couple of days. There was little concern about any separation anxiety as they had just spent over a week together on a fabulous vacation. Plus, the kids were all fond of Leona.

Monday morning, she and Leona went for their morning run, and Tami asked if she could fill in for her for a couple of days. No problem. Back at the house, she and Leona got the kids ready for school, and drove Sadie to Oakville. Her phone rang while she and her daughter were in the car, but she ignored it. When they returned, she got Leona prepared for her absence, gave her house and car keys, a credit card, and refreshed the guest bedroom.

Before going up to pack, she called AIC (agent in charge) Jensen, told him she was coming to New York, and asked if he would please forward her a copy of the Soirée tape. Her second request was a copy of the mug shot of the perp at the restaurant from the HWPD. Jensen told her she would have them electronically in a couple of hours. She then called Alaska Airlines and reserved a flight to Kennedy for that afternoon. She also called Anne Marie's mom, and they had a nice chat. She was, of course, pretty shook up but was happy Tami was coming back.

———

Tami called Malcolm, and they had a completely weird, stilted conversation.

"Sparrow here."

"Hi Malcolm, it's Tami."

"What can I do for you?"

"Why haven't you called me and asked about your phone?"

"Don't need it."

"Why?"

"I have copies."

"Nothing is as good as the original, Malcolm. You know that better than anyone."

"Don't need it."

"How did those guys get your phone in the first place?"

"I must have misplaced it."

"Malcolm are you in trouble. Did you have a problem while you were in New York?"

"No comment."

"Where did you stay in New York after you left the Plaza?"

"No comment."

"Listen pal, you better tell me where you were staying, or nobody is ever going to see that phone in this lifetime again. Plus, I can trace your location in the City from all the damn calls you made to me. Remember?"

After an awkward pause, he volunteered "The Phillips Club."

"Where's that?"

"No comment."

"Why won't you talk to me?"

"No comment."

"Well okay, goodbye then."

———

Tami could just as easily have told Malcolm she would send him the damn phone, but he was acting so strange, plus he had recorded their conversation back when under false premises. Then sold it to *Probe*, which certainly didn't have her best interests in mind either. She wasn't about to beg him to take anything back.

Her phone rang again, and she knew who was calling. "What do you want?"

"I had a deal with your agent, she and I shook on it, and I want my money."

"I don't know anything about any deal, and besides, no judge is going to uphold some kind of alleged oral deal procured under duress."

"That's why we took out an insurance policy, and if you want her back in one piece, we want the eight hundred by this Friday."

"Don't forget about the phone."

"And the phone."

"I am coming to New York this week to personally deliver the goods to you. How do you want me to get it to you?"

"You get back here, have everything, and we will tell you what to do on Friday." Click.

Tami packed, ran to the market to stock the refrigerator, made a stop at the bank for some cash, and all the while her mind was grinding. There was no doubt there were two of these guys, if not more. But how had they gotten involved in the first place? What had their assailant wanted in the Beverly Hills restaurant?" He didn't try to rob anyone. He had confronted them in a peculiar manner in a very public place. What was he doing? What was his shtick?

Jensen said he had never shown up for his arraignment, and there was a warrant out for his arrest. He didn't seem like a West Coast guy. Didn't talk like one. Could he have been associated with the mob? But what would the mob be after in the foyer of a posh Beverly Hills restaurant with all kinds of people and security around? She mentally reviewed everyone that was there that night. No one had had any secondary contact with the thug. But then someone mysteriously shows up at the Plaza with Malcolm's phone. She would have lots to think about on her flight.

AIC Jensen called before Tami left for the airport. "We caught your last call," he said.

"Good. Any thoughts you might want to share?"

"Tami, are you really coming back to New York?"

"Yes sir. I have a flight booked for this afternoon."

"I would advise you not to do that."

"You sound like my husband."

"I am not your husband, but I do care about your safety. Why do you think it's any kind of good idea for you to come to New York?"

"First of all, Anne Marie needs me. Secondly, maybe I can be of some help back there, with Anne Marie's mom if nothing else."

"Help to whom?"

"Who knows? I do seem to have a knack for finding trouble. Maybe I might be able to uncover something everyone else has missed. Thanks for the electronics by the way."

"If you insist on flying back here, I am ordering you to stand down. You don't need to be uncovering anything. The FBI will handle this investigation. We are talking about felony kidnapping and extortion. We are working with our tech people for a facial recognition ID from the Plaza Hotel lobby visit. These are some very dangerous people. Your friend is already in deep trouble, you could easily end up in the same sinking ship as her. I am going to give you the phone number of the agent in charge; please put it on your speed dial. If, by some miracle, you should uncover some detail that might assist with your friend's recovery, call it in. His name is Jensen, by the way."

"I will be very careful, Chief. And please don't worry about me; I can take pretty good care of myself."

"Tami, the New York Bureau has launched a full-scale investigation back here. These are seasoned law enforcement officers, some of the best this country has to offer. I assure you they will handle things. Please stay out of their way."

"Aye, aye, Chief."

———

Tami left to pick Sadie up from school, bought her an ice cream cone on the way home, and gave her a wet smooch goodbye before Leona bear hugged her. Tami's Uber arrived on time to take her to LAX. Ben, who was not about to discourage Tami's visit, was going to send a car and had arranged a room for her at the Plaza. The flight back was smooth, her car was waiting, and she checked in around midnight. Despite resting on the plane, sleep came easily to her, and she was dead to the world when her alarm went off at five-thirty a.m. It was too cold to run outside, so she headed down to the fitness center. Ben was joining her for breakfast at eight-thirty.

After an hour and a half on the treadmill, Tami stopped at the security desk and asked to see the security tape recording of that afternoon in mid-November when Anne Marie had received the mysterious visitor to the Plaza's lobby. She was invited downstairs and into the security offices. It took the morning staff about fifteen minutes to retrieve the film in question. Tami took a video of it with her phone, thanked the security team, and headed upstairs to get showered.

As she was getting ready, she looked at the video half a dozen times. Geo's face was obscured effectively by the surgical mask and sunglasses. But the fedora he was wearing was, of course, narrow brimmed. Therefore, she could see ears, sideburns, and an otherwise lack of facial hair. He had shaken hands with Anne Marie, but that looked more like a cordial greeting rather than a "we've got a deal" shake. He was burly, around six feet tall, carried himself with what appeared to be a military bearing. His left hand was obscured, but when he shook hands with Anne Marie, he clearly had a diamond ring of some kind on his right pinkie finger. She enlarged the picture until it blurred out, but it was clearly a manly gold diamond ring. The kind favored by certain guys who, in many cases, are desperate to portray an aura of success and power. No way was it a fraternal type of ring. He was wearing a suit, it was nice, but off the rack, no tailor job, and his tie was cheap, blocky. It was certainly not the silk tie with a Windsor knot favored by the likes of Ben Benson.

Her first impression was that of an aspiring gangster. Street smart, but not overly sophisticated. A thumper type. Smart enough to know where the Plaza was, but definitely not guest material. She finished dressing and went downstairs to meet Benson for breakfast.

Although their relationship had been strained, current circumstances overrode past differences. The breakfast was cordial, Ben caught Tami up on what was going on. Ben's relationship with Gerald Dixon had provided him with bits of inside information, which were painfully few. There were no suspects, no evidence, which required the usual defensive posturing by the Bureau.

Tami was surprised to learn of Anne Marie's new, casual relationship with Ben. But he assured her it was strictly platonic. Tami didn't care, she couldn't see what an otherwise intelligent woman might see in the man. At least he was putting her up at the Plaza and offering the use of a Town Car for the duration of her stay.

————

The first thing Tami did after breakfast that morning was go visit Anne Marie's mom. The eighty-year-old woman wasn't in the best of health anyway, and her daughter's situation had her blood pressure soaring. Tami asked if she wanted to go to the hospital and get some sedation. She assured Tami she was plenty tough and would wait at home until her daughter returned safely. "She is not too far away, mom, I can feel her presence, and I feel very good about her returning to us soon."

"Bless you, dear."

"Do the neighborhoods around here have security cameras mounted outside?" Was Tami's next question.

"Yes, they do, but I believe the FBI has already taken that up. Ben told me they saw Anne Marie being abducted, and it was one of those black SUVs the gangsters all drive. But the license plates were covered up or something."

"What time did Anne Marie go out?"

Mom told Tami about she and Anne Marie's outing in the city. "We got home around three in the afternoon, I thought it was freezing, but she decided to go running."

"Do you know where she runs?"

"I think she generally runs north to 79th and turns toward the park."

"Thank you so much. Maybe while I'm here, I can come make some dinner for us some night this week."

"Oh, that would be special, dear, but you just help those nice men find my Anne Marie."

"I will."

————

Tami googled The Phillips Club and asked the driver to take her over to the West Side. They parked in the loading zone, Tami got out and was met by a uniformed bellman outside the door.

"Are you checking in, ma'am?

"Maybe George," she said looking at his name tag. "I'm trying to reconnect with an old friend; his name is Malcolm Sparrow. Might you remember him?"

She could see the indecision on his face and reached into the side pocket of her leather jacket and pulled out a hundred-dollar bill. He accepted the money, and it seemed to jog his memory.

"Yes ma'am, I believe we had a Mister Sparrow stay here a couple of months ago."

"But isn't this a private residence hotel?"

"Yes ma'am, it is. He must have had a sponsor."

"Does anything stick out in your memory about Mr. Sparrow's visit?"

George could probably write a book about Malcolm's visit, but he wasn't sure whom he was talking to. Therefore, his brows furrowed again with indecision.

Tami reached into her jacket and pulled out a couple more Benji's and slipped them to George.

"Yes ma'am, it's all coming back to me now. He had a meeting here in September. You might want to check with the front desk. There is security footage of the lobby and the meeting room."

"And he had a meeting here in these facilities?"

"Yes ma'am, I believe he did."

Tami's pulse quickened. "Was he alone?"

"Oh no ma'am, he had a couple of bodyguards with him." Tami's blood pressure began to outrace her pulse.

"Anything else?"

"No ma'am, all's I remember is he left very, very quickly right after the meeting was over."

"Did he leave with his bodyguards?"

"Oh no ma'am. As a matter of fact, they seemed upset that he left so quickly." He leaned forward and whispered in Tami's ear, "they were actually quite pissed off."

"Who else was at the meeting?"

Indecision, another bill changed hands. George was beginning to really like this Sparrow fellow. Every time he or his name showed up, money started changing hands.

"There were two other fellas who showed up. One was a big man, around six foot three, two hundred fifty pounds, and he had a little guy with him. Looked like a gofer of some type. I parked their car, as a matter of fact. It was nice. A Jaguar sedan with Jersey plates."

"Thanks a bunch, George. I enjoyed chatting with you. Mind if the car stays around for a few minutes?"

"Not at all, ma'am. I'll take care of it"

Tami went inside and approached the front desk. There was a middle-aged woman who seemed officious and in charge. Tami introduced herself and asked if it was possible to review some old security footage.

"May I see your badge, please."

"Sorry, my name is Tami Powers, and I don't have a badge. But I sure do need to review some of your tapes from September.

"Ma'am, the privacy of our guests at The Phillips Club is of our utmost concern. Unless you have the proper credentials, you won't be able to see anything. Therefore, I must ask you to leave. Now."

Tami was ready to dig into her side pocket one more time but thought better of it.

"Ma'am, I am not trying to invade anyone's privacy at all. It's just that I have a dear friend who stayed here, and his life may be in danger. You could show me the tapes now, or I could come back with the FBI, and they would certainly be much more intrusive than I am trying to be."

The front desk manager paused for a minute and squinted at Tami's face. "What'd you say your name was?"

"Tami Powers. Maybe you have seen me on the news or on some of the recent *Cheers! America* shows?"

"Well, my goodness, you're that pretty girl that jumps around and helps people. Why didn't you say so? Wait right here." Off she disappeared back into the bowels of the Phillips Club, returning in two minutes with a youngish man in tow.

"Take Mrs. Powers down to the security room and show her anything she needs. It was a pleasure to meet you, Mrs. Powers."

"Thank you very much, and please just call me Tami."

"Can we take a quick selfie, Tami?"

"Certainly."

CHAPTER
28

Tami and the front desk assistant walked down a flight of stairs and turned left into a dark, cave-like room with thirteen screens. Tami sat by while the kid scrolled back to the first of September. She learned there was a camera on the front of the building, the lobby area, the meeting room, and one camera for each of the ten floors. He showed Tami how to operate the scanner and excused himself.

On the nineteenth of September, she saw Malcolm check into the residence club, and then go out in the afternoon. Then a disheveled Malcolm stumbled back to his room around midnight. She continued watching Monday's footage as all the fun started, intrigued by Malcolm's "bodyguards," and stopped the machine so she could view the faces closely. She recognized the guy she had decked from the Soirée restaurant, and recognized that this must be his accomplice. How long she had waited to set her eyes on their faces.

She watched the entire sequence of events; two goombahs arrive packing in a black Escalade. The meeting set-up, the arrival of the other party, their dialogue, the exchange of files, the exchange of a rather large light brown manilla envelope. Then the hastily crafted departure/escape by Malcolm. She googled the executive staff at *Probe* magazine and identified Donovan Templeton as Malcolm's guest at the club. She paused the tape and sat back for a minute to collect her thoughts.

This had to be the actual meeting when/where Malcolm sold the tape of her interview to *Probe*. But why did Malcolm ditch his mates and dash off on a motorcycle? He had to have had prior dealings with these two black leather jacketed thugs, and maybe they were expecting a cut from the fat envelope? To avoid that, he arranged a diversion and made a quick exit. That included a WBC mobile unit, so she would need to check with Ben on that one.

She still had no idea how/why Malcolm had gotten involved with the lowlifes, but he must have been the reason for their visit to the West Coast. They were after Malcolm at Soirée. *Had thug number one caused a smokescreen while thug number two was supposed to grab Malcolm? They must have gotten to him in LA. Was that where they had stolen his phone? What else had they stolen from him? Was that the reason he was so afraid to talk to her on the phone?*

Somehow/somewhere they had obtained his phone and, sly devils that they were, had given the phone back to her. Now they wanted their cuts and had kidnapped Anne Marie and locked her down for insurance. She was particularly interested in the black Escalade but could not retrieve the license plate numbers from the surveillance film.

Good questions all. Now she had to find these guys. She videoed the house security feed into her phone, froze the screen, and took numerous close-up facials of both the Italians. And paused to reflect once more.

Malcolm was staying at the Phillips Club which was on the Upper West Side. This followed their visit to *Cheers* and NYC, after which he had sold the Utah video of her. She surmised he must have gone out somewhere on the West Side and gotten sideways somehow. If that was the case, alcohol had to have been involved. Therefore, she must start poking around some of the bars in the area. And from the looks of Malcolm's friends, it was probably an Italian joint. She decided to start looking to the south, thinking it was much easier to find trouble heading towards Hell's Kitchen and past The Lincoln Center.

She left the film room, thanked everyone on her way out and settled into the back seat of the town car. This morning she had stumbled onto a bonanza of critical information, and she planned to put it to use quickly. A google search turned up an executive portrait of Malcolm along with his bio, which she texted to herself. She thought it would raise less suspicion when she started trolling, to ask about Malcolm rather than two local toughs. They would be connected and would quickly hear about some white girl who was asking questions. If she could find someone who recognized Malcolm, that could very well lead her to what she was looking for.

She knew this might be like looking for a needle in a haystack, but she also knew from her days back on the farm in Idaho that haystacks come in a lot of different sizes.

She started out working her way south on Columbus Ave, hit half a dozen spots, before they edged out to the west, and stopped in front of Luca's place. By now it was getting close to dusk and therefore happy hour. Her driver was dressed casually, so she invited him in with her, and told him if there was any kind of trouble to video it. They walked past a quiet dining room and took the last two seats at the bar.

Tami whispered to the driver to order a real drink, just before Mick came over and grunted at them for an order. He was back a minute later with a lite beer and a glass of pinot grigio for Tami. They sat and sipped for a few minutes until the bartender had a break, Tami motioned him over.

"Hi, I'm visiting the city for a few days and am trying to locate an old friend. He used to live on the West Side, I wonder if you might have ever seen him in here." She flashed the corporate head shot of Malcolm and noticed him flinch imperceptibly.

Mick looked up and squinted his eyes at Tami and her escort. She didn't smell like a cop, maybe she was legit, maybe not, but he wasn't taking any chances. "Nah, I ain't never seen nobody look like him in here."

"You're sure? I thought I might have heard him mention this place."

Mick didn't take time to reply, he turned his back and went over to pour a couple more pints of Peroni's. Tami didn't need an answer, her radar and Mick's second squint told her she had the right place. Three or four of the other bartenders had taken a long look at Malcolm's pic, asked his name, what he did for a living, his physical description. Luca's was all business. She didn't want to attract any attention, so she chatted with the driver, they finished their drinks, and asked for the check. She knew cops weren't the biggest tippers, but she didn't want to raise any suspicion either, so she paid in cash, left 20% and walked out holding hands with the surprised driver.

"Sorry, I didn't mean to get personal, it just wasn't a good time to attract any attention."

"No problem."

————

The Lincoln was parked across the street from Luca's, and Tami told the driver she wanted to sit for a while and see if her friend showed up. The driver knew she was up to something, but he worked for her, so he sat. After a couple of hours, he volunteered to walk up the street and get some Chinese to go. She gave him a hundred bucks and turned her eyes back toward Luca's.

Stakeouts are a tedious business and takeout food on the job is not usually a good thing, as food tends to make one sleepy. But Tami stayed on it for another couple of hours before bailing. The driver had already had a long enough day, so he dropped her at the Plaza and headed back to headquarters.

————

After checking the car in, he went up to reception where he called Ben Benson's personal cell as instructed on one of the house phones. "Hey boss, I just dropped her off."

"Wow, long day."

"Yeah, we was all over town. She went to the mom's place first, then some hotel on the West Side, finally we went into a bar on West 31st and she asked the bartender about some guy. The barman said he didn't know him, and we sat outside for about four hours watching the restaurant."

"What bar?"

"Then we musta stopped at six West-Side bars until we ended up this joint called Luca's."

"Hmm, Luca's. Never heard of it."

"It's an Italian of course, restaurant and bar. Okay place, we had a drink."

"What time are you picking her up tomorrow morning?"

"She didn't say."

"Like she doesn't need you tomorrow?"

"She didn't say nothin', boss."

"I'll call you in the morning. Hang tight, she's an insomniac or something, so it may be early."

"Got it."

———

Benson called Jensen's number and the FBI AIC also answered from home, "What's up?"

"I think our lady friend may be onto something."

"What?"

"Well, she had my driver taking her all over town today, and finally made him stop at some Italian joint in lower midtown. She's looking for someone."

"Who?"

"I don't know, but it definitely seems like she might have found a clue or two."

"Damn it, this woman is going to get herself killed. I'm going to put a team on her tomorrow. What time is your driver picking her up?"

"She didn't say. I don't think she wants him tomorrow."

"No problem. We'll follow her from the Plaza and stay on her from now on."

"Thanks, I think that's the smart thing to do. If she calls, I'll let you know."

———

Tami was glad to be back at her temporary home. She couldn't have asked for a better start to her New York trip. She checked with the concierge to see if a town car was available tomorrow, reserved it and a driver, then went into the bar and ordered a glass of chardonnay.

Sitting at a small corner table of the bar discouraged company, and she began to reflect on her day. Had she missed anything? Was her construct and timeline of September's events correct? *I'll probably know by tomorrow,* she thought. At least she knew she had her guys.

———

It was almost eleven o'clock, which made it the perfect time to call Scott and the kids on the West Coast. Everybody was doing great, Sadie gave her phone kisses, and told her how much fun she had had combing out Leona's afro that afternoon. Scott was glad to hear from her and again advised her to be very careful and let the FBI run the show. She assured him she was lying low.

Lying low, lying schmo, he thought.

CHAPTER
29

Wednesday morning Tami was up at six-thirty and ran for an hour and a half in the exercise room. She had adjusted to the jet lag and had also begun to get used to the bitter cold front that was settling over eastern New York. Back upstairs, she showered, dressed in jeans and runners, and went down for some breakfast. To her surprise Ben Benson and Agent Jensen were sitting in a booth and waved to her.

"Good morning, Tami. Would you care to join us?"

"Sure, thanks for the invite."

"What time will you be needing the car today?"

"Oh, I'm good for today. I'm not doing much, maybe go spend some time with Anne Marie's mom. Any news on anything?"

"Not much. How about you?"

"I'm glad you're here Agent Jensen. I found out some interesting information yesterday."

Not smugly, but with a certain note of distain in his voice, AIC Jensen asked "Whatcha got there, Tami?"

"Well, I found out who our dudes are; I just don't know their names." She pulled out her cell phone and showed them pictures of Geo and Alfonzo.

"That's him," Ben blurted when he saw the picture of Alfonzo. "That's the thug who assaulted my wife at Soirée last September."

"I believe the other guy was also there. They may have been after Malcolm, that's probably where they got his phone. Also, I think this one is the person calling me Mr. Jensen," she said and pointed at Geo.

Maybe you can run their visuals through your database and ID them. Plus, I'm due for my morning call from our friends any minute now."

AIC Jensen was stunned. Tami had turned up more information in one day than his agents had all week. "Tami, I will get someone on this immediately as soon as you forward the facials to me. Also, I don't know what your plans are today, but I want to have one of my units follow you."

"Oh, that won't be necessary."

"I know you don't think it is, but these are some dangerous men we are dealing with. If they feel cornered for any reason, they could turn violent in a nano second. This is for your safety, believe me." *And you better not get to these damn guys before we do,* he thought in frustration.

"Whatever, but I'm taking off right after breakfast," she said as the waitress dropped off her lite breakfast meal.

"No problem. I've got two agents outside in a mobile unit. They can follow you, and Ben will take me back to headquarters."

"Tail me if you want to, but they're not with me, and I am leaving in fifteen minutes," Tami said between mouthfuls.

"Be reasonable, Tami," Ben interjected.

"I am, Ben."

"Tami, why don't you let us escort you today," Jensen continued while he forwarded Tami's pictures to his tech team at headquarters. "My agents would be at your direction. You would have two trained operatives with you all day. You would have a level of protection around you that could very well save your life."

"Sorry but I gotta go." Tami slid out of the booth, grabbed her jacket, neck scarf, told the server to add a 25% gratuity and sign her off. With that, she pivoted and headed for the exit. Jensen scrambled for his phone and notified the agents she was coming.

"Jensen here, Mrs. Powers is headed for the lobby door of the hotel right now, and I want you on her all day. Do not lose her. I repeat, do not under any circumstances lose that woman. 10/4?"

"Got it Chief, here she comes now."

Jensen turned to Ben Benson and said, "Doesn't that broad work for you?"

"Well, in theory yes. In practice, not so much."

"Must be frustrating."

"Not really. She's the network's cash cow right now and, so far, her judgment has been pretty damn spot on."

————

Tami had an inspiration and was anxious to get rolling. Her town car was waiting in front of the hotel, and the driver had been programed by the concierge as to whom he about to squire around town.

"Don't let her out of your sight and have your phone ready to start filming. This woman is bionic and has a nose for trouble." Also, knowing Benson was a major patron of the Plaza, she told the driver if anything happens, if you shoot some video, don't talk to anyone but WBC people. The driver was excited by his assignment and assured the concierge he was up to the task.

Tami sat calmly in the back seat as her mind deliberated. She was surprised not to have received her call from Geo by now. Which meant they were getting a late start. She had already done a mental analysis of their personas, and decided the best place to start looking for them was Brooklyn, and work her way north if she had to. She couldn't rationalize these guys living in or originating from Manhattan. If they had at one time, the way the city had gentrified, the suburbs were certainly more affordable, and offered more latitude for them to function now. After all, a couple of up-and-coming operators definitely need space to operate.

If they were running late, her timing was perfect, and she could only speculate, but where else would a couple of thirty-something kidnappers start their morning but in a coffee house? What would they want to start the day off with other than a couple of double espressos? So, she directed her driver past a half dozen Dunkin' Donuts and one

Starbucks, nothing on her antenna, until she finally saw a black Escalade parked in front of the oldest java joint in Brooklyn. Caffe Carolina. Carolina was a highly rated, third-generation Italian coffee house on Fifth Avenue. And she told her driver to park the car.

He pulled up in front of the shop, parked, and they got out. The agents behind her had to slow, and one of them jumped out while his partner found parking on the street. She and her driver were already walking in the door of the caffe, and there they were, pretty as a Picasso. Geo stood in front of Alfonzo both men waiting in the barista's line.

The coffee shop was a square shaped room in an older, high ceilinged brick building. The service area was set back into the room. There were tables and chairs in the central area. Customers entered and walked in to form a queue on the right side of the coffee bar, processing through to the left for their morning fix.

The last customer before Geo and Alfonzo stepped to the left to pick up her order, and as they moved past the pastry case and to the order counter, the barista greeted them by name and winked at Geo. She then turned away and began loading the espresso machine. Alfonzo casually looked over his shoulder when he heard the door open, and almost had a gastrointestinal event when he saw Tami. He bumped Geo while he was spinning around and started to stutter something. Geo saw the look on his partner's face and automatically reached for his shoulder holster as he turned.

Tami said, "well lookie who's here," and to the barista, "you can cancel that order."

———

With the two agents approaching from outside and looking in through the glassed-in façade of the coffee house, Geo's hand closed around the grip of his handgun. When it the weapon was halfway out of his leather jacket, Tami took a hop step and sprang up and across the room to her right. In a split second she kicked high off of the solid, brick wall and from fifteen feet up, did a one-eighty pivot in midair and for the second time in his life, landed a drop kick flush on Alonzo's jaw. Her descending momentum was significant, and knocked him back into Geo, who lost his balance. He recovered quickly and as he began to raise his weapon, Tami, who had landed on the balls of her feet, sidestepped the fallen Alfonzo and kicked Geo's right hand and the butt of his sidearm. The Glock pistol flew through the air and was clattering around on the floor as the agents burst into the room. With their weapons drawn, they both shouted, "Freeze, FBI!"

Geo cursed and raised his hands. Alfonzo was still lying unconscious on the floor at his partner's feet. Geo managed to spit out, "arrest her ass, she attacked both of us for no reason."

Agent Dixon turned Geo around and cuffed him. "You are under arrest for suspicion of kidnapping and extorsion, anything you say can and will be used against you in a court of law."

He asked the barista for a cold, wet towel to revive Alfonzo. Several of the astonished customers had called 911, sirens began to scream outside, and a crowd was gathering.

———

Ben Benson was still with AIC Jensen when the call came in that the two perps had been arrested in Brooklyn. Benson grabbed his cell phone and immediately called his ops manager at WNY12, identified himself and screamed for the young woman to get a team out to Brooklyn.

"We're already there, Chief. We sent our Brooklyn reporter as soon as the scanner picked up the disturbance. Apparently, Tami's driver went into the caffe with her and filmed the whole incident on his phone. He has already forwarded his tape to our guy. Says we owe him five grand. You are going to have some spectacular footage for national tonight. Apparently, Tami jumped, across the room pretty high in the air, then kicked off the wall, hurtled back across the room and knocked one guy out, then disarmed the other guy."

"Fuck me, that woman is out of her mind. What is your name again?"

"Sharon Young, and what should we do with the driver?"

"Not to worry, I will personally take care of him. Please let him know that, and good work, Sharon."

"Thank you, sir."

"Tell your reporter and the driver to get Tami out of there as soon as possible. We've got to get her here to the studio and start recording her on what happened to accompany that video tonight."

"Will do."

Benson turned to Jensen, "that broad, as you so crassly refer to her, is sure making you guys look good." Jensen grunted, and Benson picked up his phone again and rang Tami. Amazingly she picked up the call.

"Hi Tami, this is Benson. You okay? I just heard about what happened."

"I'm fine Ben. I'm sure you want me at the studio for an interview."

"How can you be so calm after taking out two organized crime guys and possibly saving your best friends life?"

"All in a day's work, boss. I think my driver has some footage for you."

"Yes, I heard. The important thing is you're okay."

"I'm great, thanks. I'll see you as soon as I can get out of here."

"I'll be in my office."

The crowd at Carolina's dispersed after the agents hauled Geo and a woozy Alfonzo away.

Tami spoke to the reporters enough to give them a teaser, then scrambled into her town car with the reporter from WNY12 and her driver headed back across the Brooklyn Bridge to midtown Manhattan.

The FBI hustled their suspects into headquarters and immediately into an interrogation room.

Agent Jensen was there to begin the interview. "Where are you keeping Ms. Stein?"

"Who is that?"

"We've got you on tape talking to Mrs. Powers about a payout to ransom her business agent. Your phone here confirms those calls."

"I want to speak to my lawyer."

When Agent Jensen removed Geo and Alfonzo's personal belongings, he finally had their ID problem solved.

"What about you, Mr. DeNardo?"

"I would like to speak to my lawyer."

That was as far as Jensen and his trained team got with their prisoners. Arraignment was set for Friday morning, and mysteriously, after Geo had made his phone call from the station, Anne Marie appeared six hours later on the streets of Queens, outside of the NY Met's Citi Field Stadium. They returned her handbag, so she was able to call for a ride. Her reappearance was a joyous occasion for all involved and she seemed none the worse for wear, except she had missed the extraordinary WBC News coverage of the capture of her tormentors.

Tonight, Tami gleamed brightly from the local WNY12 broadcast. Then starred on the national news show. WBC also did a special half hour segment after both news broadcasts were over, which included a collage of all of her rescue scenes with extensive narration.

The latest episode, having again occurred right here in NYC, ranked up there with the Grand Canyon. Not that many New Yorkers hiked in the Canyon, but they sure could relate to a beautiful, athletic young woman taking down two burly ex Rangers of questionable character. And right in the heart of Brooklyn.

There were City luminaries in the studio for the special program including several Chiefs of Police and the FBI who begrudgingly sang Tami's praises and recognized her heroism. The mayor of Manhattan was present and presented her with a dozen long stem red roses, and a key to the city.

During the show WBC posted a survey on their website, show-ing all of Tami's episodes, and set up a vote to rank her interventions. Before Tami got back to her hotel room, there were three point seven million hits on the website.

————

She had called her family twice a day and told them how much she missed them. The boys wanted swag from all the shows, Sadie wanted something big and stuffed from FAO Schwartz, Carrie was ready to start her intern-ship yesterday, and Scott just wanted her home safely. Anne Marie was in tears every time they talked and couldn't thank her friend enough. They agreed she would return to the West Coast as soon as possible.

Because of the key-to-the-City thing, Tami was forced to stay an extra day in NYC. Anne Marie would spend some extra time with her mom and wrap up her East Coast business. Tami and an aide from the Mayor's office toured City Hall and shared a pizza with her honor for lunch. She, Anne Marie and mom had comp seats to the theatre for *Moulin Rouge.* Then Katherine invited her for a hosted dinner at the Hard Rock Hotel's Roof Top Room in exchange for some photo ops.

Before you knew it, Tami was up at six o'clock for her morning run on Saturday morning, had one last breakfast at the Plaza, and was settling into her first-class seat for the trip home. AIC Jensen insisted they send an agent along to ensure her safe travel, she sat up front with the stews.

Probably good to have an escort because there was a phalanx of reporters waiting when she touched down in LA. The agent escorted her through the foot traffic, and out to her family who waited for her in the Beamer.

————

"Gee mom, you are bigger than that Tesla guy. There have been report-ers hanging around the house all week. We had to ask them what they wanted, and told 'em you were in New York."

"Hey, let's go to the ocean and stay overnight. Try to avoid all of that. Wanna?"

"Sure, Mom."

———

They checked into the Malibu Beach Inn and watched a spectacular sunset while strolling along the sand at the water's edge. Got sundries from the front desk for the night and enjoyed a lovely dinner while serenaded by the roar of the surf. Tami gave out all of her various swag and presents, and then everyone drifted back to their rooms. When they were alone Tami gave Scott a deep kiss, and they hugged.

"I've missed you so much, babe. You're safe and home and Anne Marie is also okay. Plus, it almost drove me crazy watching all the gorgeous LA weather babes on TV this week."

"Don't you even think about them. You come with me," Tami said as she took his hand and led him into their bedroom suite.

CHAPTER 30

The Powers had some fun splashing around in the morning surf, and later on Scott wanted to take everyone to Venice Beach. Tami was free of her FBI escorts, so they left around one and headed down the coast. After a brief stop in Santa Monica for fish tacos, they left for crazy town Venice Beach. That short strip of SoCal waterfront is the California version of the San Diego Zoo gone psycho. Scott knew his kids would get a fun buzz off the place.

Throngs of people, pets, skateboarders crowded the massive skate flow park and the "I Heart Everything Venice" tourist shops. A fat guy was playing a grand piano on the promenade in a speedo. There were medical marijuana stores two to a block; the body builders were a show in themselves. There were jugglers, artists, mimes, and a dog show. A young woman played the violin so beautifully she started crying. The kids loved the activity. Tami was concerned Sadie might be scarred for life, but they made an afternoon of it and headed home around four.

Back in La Canada, they found very few media types around. Studio security personnel were there, and some paparazzi still slouched on their cars. Tami waved to them, and the family went inside for the evening. Tomorrow was another day, and she was looking forward to running with Leona. Then a drop in at headquarters to see Carl was scheduled. Work and school called for the rest of the family.

Next Thursday was Thanksgiving and Christmas would be here before you knew it. Anne Marie was staying in New York until the

New Year. By then her mom would be in assisted care and she'd be headed back to the left coast. She and Tami would get ultra-serious about training for the Universal Marathon Trials in Orlando.

The Thanksgiving holiday would be relatively quiet for the Powers family—just the immediate family—and she had invited Leona, her boyfriend, Carl, and his wife. Tami loved to cook for family and friends, and what better time for it than the late fall season. She loved a warm cozy home full of cooking aromas, friends, and family. And she had all day Wednesday to shop.

For Christmas, they had been invited to her parents' home in Idaho Falls. Retired for about ten years, her parents now lived in this small Idaho town, and her brothers ran the farm east of Pocatello. They would fly to Boise, take a short hop over to her parent's, and the whole family would be together for Tami's favorite holiday. On the 26th, they would fly back to Sacramento, rent a Suburban, and drive up to see Scott's folks in Incline Village, Nevada. There they would have almost a week to visit Scott's side of the fam, and during the daytime check out the world-class skiing of the Tahoe Basin.

———————

Before they left, Tami wanted to do something for her community to celebrate the holidays. She and Leona put together a kid's gift giveaway in Leona's old South Central Los Angeles neighborhood. Anne Marie got busy on the phone to Walmart, Costco, and Target, etc., and found some super at-cost prices and contributions. Pretty soon there was a semi-truck at a Riverside warehouse filled with toys and books and stuff for kids.

Leona chose the Greater New Canaan Baptist Church on Brentwood Street, a tiny one city block long stretch right around the corner from Slauson and Broadway Streets. There they had plenty of room to set up their distribution center. The small church was perched on a large, double lot set back from Slauson and afforded plenty of open, albeit asphalt-covered space.

There would be a squad of male and female officers from the 77th Street Station to help pass out gifts and be around if needed. A backpack awaited every kid with a cool book or toy and a couple of twenty-dollar bills in it. There was also a bonfire with marshmallows and hot chocolate for the youngsters. A couple of complimentary taco trucks for everyone's pleasure, and a barista station for the adults. The world-famous Ebenezer Baptist Church Youth Choir, all fifty-two strong of them, would be there to entertain at two p.m. Carl had WLA12 coming for a low-key holiday feel good shoot in the afternoon.

Tami and Leona stood and greeted every one of the families as they filed through the line for their goodies. There were lots of hugs and selfies for everyone. Scott and the kids, along with volunteers from the GNCCG congregation, the 77th's group, and some of WBC's rank and file handled the gift give line.

After starting at noon, the semi-truck was empty by two-thirty, then the choir began singing, and their powerful, award-winning spirituals rocked South Central. Around five the crowds began to dissipate.

Tami and Leona thanked the pastor of New Canaan for his hospitality, and he invited them back again next year. Tami slipped him a nice check to help keep the lights on, and they all stayed until cleanup was wrapped.

The Powers family got home tired but feeling merry. Lots of South-Central kids went home full and cherry. A wonderful holiday season awaited her family, and Tami was delighted to reach out, and also have her children be involved.

———

In a blink, it seemed like the New Year was here. Tami and her crew were back home in LA, although open country horseback riding in Idaho, skiing Heavenly Valley on Lake Tahoe's south shore and then hitting Palisades Tahoe (aka Squaw Valley) were definite highlights of the trip. WBC still provided security at their home, but Scott and a realtor were looking for a new place in a gated community.

Anne Marie was back, and she and Tami were starting to do some serious road work. The February Universal Games Trials in Orlando were a little over a month away, and Tami, Anne Marie and Leona were sticking mainly to trails in the San Gabriels. First for the altitude work, secondly to stay out of the limelight and avoid situations that would involve Tami and the media, police and/or heroic rescue attempts.

Anne Marie continued to approach Tami about commercial opportunities. "Tami, I am going to start a YouTube channel for you. Sponsors will be willing to pay as much as a hundred grand a month if not more, once you start to amass some numbers. All you would need to do is a half hour weekly segment, and you could build a massive following. Hey, put on a GoPro and detail our weekly work outs. Add some dialogue. Have face time with your kids, cook your training menu for dinner, whatever you want and Bam, there you go. I'm sure one of the WBC guys would help you on the tech side.

"Also, I am getting lots of inquiries from the likes of running shoe companies, athletic wear, Coca-Cola, supplement companies, fitness groups, insurance people, etc. You've got to strike while the iron is hot, right? And the kicker of all this, is an invitation from Oprah herself to come with your family for a weekend visit to her ranch."

"I'll think about the commercial stuff, but I don't want it to interfere with my normal routines. We would love to go for a visit with Oprah. Would you come along and go with us?"

———

February was rapidly approaching, and Tami asked Scott if he would mind staying with the kids so Leona and Anne Marie could go back to Orlando with her.

"Sure babe, don't mind at all." They were happy to share child duties. Scott appreciated all Tami did as far as running the household and was happy to reciprocate when she needed him.

———————

The trio of fleet footed women took off Tuesday morning, the eighth of February from LAX for Orlando International. They had a suite reserved at the downtown Orlando Marriott on Livingston Street. Getting in on Tuesday afternoon would give them plenty of time to acclimate to the new time zone, prep and research the course. Keep the workouts on the lighter side and peak for the race.

February climes in Orlando are some of the most pleasant of their year. Cool, with much less humidity than the scorching summers, and Tami was excited to challenge the rumored to be fast/ flat course. All three women knew their speed work, as well as all the endurance running would payoff soon.

Anne Marie sat Tami and Leona down after their morning run and over sauteed veggie omelets, informed her client it was time to schedule a business meeting. "Tami, the offers are piling up. What do you want me to do with them? It's time for you to stop dragging your feet on this and make some decisions."

"Okay, okay, then you can stop bugging me. I don't want to have more than three endorsements. New Balance shoes would be a good one, a women's apparel company, and maybe Coca-Cola. Could we pay Leona to handle the YouTube channel if she was interested? Maybe Carrie could help. If this thing gets off the ground, perhaps Carl could lend a hand. And one more thing, I hope you realize how much I am looking forward to getting back to LA on Monday and spending Valentine's Day with Scott and my kids."

Anne Marie paused for a pregnant moment and said "I'm on it. Trust me, this will prove to be the shortest business meeting with the biggest pay back in recent American history. And don't worry about Valentine's Day."

"Anne Marie, you know all this commercial stuff can basically be damned in my opinion. If a situation should present itself, and my mind is off on some commercial shoot, I might not be able to respond properly, which could be catastrophic. You know I just want to stay soul centric, then there is Scott, my babies and that is my value system. I will do the commercial stuff on a limited basis, but it will not conflict with my life and my values. If New Balance wants me to fly somewhere and make an appearance, and Charlie has a baseball game or Carrie has a volleyball game, New Balance loses. We understand each other, right?"

"Succinctly. What we should be striving for is a contracted number of commercial shoots, and a severely limited number of personal appearances."

"Here's another thing, if we get too busy on the commercial side, I think we should talk to WBC and rethink our relationship with them. I might be so busy with these new responsibilities and my family; I will have zero time to fulfill my commitment with WBC."

"Well girlfriend, I have already had extended conversations with both Carl and Ben. Ben wants to keep you around strictly in a PR role and forget about the damn cost analysis. He mentioned that your annual review was coming up, and you were due for a substantial raise.

Carl communicated to me, very confidentially, that Ben is researching the possibility of an afternoon variety-type show for you. It would air right after *Cheers! America*, and star you as host/moderator with a format of good news and profiling people of all races and walks of life. It would be broadcast from their studios here on the West Coast so you wouldn't have to travel. The show would feature you interacting with people who have risen above their personal circumstances and are succeeding in life. It would be a show of hope, family and love."

"Hmmm, that sounds interesting."

"Here's something else to keep in mind: All this commercial income is going to do nothing but underwrite the fund you are wanting to set up."

"That's true. I just don't want that side to get out of control, right?"

"I get it."

———————

The marathon layout was still open to public traffic until it closed on Friday for set-up and Sunday's race. Wednesday afternoon the contestants were able to drive it and mark out their mileage posts and hydration spots. They could work on their scheduled pace and timing goals, making sure they had their starting times and access organized.

This race was the first Universal Games qualifier hosted by Orlando, or any city in Florida for that matter. The City Fathers wanted the event to reflect the values and achievements of the city itself, but still include their major friend and neighbor at Disney World.

The race would start at Lake Eola Park, Orlando's signature downtown recreational activity center. Then wind through numerous city neighborhoods and finish back at the lake. Although the race was organized and managed by some experienced marathon staging veterans, Tami was taking no chances with first time miscues. One great thing about this marathon was that the US Track and Field organizers had raised the qualification standards. There would be less than half of the field (231 runners) as the last qualifier (567 runners). This would definitely eliminate a lot of congestion during the race.

Tami and Leona spent more time together than they did with Anne Marie, who was busy working the phones and setting up appointments for the rest of the week. The two non-working teammates leisure time was casual and pleasantly spent. They lunched, shopped and played tourists. The city was crowded with visitors and racers peaking toward the weekend.

Leona suggested a quick trip over to Daytona Beach which sat a little over an hour to the northeast. "For one thing, Daytona is great for running on its flat and firm sandy beach front." It was fun and relaxing for Tami to spend time with an accomplished young athlete who was not only a great running mate, but also an easy travel partner.

———

Finally, it was D-Day. Tami had hydrated and carbed up thoroughly on Saturday and was out of bed at six on Sunday morning. She ate a banana and half a bagel about quarter to seven. and wouldn't start rehydrating during the race until about mile fourteen. Anne Marie was scheduled to be at mile sixteen with some sports beans for her. Her music was all set; fast/upbeat for the first hour, moderate tempo for the middle set, and finish on the upbeat side. Now to pass the next hour, she stretched, did some breathing exercises. She meditated to calm her mind and strengthen her body. Then it would be time to roll.

———

Tami's number thirty-two seeding put her toward the middle of the first flight. She was concerned with grouping as always and had to steady herself a couple of times. Nothing more than her hands going up to balance herself against other closely packed runners at the start of the race. But by mile number five she had passed a lot of racers and was hitting her one-mile splits right at 5:58.

The field was thinning, and she was pleased with both her pace and position. The leaders had stretched out some but were still in sight and that encouraged her. Feeling strong and relaxed, her gait was fluid and smooth. She loved the conditions, and if she could keep the leaders in sight and let them set the pace, she was confident her training would allow her to close strongly. The crowds were tremendous, packed the course, and were shouting encouragement and helping build excitement. A top three finish beckoned.

After all her running experience and her many, many marathons, she still knew she would hit the wall. By mile twenty-three it would be a mental battle to overcome the pain in her body and push on to the finish line.

Also, this was the first ultra-competitive race she had run, where she was definitely challenging other world class athletes. Where she was running competitively to continue on to the next level. All of her marathons had been hobby runs, and while they were timed, she had basically been running against the clock. But competing against the best in the country was definitely a motivating factor.

If she ever qualified to represent the United States of America it would be the biggest thrill (after marriage and childbirth) of her life. Couple that with running for her family and country, and after all the work she and her team had put in; this was Tami running at her absolute optimum level. She would never again be at this moment in her life, nor this finely tuned in her running career.

And don't forget she was running against professionals who were anywhere from eight to twelve years younger. But her shot at keeping pace would come from her superior training and physical conditioning. She hoped.

———

The early miles clicked off. Mile fourteen came and went. She grabbed a cup of electrolyzed sports drink and knew the water stations would be coming more frequently now. Anne Marie would be there for her within a couple of miles, with her sports (coffee) beans and a strategic update. The leaders of the race remained ahead by only fifty yards.

Her best friend and agent was there in her volunteer bib as expected at mile sixteen. Gave her a huge smile with a double thumbs up (which meant she was on her times), passed off the beans, and screamed at her to get her ass in gear. Thanks for nothing. Leona would be there at mile twenty-two. She had rented a moped to run back and forth, and then pick up Anne Marie so they could meet Tami at the finish line.

———

The running Gods were with her, and the wall didn't really hit until mile twenty-two, but Tami kept her stride steady and pressed on. A couple of the pace setters had fallen back and were passed by Tami. Now there were four runners forty yards ahead of her, and she only had to beat two of them to get in.

She caught up with Leona, who yelled encouragement and again signaled that she was on schedule. That kept her going for another couple of miles, and the goal of starting her kick at mile twenty-five was nearing. She was hurting as usual, but her feet, knees and hamstrings were holding up, and she didn't feel any other external pain. Except her lungs being ready to explode. It was going to be all mental discipline from now to the finish line.

As her kick point passed, Tami began to ramp it up. Timed splits were no longer important, she was now running strictly against the competition. Her times dropped slightly, even though this was as fast as she had ever run this late in a race. She was gradually covering, but realized the leaders were also kicking and holding on. At the twenty-five and three quarters mile mark, she was still twenty yards behind, but saw one of the four leaders fading.

She knew there was less than half a mile to go, and by this time the crowds were thick, and the air pulsed from crowd noise. She kicked harder and felt lightheaded. Dehydration smacked her in the face. Her stomach was cramping as the temperature had now risen into the mid-seventies.

Mile twenty-six approached, and she passed racer number four. She had two tenths of a mile to catch number three, who was still five or six yards ahead of her. She couldn't really tell, as her vision was now so blurry, she could hardly see the finish line.

And then the race was over. She felt someone's arm around her and had finished fourth. Five yards from glory. Five yards from achieving the dream of a lifetime. But she was too exhausted to be disappointed. Someone else threw a logo blanket over her shoulders and gave her an energy beverage. She slumped into a chair to rest her feet for a moment, then got back up and kept walking to keep from cramping.

Soon Anne Marie and Leona had fought their way to the edge of the staging area, caught Tami's attention while they were hanging over the yellow rope. Scott called Anne Marie who handed the phone to Tami and he and the kids screamed out their love and excitement to her. They had all gotten up to watch the race on TV, and Scott had Charlie tape the action. She thanked them and agreed to talk again with Scott in an hour when things calmed down. Anne Marie told her to go get a quick massage before the tables crowded up. She said they would be right here and a WO12 reporter and cameraperson were coming.

Tami felt like an hour and a half massage would be just about right, but ten minutes was the time limit, so she got up, snarfed a couple of peanut butter bars, and went to the registration table to pick up her finishing certificate and an "I Ran" accreditation on a lanyard. The registrar told her that as fourth place finisher she was first alternate to the Games, and the organizers would be in touch.

As she was still halfway out of it, this came as a pleasant surprise. Then it was back to her girlfriends. She was disappointed, but Anne Marie was ecstatic to mention she had finished in 2:19.33, by far her best time ever. And since she was the first alternate, would be going to the games anyway. In case injury or anything else should prevent one of the qualifiers from competing, she would be running.

Hearing it said twice buoyed her spirits and gave her some incentive to speak with the media rep. She turned out to be an excited young woman, who introduced herself as Myndee, and congratulated Tami on a spectacular race. She patiently tolerated Tami's chugging Diet Coke throughout their chat. They even got a picture of her doing her chug thing for national TV. The reporter told her how proud her WBC family were of her, asked how the race had gone. Any health or logistical problems along the way? Too bad the distance wasn't twenty-six-point four miles, because she would have won it, etc.

In closing Michelle asked one penetrating question which came out of the blue, "Tami, there is a rumor going around relating to one of your interventions, I believe it was the one where you single hand-edly overpowered, was it eight thugs, and captured the gang who was causing trouble for the Asian community in LA. During this event you seemed to actually disappear from sight while doing your rescue thing. You became invisible. Any comments on that?"

Tami paused, then replied with a response she and Scott had created, relating back to/from their respective college Physics 101 Classes, "Michelle for all I know, it could have been a photoelectric diffraction of light or some other local disruption. I really couldn't say with any surety. Thank you for your time." Tami turned away, the interview was over, and Anne Marie bade Myndee adieu.

————

As she stepped away, a tall man in a grey suit with credentials dangling from his neck approached. He introduced himself as Robert Thompson.

"Tami, I am with the Diplomatic Security Service, the DSS, and I wonder if I might give you a call later this afternoon or tomorrow morning?"

"In regard to?"

"Since you have qualified as first alternate in the Universal Games marathon race, we would like to invite you to join forces with our security team for the Games."

"Cool. This is my representative Anne Marie Stein; she can speak with you and will communicate with me."

"Thank you so much, Tami" and Robert turned to AM and took out his phone.

————

"Let's go get something to eat, I'm starving," and they went to a Mexican/Cuban Restaurant Tami and Leona had scoped out. Tami again amazed everyone with how much food she could put away in one sitting.

"Whadda ya think, Tami girl? Want to help protect our athletes?"

"Heck yes, I do."

When the food was gone, Tami ordered three margaritas for a final toast, and then it was time to get out of there and pack up for home. Leona had to follow them on the moped for a drop off, and when they were in the car alone, Anne Marie teared up and told her "I am so proud of you."

"Couldn't have done it without you, partner."

They picked Leona up, and she wondered why they both had been crying. After fighting through downtown traffic for what =seemed like hours, they finally pulled back under the canopied hotel entrance.

————

Tami was no sooner in her room than her phone pinged with an incoming call from Scott.

"Hi baby, is this a good time?"

"Sure, I just got back to my room, and was about to chill for an hour."

"Wow, you just killed your best time ever today. We are so proud of you."

"Thanks, it was tiring, but I got through it. Did you hear, I finished fourth. I'm the first alternate. Then a guy came up to us after the race and wants me to help out with security for the US team at the Games."

"Well, that'll be another challenge. I also have some news. I've got to be in New York City for some business on Tuesday. I'll probably catch a redeye Monday night and go straight to Midtown. Could you come home via New York, and I'll meet you at the Plaza late morning?"

"What about the kids?"

"Don't worry, I already talked to them. They gave us special dispensation to go out on the town. We can make it up to them when we get back."

"Scott, I don't want to leave them alone without us."

"I know baby, but it's Valentine's Day. If Leona or Anne Marie were getting home on Sunday, they could come over and hold down the fort for a day. I would so much love to spend some time alone with you, my love. And on such a special day."

"Owoo, if you put it that way. I'll check with them. Call you back tonight."

"Love you."

"Ditto, only more."

CHAPTER
31

Tami hung up and called Anne Marie. "Hi Tami, oh you know I would be delighted to help out with the kids. Let me rearrange your return flights, and you can come back on Wednesday from Kennedy. Does that work?"

"I've got to talk to Scott and see what he has planned. Are you okay to ride herd for that long?"

"No problem, I'll be at the house anyway, and Carrie is always a jewel. Oh, there is one more thing, *Cheers* has been bugging me to have you drop by and say hello while you are on the East Coast. Would you mind a short pop in with them on Tuesday afternoon?"

"Okay, but please tell them to keep it short. And be sure to tape the show when you get home so the kids can see me say Happy Valentine's Day to them on TV. And don't forget that Sadie has special needs at school."

"For sure I'll make it short with *Cheers* and be sure to walk Sadie into class. Let me call my contact at the studio, and I'll get back to you. Why don't you buzz Scott and check on his schedule."

––––––––––

"Hi again."

"Hello."

"Anne Marie is good to hold down the fort. I assume we will stay at the Plaza and return on Wednesday. Then AM said *Cheers* wants me for a pop in to start the show on Tuesday. Would that be a problem?"

"Not at all; my meetings should wrap up by noon on Tuesday. Hey why don't I just grab a quick bite and meet you at the studio. Then we could go onward and upward and fly out on Wednesday afternoon. I'll call Anne Marie and give her my information. She can coordinate everything."

"Good call. AM should be back in LA tonight. I'll pick her up at LAX and I'll see you on Tuesday."

"Right on, this is going to be fun."

———

"Hi Scott, AM here, yep I've got this, don't worry about anything."

———

Anne Marie and Leona bid Tami goodbye and headed for the airport. Tami felt kind of weird being alone on such short notice, but she was looking forward to resting up. Then she would fly to Kennedy tomorrow morning and have some quality museum time tomorrow. *Wow, almost two days to myself,* she thought.

Late Sunday afternoon Anne Marie called and filled Tami in on her Orlando flight. Take an Uber from the airport to the Plaza, but a limo from the studio will pick you up at eleven on Tuesday morning. "Don't be late, America will be waiting for you."

"Anne Marie, you don't have to send a stupid limo for me. I can just as easily walk down to Times Square, it probably isn't even a mile away."

"Great, show up and be all pitted out for national TV."

"I could freshen up."

"I know you could, but the studio insisted. You know how they are, because they are live, they can't relax until you are actually on the premises. Plus, you want to look hot for Scott, don't you? Leona is driving him to LAX on Monday night. She said he was really excited to spend some adult time with you.

———

Monday was forecast to be clear and warm. Tami slept in until seven, took a day off from running, and left for the airport at ten. She would arrive in Queens around two and had called ahead to the Plaza and scheduled a massage in the Spa.

Her flight was smooth and on time. She felt on top of the world stepping into the Plaza lobby. Checked in and headed for the elevators and the twelfth floor. Stowing her bags, she freshened up, and went right back downstairs and headed to the salon.

Tami didn't really have any formal wear with her for the show, but she found a pair of dressy black slacks, a brilliant emerald green, silk blouse, some comfortable pumps and slinky lingerie in the Plaza boutiques before dinner. They would have to make do with her full-length black parka for outer wear.

She ordered a quiet dinner from room service, and was determined to finish reading *The Boys in the Boat* before falling asleep in the luxury of her king-sized Plaza bed. As most of the museums were closed on Monday, she called KK and arranged a late luncheon with her.

Tuesday morning, she got up late (for her) again, did fifteen miles in the gym, grabbed a bite of breakfast in the Pump Room, then rode back up to get ready.

After dressing and approving of herself, she dabbed on a touch of some French perfume from the sample the salon girls had gifted her, and it was time to head for Times Square. She floated through the elegant marble and potted palm tree filled lobby. Her driver was waiting for her with an open door. Feeling great, and looking like a starlet, she was excited to see Scott soon. She slipped her sunglasses on, jumped in the limo, and headed off on this special day to meet her old friends at *Cheers! America.*

———

She did actually feel guilty riding such a short distance, but the driver dropped her at seventh and Broadway and the doorman ushered her through all the bright lights on the facade of the building and into the studio. A receptionist welcomed her, and walked her back to a production manager who escorted her to make up. He communicated that she was first up on today's call sheet.

"I hope this will be short and sweet," she replied. "By the way, my husband Scott is supposed to meet me here at the studio. I not sure what time he is coming, so could someone please keep an eye out for him?"

"Certainly Mrs. Powers, I will call the reception desk for you."

Makeup took less time than usual. The techs airbrushed a bit more color on her cheeks, brightened her lip gloss, dusted her forehead and Tami found herself following someone else into the Green Room. They turned away and now she was alone, which she found a little weird. No one other than herself was waiting in there. But she sat down and picked up a *Runner's World* magazine to browse until they called for her. It was now past two, and she wasn't sure why she couldn't see or hear the programming on the green room monitor. *Maybe it's a technical problem,* she thought.

The same production assistant came back to the GR twenty minutes later. "Mrs. Powers we are through with the daily stuff. If you are ready, let's do it."

"Okay, and please call me Tami."

"Yes, ma'am."

"Yes who?"

"Yes, Tami."

"Thank you."

———

Tami was escorted onto the live social lounge set of the national *Cheers! America* show and her world stopped on a dime. The anthem portion of Black-Eyed Peas' "Let's Get It Started" was blasting on the house sound system, her husband and her kids along with Anne Marie, Leona and Katherine Katz, as well as their TV hosts, were standing on the set and clapping a welcome for her.

If a feather floated down and landed on her shoulder, it would have knocked her down, maybe out. Not only did she feel the all-consuming shock of being caught pants down and completely surprised, but it was also happening live and on national television. She raised her right hand to her mouth, and wasn't sure who she should kill first, Anne Marie or her husband. Then Sadie ran up to her mom, jumped into her arms and her maternal instincts took over. She joined the group, hugged her kids, then Scott and was laughing and crying all at once.

Michelle and Lara took over and bent over backwards to get her seated and comfortable. With her family surrounding her, it wasn't too hard. Her hosts welcomed her, wished her a Happy Valentine's Day and related that this was a very special program. The duration of that day's show was dedicated to honoring her. Michelle also announced that since the show was such a surprise by nature, the network would be rerunning this edition of *Cheers* to a national audience this Thursday evening where they could promo it properly.

"Tami," Michelle began, "what a year this has been for you! Since last July north of Zion National Park and your first intervention, you have saved numerous lives, and singlehandedly corralled a number of bad guys. Later in the year, you flew through space to save a life at the Grand Canyon, then calmed an ugly situation at your daughter's school and in your own Asian community."

"Speaking of the Grand Canyon, Tami," chimed in Lara we have a special guest who has flown here in your honor." And Jessie emerged from backstage with a dozen long-stem roses in her arms. She presented the roses to Tami, they hugged, and hugged some more.

"Do you have anything to say to Tami, Jessie?"

"Tami, how can I ever thank you enough for being there that day for me? You saved my life, and I will never, ever forget you."

"I'm so glad we were there for you. Since you have survived that ordeal, take your life and run with it. Make something of yourself."

"Well, I'm working full time now, and going to school at night studying Cosmetology. I want to be an esthetician or work in make up on TV or for a studio."

"That's wonderful, Jessie; I am so proud of you."

Mara intoned, "Jessie, we may be able to help out there. One of our program managers would like to speak with you after the show and make an internship available for you at one of our local affiliates." Jessie burst into tears, and Tami gave her another hug.

"Tami, we have another friend of yours here today, Mei can you come on out?" And Mei Chun arrived on stage, hugged Tami, then Anne Marie and Leona. She related how Tami had singlehandedly subdued eight grown men, and the second wave to attack her were carrying guns and knives; some major deadly weaponry. The audience applauded wildly, Tami bowed, and again related to everyone what a blessing it was to be able to help someone, and how thankful she is to have the God given talent to intervene when possible.

"Tami," George spoke up "I know you've been asked this many times, but how do you manage to do what you do?"

"George, I'm beginning to think of it as my Quantum Burst. When confronted, I seem to pause as all of the microscopic molecules, waves, particles, electrons, quarks, whatever organic matter, seems to synthesize itself in my mind and body. It feels like they cube their density, and I am temporarily transformed. This Physiological Burst enables me to achieve what would not be capable of another person. I feel like this transformation developed through my running regimen. Running daily empowers me, not to the extent of an intervention, but during and after my early morning runs, the feelings I experience are euphoria. I am ultra positive, feel super productive and have a deep and abiding gratitude for my life, my family, our planet. People say to me, "You must be exhausted, getting up so early and doing what you do." But just the opposite is true. It empowers me. No pun intended. Does that answer your question?"

"That is as definitive an answer as I have heard you give, thank you. Tami, you have qualified as a first alternate for the Universal Games, do you feel like your Quantum Burst as you call it, helps you achieve better times in your marathon qualifying races?"

"Absolutely not George. My normal daily runs are totally unrelated to any paranormal talent that might visit me periodically. And thank you for asking this question so I can unequivocally assure everyone, and I mean everyone, that any success I might achieve in running is the result of daily physical workouts and training on roads and trails wherever I might find myself."

"Thank you, Tami. another question, we understand you have been invited to work with the Diplomatic Security Service. Do you know in what capacity you might be of use to that organization?"

"No sir, I do not. Except to say that I have begun to have prescient feelings sometimes when there might be an intervention approaching. If I can do anything to help prevent any problems at the Games, I would be honored to assist."

"Thank you, Tami."

———

Mara again, Tami lets go back to the beginning, to that fateful day in Southern Utah, and here are a few more friends who want to say hello. Images of Amanda, Linda and Todd appeared on a drop-down screen from a live feed. The three old friends were able to share their experiences from that ugly day on the set. Of course, the aspiring young actresses were effusive in their praise of Tami's first rescue.

"Don't look away just yet, Tami" and the Upper East-Cide couple whose baby Tami had saved from disaster appeared on the same screen as the Zion cast faded out. They too were lavish in their praise for Tami and her help.

Lara continued the celebration by summarizing Tami's recent victory in her court battle, the culmination of which was aired nationally here on our *Cheers* show. She described how Tami had undertaken the case against some prominent legal advice and fought considerable odds to miraculously win the trial. Some might say it was the trial of the decade. More applause.

"Then you flew to New York City on your own dime, to help capture some bad guys who were up to no good. " Unfortunately Geo and Alfonzo were not invited to attend the show, either in person or on a drop screen.

As time was beginning to run out, and Sadie was starting to fidget on Tami's lap, Michelle said, "Tami, what more could we possibly share with you today?"

"Gee, Michelle, you've got me there."

"Well, we'd like you to know of one more thing, and that would be how hard Scott, Anne Marie and Carl have been working in the background for you. Scott, would you like to do the honors?"

"Thank you, Michelle. Tami my love, on behalf of a lot of people, Anne Marie, Carl and myself, but also Ben Benson, the legal team at WBC headquarters, Carrie, Leona, your dream of creating the Tami Powers Endowment Fund has been fully, realized, established, funded, and is ready to rock and roll!"

Michelle took the floor back and announced, "Tami, WBC has matched your contribution of one million dollars. Also, we have started a Go Fund Me Campaign so that anyone from our audience can contribute to your scholarship efforts to help underserved youth from all of our communities get a strong start in life. As we mentioned earlier, WBC is going to re-air this program in its entirety on Thursday evening. By then we will be able to promote the show properly, and give you an update on the Go Fund Me Campaign."

Tami stood trembling with emotion, while holding Sadie in her arms, and said, "Thank you everyone from the very bottom of my heart and soul. I was sooo surprised today; I knew nothing about any of this. I would especially like to thank my family, my management team, the

Cheers team, also my extended family here at WBC, and lastly each and every one of you out there in our viewing audience.

I promise you we will stretch each and every dollar in the foundation to help people, and it simply thrills me to my core to be able to share some of God's goodness to me with all of you. Thank you again so very, very much." Tami waved to the audience, wiped a tear from her eye with Sadie's pigtail, turned, and sat down between Scott and Anne Marie.

The End

ACKNOWLEDGMENTS

To Tami Christensen, whose life of purpose and determination, whose friendship and willingness to share concepts and content from her book, *Life on the Run* (available through Amazon Books), were the inspiration for this book.

The author would like to thank his early readers: Marianne Jorgenson, Geraldine Warner, Linda Linehan, Linda Collins, and Sally Middleton.

Arlyn Lawrence, President of Inspira Literary Solutions, whose help in the publishing process was indispensable to the completion of *Power Woman*.

Jerry Pugnetti for his much-appreciated editorial input, as well as his friendship, encouragement, and willingness to share his professional writing experiences.

To Wikipedia for their always solid, timely, accessible, accurate content.

Don Snowdon and Molly Brahmer for their work in helping design the cover art for *Power Woman*.

To the authors and artisans who have taken the time to read and endorse this book, please know how deeply grateful I am.

ABOUT THE AUTHOR

Lee Jorgenson's second book, *LPGA Minus One,* was one of three nominees for best new work of fiction in the State of Washington. He grew up in Orange County, California, attended Northern Arizona University, served a tour of duty with the 199th Light Infantry Brigade in Vietnam, and now resides in Gig Harbor, Washington. After founding and managing his restaurant and catering company for over thirty years, he is retired and enjoys spending time with his family, the cinema, reading, writing, cooking, fishing, and is an avid golfer.

Please feel free to contact him: leejorgo12@gmail.com.